Albert S. Cook

The Defense of Poesy

Otherwise Known as an Apology for Poetry

Albert S. Cook

The Defense of Poesy
Otherwise Known as an Apology for Poetry

ISBN/EAN: 9783744786836

Printed in Europe, USA, Canada, Australia, Japan

Cover: Foto ©Andreas Hilbeck / pixelio.de

More available books at **www.hansebooks.com**

Sir Philip Sidney

THE DEFENSE OF POESY

OTHERWISE KNOWN AS

AN APOLOGY FOR POETRY

EDITED

WITH INTRODUCTION AND NOTES

BY

ALBERT S. COOK

PROFESSOR OF THE ENGLISH LANGUAGE AND LITERATURE
IN YALE UNIVERSITY

GINN AND COMPANY

BOSTON · NEW YORK · CHICAGO · LONDON
ATLANTA · DALLAS · COLUMBUS · SAN FRANCISCO

TO

MINTON WARREN

IN FRIENDSHIP AND GRATITUDE

PREFACE.

SIDNEY's estimate of poetry heralded such poetic achievement as the world had only once or twice witnessed. What Sidney outlined, Spenser and Shakespeare executed, though not always in the precise forms which he himself would have approved. In this essay he appears as a link between the soundest theory of ancient times and the romantic production of the modern era, as a humanist actuated by ethical convictions, as a man of affairs discharging the function of the scholar with the imaginative insight of the poet. To assist in placing the student of English literature at the point of view from which he can rightly judge of the merits and relations of Sidney's immortal disquisition is the object of the present editor's labors.

In modernizing the spelling and punctuation of the text, I have been guided by the principles which have been well expressed by Dr. Edwin A. Abbott, in the Preface to his edition of Bacon's Essays, pp. iii–iv : " As regards spelling, the principle adopted in the following pages is this : whatever quotations or extracts are made for critical or antiquarian purposes are printed with the old spelling, but the Essays themselves are placed on the same footing as the Bible and Shakespeare ; and, as being not for an age but for all ages, they are spelt with the spelling of this age.

Still less scruple has been felt in departing from the old punctuation; it has no right to be considered Bacon's; it often makes absolute nonsense of a passage; it sometimes produces ambiguities that may well cause perplexities even to intelligent readers; and its retention can only be valuable to archæologists as showing how little importance should be attached to the commas and colons scattered at random through their pages by the Elizabethan compositors."

My obligations to various scholars will be found recorded in their proper places in the Notes; but I take pleasure in bringing together, in the order of their citation, the names of Dr. J. A. H. Murray of Oxford, Mr. Ralph O. Williams of New Haven, Prof. T. F. Crane of Cornell University, Prof. Daniel G. Brinton of the University of Pennsylvania, Prof. Bernadotte Perrin of Adelbert University, and Prof. Thomas D. Goodell of Yale University.

A. S. C.

New Haven, July 4, 1890.

CONTENTS.

———◦◦◦———

INTRODUCTION.

1. SKETCH OF SIDNEY'S LIFE.

(Adapted from the Chronicle in Arber's edition.)

PHILIP SIDNEY "was son of Sir Henry Sidney by the Lady Mary his wife, eldest daughter of John Dudley, Duke of Northumberland; was born, as 'tis supposed, at Penhurst in Kent, 29 November, 1554, and had his Christian name given to him by his father from King Philip, then lately married to Queen Mary" (Wood, *Athenæ Oxonienses*). He was the eldest of three sons and four daughters. Philip Sidney and Fulke Greville, both of the same age (nine years), and afterwards friends for life, enter Shrewsbury School on the same day, Oct. 17, 1564. Fulke Greville thus testifies of his schoolfellow: "Of whose youth I will report no other wonder but thus, that though I lived with him, and knew him from a child, yet I never knew him other than a man; with such staidness of mind, lovely and familiar gravity, as carried grace and reverence above greater years. His talk ever of knowledge, and his very play tending to enrich his mind, so as even his teachers found something in him to observe and learn, above that which they had usually read or taught; which eminence by nature and industry made his worthy father style Sir Philip in my hearing (though I unseen) *Lumen familiæ suæ*" [the light of his family]. "While he was very young, he was sent to Christ Church to be improved in all sorts of learning . . . where continuing till he was about 17 years of age" . . . (Wood, *Athenæ Oxonienses*). This settlement at Oxford was made when

he was 13 years old.   On May 25, 1572, the Queen grants
Philip Sidney license to go abroad with three servants and
four horses.   On May 26 he leaves London in the train of
the Earl of Lincoln, Ambassador to the French King.
August 9, Charles IX makes him one of the Gentlemen of
his Chamber.   August 24, the Massacre of St. Bartholomew;
Sidney, being in the house of the English Ambassador, Sir
Francis Walsingham, is safe.   He however soon leaves
Paris, and journeys by Heidelberg to Frankfort, where he
meets Hubert Languet, aged 54.   He stays at Frankfort
about nine months.   They two then go to Vienna, where,
after some trips to Hungary, Sidney leaves Languet, and
spends eight months in Italy, chiefly in Venice, Padua, and
Genoa.   He returns to Vienna in November, spends his
winter there, and, coming home through the Low Countries,
reaches England on May 31, 1575, having been absent a
trifle over three years, from the age of 17 till that of 20.
In the same year introduced to Court by his uncle, the Earl
of Leicester.   July 9–27, 1575, is at the famous reception
given by Leicester to the Queen, at Kenilworth.   The Court
moves to Chartley Castle, where Philip is supposed first to
have seen 'Stella' (Penelope, daughter of Lord Essex, then
aged 13; afterwards Lady Rich).   The sonnets of *Astrophel
and Stella* go on for the next five or six years.   In 1577, at
the age of 22, is sent as Ambassador with messages of con-
dolence to Rodolph II, the new emperor of Germany, at
Prague, and to the two sons of Frederic III, late Elector
Palatine, viz., Lewis (now Elector) and John Casimir, at
Heidelberg.   In May of 1578, on the coming of the Court
to his uncle's at Wanstead, Sidney writes a masque entitled
The Lady of May.   About this time Sidney becomes
acquainted with Gabriel Harvey, and through him with
Edmund Spenser.   In August, 1579, Stephen Gosson pub-
lishes *The School of Abuse,* and on Oct. 16 Spenser writes
to Harvey Sidney's idea of it.   Soon after (Dec. 5)

Spenser's *Shepherd's Calendar* is entered at Stationer's Hall. In 1580 Sidney writes to the Queen against her marrying the Duke of Anjou, and while virtually banished from Court writes the *Arcadia*, and, jointly with his sister, translates the Psalms. Early in 1581 Sidney is a member of Parliament, and on Sept. 30 Languet dies at Antwerp. On Jan. 8, 1583 the Queen knights him, and soon after he marries Frances, daughter of Sir Francis Walsingham. In this year he probably writes the *Defense of Poesy*. During the winter of 1584–5 he is a second time member of Parliament. His daughter Elizabeth, afterward Countess of Rutland, is born in 1585, and Sidney projects an expedition to America with Sir Francis Drake. On Nov. 7, 1585 he is appointed Governor of Flushing, on Nov. 16 leaves England for the last time, and on Nov. 21 assumes his office. In 1586 his father and mother both die. On Sept. 22 of this year the fight at Zutphen occurs. According to the Earl of Leicester's account, Sidney "received a sore wound upon his thigh, three fingers above his knee, the bone broken quite in pieces." Sidney lingered twenty-six days, his last words being these, which were addressed to his brother: "Love my memory, cherish my friends; their faith to me may assure you they were honest. But, above all, govern your will and affections by the will and word of your Creator, in me beholding the end of this world with all her vanities." He died when he had not quite attained his thirty-second year. On Oct. 24 his body was removed to Flushing, embarked there for conveyance to London on Nov. 1, landed at Tower Hill on Nov. 5, and taken to a house in the Minories, without Aldgate, where it remained until the public funeral at St. Paul's on Feb. 16, 1587. "Volumes," says Fox Bourne (*Memoir*, p. 534), "would be filled were I to collect all the praise uttered in prose, and still more extensively in verse, by Sir Philip Sidney's contemporaries or his immediate successors."

2. Date of Composition and Publication.

As Sidney refers to the *Shepherd's Calendar* of Spenser (47 14), the *Defense* must have been written subsequent to the publication of that work, which was entered at Stationer's Hall on Dec. 5, 1579. Moreover, the *Defense* was in some measure . intended as a reply to Gosson's *School of Abuse*, which appeared about August, 1579, and which had certainly been examined by Sidney before the middle of October of that year, as appears from Spenser's letter to Harvey.

After Sidney's departure from England to serve in the Low Countries, Nov. 16, 1585, he would have had no leisure for the composition of such a work. Accordingly it must have been written between 1579 and 1585. Arber thinks "that the vindication followed soon upon the attack," and is therefore disposed to fix the date of the *Defense* in 1581. Fox Bourne says (*Memoir*, p. 407) : "*The Defense of Poesie*, written after *The Arcadia* and *Astrophel and Stella*, and therefore probably not until the year 1583." In explanation of this, it must be remembered that the *Arcadia* was begun, and the most of it probably written, in 1580. Fox Bourne says of it (*Memoir*, p. 345) : "Having commenced his romance in the summer of 1580, I infer that Sidney had written about three-quarters of the whole, and all which has come down to us in a finished state, by the autumn of 1581." Some time must be allowed for the change in Sidney's style, the abandonment of a florid and sentimental manner of writing, and the acquisition of that sobriety and solidity of diction which reflects a maturer manhood. This progress toward maturity is noted by Fox Bourne (p. 347) : "His journey to Flanders, in the early spring of 1582, must have interrupted his literary work. After that there was a marked change in his temper. Honest purposes were rising in him which little accorded with many sentiments in the half-written romance." The argument derived from the change in Sidney's style, the index of a corresponding change in his temper and views, seems to me irresistible, and I am therefore inclined to place the *Defense* as late as 1583. The quiet happiness of the first months succeeding his marriage may have been especially favorable to such thoughtful composition.

Even more conducive to the philosophical meditation which the authorship of this tractate required may have been his friendship with a famous philosopher and highly gifted nature, who in that year came to England and entered the circle composed of Sidney and his most intimate friends. I refer to the poet and mystic, Giordano Bruno, a precursor of Bacon and martyr of the Inquisition. The preparation for the *Defense* necessitated a comparison of the doctrines of Plato and Aristotle touching poetry, and nothing could well have served as a more urgent stimulus to such philosophical study than familiar intercourse with Bruno, at home in Platonism and Neoplatonism, and a vigorous assailant of the exclusive authority of Aristotle. Who can fail to recognize the substantial identity of Sidney's reflection on the loveliness of virtue (30 20-22), not only with the common source in Plato, but also with the following sentiment taken from Bruno's *Heroic Rapture*, which was dedicated to Sidney (quoted in Frith's Life of Giordano Bruno, p. 125) : " For I am assured that Nature has endowed me with an inward sense by which I reason from the beauty before my eyes to the light and eminence of more excellent spiritual beauty, which is light, majesty, and divinity." The impulse given by Bruno would be precisely that which Sidney needed in order to urge him to clarify his ideas, and reduce them to the orderly form in which they are presented in the *Defense*. On the hypothesis that this intimacy with Bruno did mark a distinct stage in Sidney's spiritual development, we can more readily comprehend how he was led to undertake the

translation of Duplessis Mornay's book on the Truth of the
Christian Religion, a work abounding in the Neoplatonic
views with which Bruno's philosophy is surcharged.

The reason for assigning the *Defense* to the year 1581
has less weight when we discover that it is much more than
a reply to Gosson, that the "argument of abuse" occupies
a comparatively small part of the whole treatise, and that
the positive, constructive, and critical element of it is what
constitutes its chief value. Were we to assume, with Grosart (see p. xxxviii), that Spenser, perhaps before Gosson's
attack was issued, suggested such a positive and constructive
work to Sidney, if he did not actually have a hand in the
planning of Sidney's own tract, there would be still less
ground for believing that Sidney hastened to reply, especially as there had been at least one confutation of Gosson's
pamphlet attempted in the year 1579, under the title of
Honest Excuses. In Gosson's *Apology of the School of
Abuse* (Arber's ed., p. 73), we read: "It is told me that
they have got one in London to write certain *Honest
Excuses*, so they term it, to their dishonest abuses which I
revealed." This *Apology* was written in 1579, and within
a year or so Thomas Lodge had written his *Defense*, unless
we assume that this is identical with the *Honest Excuses*, as
has been done by some. In any event, we may be sure
that there was no lack of ephemeral strictures, conceived in
the same kind as the *School of Abuse* itself. What was
wanted was a dignified discussion of the whole subject,
based upon a profound and dispassionate view of the principles involved, and this, so different in every way from a
hasty compilation, spiced with virulent epigrams, or what
passed for such, Sidney would have been in no haste to
publish. To these considerations in favor of the later date
may be added the opinion of Collier (*Hist. Eng. Dram.
Poetry*, 2. 422–3 and 3. 374), who believes it to have been
written "about the year 1583."

The *Defense* was not published till 1595, and then by two different printers, Olney and Ponsonby. The former gave it the title, *An Apologie for Poetrie;* the latter, *The Defence of Poesie.* It is doubtful which of these appeared the earlier (Flügel's ed., pp. 65, 66). Sidney himself refers to the treatise as "a pitiful defense of poor poetry" (but cf. p. xxxix).

3. LEARNING.

Like Bacon and Shakespeare, Sidney was a diligent student of Plutarch, and scarcely less of the *Morals* than of the *Lives.* On the 19th of December, 1573, he wrote from Venice to his friend Languet, asking for a copy of Plutarch in French. The indications accordingly are that he did not then read Greek with much fluency. His words are (Fox Bourne, *Memoir*, p. 74) : "If you can pick them up in Vienna, I wish you would send me Plutarch's works translated into French. I would willingly pay five times their value for them." Languet replied "that for all the money in the world he could not buy a copy of Plutarch, though perhaps he might borrow one" (Fox Bourne, p. 75). This answer is not a little surprising, seeing that Amyot's French translation of the *Lives*, from which the English rendering by North was afterward made, appeared in 1559, that of the *Morals* not being published, however, till 1574. North's version was issued in 1579, but long before this time Sidney was no doubt able to read Greek with much greater ease, and in any case must have familiarized himself with the matter of Plutarch. No one among the ancients was so abundant a source of illustration to the moralists and essayists of the sixteenth century. It is for his store of anecdote and his living traits of the great men of antiquity that Sidney chiefly uses him, though it is clear that he had likewise become strongly imbued with Plutarch's ethical sentiments, except in so far as they were condemned or superseded by the purer tenets of Christianity.

Sidney's favorite among the Latin prosaists was unques-
tionably Cicero. To him, as to the men of the literary
Renaissance generally, Cicero was the unrivalled model of
style. Sidney's ear was charmed by the harmonious cadences of the great rhetorician, while his imagination was
fired by Cicero's ostensible fervor of patriotism, his oratorical indignation or zeal, his prodigality of information and
allusion, and, perhaps beyond everything else, by the reflected glories of the ancient Roman State. If the style of
the master partakes somewhat too much of Asiatic grandil-
oquence and floridity, and somewhat too little of Attic re-
finement and moderation, we should not be greatly surprised
if we find the pupil occasionally proving his aptness by a
clever imitation of the blemishes, as well as the beauties, of
his original. We must not be unjust to Sidney because the
sounding brass of Cicero sometimes gave forth in his hands
the tone of the clanging cymbal. It must be remembered
that the mind of England had been largely nourished upon
the Psalmists and Prophets of the Old Testament, and had
thus acquired a certain liking for the splendor of Oriental
imagery, as well as the pomp and harmonies of Oriental
language. To this must be added the familiarity with the
mediæval romances which came in the train of the Crusades,
many of which were fragrant with the breath of the East.
Finally, a fresh wave of Orientalism was now pouring upon
France and England from the land of chivalrous thoughts
and high emprise, the Spain of the Moors and the Castilian
kings, of Guevara and Montemayor. Instead of wondering,
therefore, that Sidney could endure, much less imitate, the
Asianism with which Cicero's style, notwithstanding its many
beauties, is still infected, we should rather wonder that he
possessed the vigor of understanding and sense of form
which are unmistakable in his theory and in the best of his
practice, and that he was able to make so firm a stand
against those tendencies of his time which resulted in the
pedantries and imbecilities of Euphuism.

Languet, Sidney's early and revered friend, is to be held partly responsible for his application to Cicero, as well as for any undue attachment to the Latin writers in general. In response to Sidney's letter quoted above, penned when Sidney was but 19, Languet wrote : "You ask me how you ought to form a style of writing. In my opinion you cannot do better than give careful study to all Cicero's letters, not only for the sake of the graceful Latin, but also on account of the weighty truths which they contain. . . . But take care of slipping into the heresy of those who believe that Cicero-nianism is the summum bonum, and who will spend a life-time in aiming after it. . . . When you begin to read Cicero's letters you will hardly need Plutarch " (Fox Bourne, pp. 74–5). This was soon followed by more counsel of similar tenor : "Greek literature, again, is a very beautiful study ; but I fear you will have no leisure to follow it through, and whatever time you give to it you steal from Latin, which, though less elegant than Greek, is far better worth your knowing " (Fox Bourne, p. 76). Fortunately, as we shall see, Sidney was too wise to yield implicit obedience to his Mentor with reference to the neglect of Greek literature, and, even before writing the *Defense*, his eyes had been opened to the folly of excessive devotion to the niceties of Latin style. In 1580, when he had reached the age of 25, he wrote to his brother Robert : " So you can speak and write Latin not barbarously, I never require great study in Ciceronianism, the chief abuse of Oxford, *qui, dum verba sectantur, res ipsas negligunt*" [who, in their application to words, neglect the things themselves]. This sounds like an anticipation of Bacon's judgment (*Adv. Learning*, 1. 4. 2, 3) : " This grew speedily to an excess ; for men began to hunt more after words than matter ; more after the choiceness of the phrase, and the round and clean composition of the sentence, and the sweet falling of the clauses, and the vary-ing and illustration of their works with tropes and figures, than after the weight of matter, worth of subject, soundness of argument, life of invention, or depth of judgment. . . . Here, therefore, is the first distemper of learning, when men study words and not matter." Yet, notwithstanding Sidney's discernment of this weighty truth, and the progress in simplicity made between the writing of the *Arcadia* and that of the *Defense*, it is but too evident that what may be called the vices of Ciceronianism still continued to corrupt his style in an appreciable degree, or else that the element of purer Atticism in it had not been an effectual antidote against the Asianism derived from other sources.

In one respect the study of Cicero was an almost unmixed benefit to Sidney. More than any other author except Plutarch, Cicero seems to have acquainted him with the history of the ancient world. He was to Sidney a mine of information about all sorts of subjects — lives of men, traits of manners, and philosophies — besides supplying him with more than one epigrammatic sally which only needed to be translated into English, and deftly introduced, to adorn the page on which it appeared.

With the two chief epic poets of antiquity, Homer and Virgil, Sidney had a familiar acquaintance. Virgil occupies the first place in his affections, but he is by no means insensible to the superior loftiness and naturalness of Homer. As a highly educated man of that day, he knew well his Horace and Ovid, the dramatists Plautus and Terence, the satirists Juvenal and Persius, the historians Livy, Suetonius, Justin, and even the authors of the Augustan Histories, moralists like Seneca and the Pseudo-Cato, and perhaps Lucretius and Quintilian. Of these the first four were perhaps preferred to the others. More remarkable, because less usual at that day, was his knowledge of the Greeks. Besides Plutarch and Homer, who have already been mentioned, he admires and repeatedly mentions the *Cyropædia* of Xenophon. Of the three tragedians, he was apparently best acquainted with Euripides, though typical plays of both Sophocles and Æschylus had been included in his reading. Of Plato and Aristotle I speak under another head, that of Sidney's Theory of Poetry. Here it is sufficient to say that the dialogues of Plato which he had apparently studied with most care are the *Ion, Symposium, Phædrus, Sophist, Phædo,* and *Republic*, and that he was conversant with at least the *Poetics* and *Ethics* of Aristotle, and perhaps with the *Rhetoric.*

The incidental mention of such authors as Solon, Tyrtæus, and others, proves nothing as to Sidney's personal knowledge of their writings. Many of these names, like those of Orpheus and Musæus, were freely introduced into literary works and learned discussions, merely on the strength of similar mention of them in ancient writings of a relatively late period, and the commonplaces concerning them are therefore to be expected in any sixteenth century pamphlet or treatise on the subject of poetry or literary history. But there are others, such as Herodotus and Theocritus, whom Sidney mentions in such a way as to lead us to believe that he knew them otherwise than from mere hearsay. Even the Greeks of the post-classical age were not beyond the pale of his curiosity, as is shown by his praise of the romance of Heliodorus.

In his quotations from the ancients Sidney is frequently inaccurate. We should not infer that in this respect he is singular among the Elizabethans; Bacon, not to mention others, does not always adhere strictly to the phraseology of his author. Such inaccuracy is of doubtful interpretation in an age not distinguished for scientific exactness. It may indicate either a deficiency or a plenitude of scholarship, and our decision in favor of the one or the other should depend upon collateral evidence. Evidence of this nature is not altogether wanting as respects the fulness and essential justness of Sidney's learning. It is found in his general

mastery of a difficult subject, but also in his manner of handling, and as it were playing with, some of the quotations
he employs. Now he changes the form of a verb from the
second person to the first, in order to appropriate to himself
a citation from Horace. Again for two nouns he substitutes
their antonyms, that he may adapt a line from Ovid to his
purpose. In these and similar cases his learning seems to
be so entirely at command that he can mold and twist it
to suit all the vagaries of a sportive humor. Less conclusive
is his amplification of the famous apostrophe in the First
Oration against Catiline (53 24, note). Here, in his endeavor to illustrate a rhetorical artifice, he appears to extend.
the quotation in order to make the illustration more telling.
Unless the Elizabethan text of Cicero differed materially from
that now accepted, this variation must be laid to the account.
of dishonesty or to that of a treacherous memory. No one
who has formed an opinion concerning Sidney's character
would accuse him of deliberate dishonesty, and hence we
have no alternative except to suppose that his verbal memory
was at times untrustworthy. All things considered, the accuracy of his learning could probably be impeached, and has
perhaps often been surpassed, by the best of our contemporary writers ; yet it is none the less true that the extent
of his reading, and the degree to which he rendered the
substance of books tributary to the expression of his own
convictions and essential manhood, might well put to shame
many who are rightly esteemed his superiors in technical
and minute scholarship.

Sidney refers to numerous contemporary humanists, Italian, German, French, and English, whose names it would be
tedious and unprofitable to enumerate, especially as they are
all contained in the Index of Proper Names. An exception
must be made in favor of the elder Scaliger, to whose *Poetics* Sidney's indebtedness is not inconsiderable. In Italian
literature his range is from Dante to Ariosto, and in English

from Chaucer to his personal friend Spenser. How lively was his interest in Italian authors we may infer from his friendship with Giordano Bruno, and the terms in which the latter dedicates to him two of his important works. Sidney read Spanish with ease, as we may infer not only from his imitation of Montemayor, but from his use of Oviedo, though it is just possible that the latter may have been accessible to him in translation. With respect to poetry there appears to have been a substantial identity of opinion on many points between himself and Cervantes, and, in a less degree, between himself and Lope de Vega. Of his love for all that illustrated the riches of the English tongue, and of his ardent desire that the glories of its literature should be still further enhanced, these pages furnish ample proof.

Finally, Sidney was a diligent and enthusiastic student of the Scriptures of the Old and New Testaments, both in themselves and in commentaries upon them. Not only did he endeavor to guide his life according to their precepts, but he delighted in them as literature. His appreciation of the poetry of the Bible is shown by his translation of the first forty-three Psalms, and not less by his glowing, yet reverent, estimates of the parables of Christ, the hymns of Moses and Deborah, the dramatic poem of Job, and the lyric or didactic compositions of Solomon. In the Sacred Writings he discovered something that corresponded to every element of his manhood, and while their beauty and sublimity enthralled his æsthetic sensibility, he was ready to acknowledge in them a diviner efficacy which transcended the efforts of the human spirit to fathom, as when he exclaimed upon his death-bed, "How unsearchable the mysteries of God's Word are!" (Fox Bourne, p. 512.)

4. STYLE.

Sidney has sometimes been called a Euphuist. This term has been so loosely employed that it would be unprofitable to examine the appropriateness of the designation without first defining what is to be understood by Euphuism. Fortunately, substantial unanimity has been reached by the competent investigators of the subject, and it is possible to utilize, without lengthy beating of the air, the labors of a scholar who is recognized as one of the foremost expounders of the modern theory of Euphuism. This authority, Dr. Frederick Landmann, has formulated the law of Euphuism in the following brief sentence (*Euphues*, Heilbronn 1887, Introduction, p. xv, note) : "I consider transverse alliteration in parisonic antithetical or parallel clauses as the indispensable criterion of the presence of Euphuism."

This sentence is enigmatic in proportion to its brevity, and demands a commentary to make it intelligible. The commentary, which will be extracted from the same work, adds to the criterion already given a third peculiarity, which Landmann seems to regard as inferior in importance to the one, or rather two, comprised in the sentence already quoted (Landmann, pp. xv–xvi) : "We here have the most elaborate antithesis not only of well-balanced sentences, but also of words, often even of syllables. . . . Even when he uses a single sentence, he opposes the words within this clause to each other. When we find a principal and a subordinate clause we may be sure that two, three or all of the words of the former are opposed to an equal number in the latter. This we call parisonic antithesis. . . . The second class of elements peculiar to Lyly's style are alliteration, consonance, rhyme, playing upon words, and the use of syllables sounding alike. These embellishments he uses to point out the respective corresponding words in his antithetical clauses. It is not continuous alliteration as we have it in almost every writer of the sixteenth century from Surrey to Spenser, which was condemned by Wilson, Puttenham, and others, but *transverse*, as it has been very aptly termed by Weymouth : e.g. 'Although hetherto Euphues I have *sh*rined thee in my *h*eart for a *tr*ustie *f*riende, I will *sh*unne thee *h*eerafter as a *tr*othles *f*oe.' The third distinctive element of Euphuism is the tendency to confirm a statement by a long series of illustrations, comparisons, *exempla* and short similes, nearly always introduced by ' for as — ' ; these he takes from ancient history and mythology, from daily life, and, last but not least, from Pliny's fabulous natural history, translating Pliny literally in the latter case." }

Landmann's opinion concerning Sidney's style is based upon the *Arcadia*, and it is in this, rather than in the *Defense*, that we should expect to find the distinctive marks of Euphuism. Notwithstanding, Landmann denies that Sidney belongs to this school (p. xxx) : " But we see that Sidney avoided Lyly's artificial combination of parisonic antithesis with transverse alliteration, as well as his absurd similes taken from Pliny ; in other words, the most characteristic elements of Euphuism." The statement concerning the similes from natural and unnatural history is confirmed by the quotation from Drayton, cited in the note to 54 12. In only one sentence of the *Defense* (2 24-27) is there any indication to the contrary, and this I surmise to have been intended as a parody of Gosson's manner (see the note on this passage).

The stylistic peculiarities of Sidney's romance Landmann comprehends under the term Arcadianism, which he thus describes (p. xxviii) : " The elements of style in Sidney's *Arcadia* are different from those of Euphuism. In brief, they consist in endless tedious sentences, one sometimes filling a whole page, in the fondness for details, and in the description of the beauties of rural scenery. Instead of Lyly's *exempla* and shortened similes with ' for as — so,' we here have minutely worked out comparisons and conceits couched in excessively metaphorical language, quaint circumlocutions for simple expressions, and bold personifications of inanimate objects. Besides, Sidney is fond of playing upon words, and is not averse to *simple* alliteration."

Having thus distinguished Arcadianism from Euphuism, Landmann affords us no further aid in determining to what extent, if at all, the style of the *Defense* is Arcadian. This, however, we can readily do for ourselves. Of the characteristics noted by Landmann, we may at once dismiss all except the very last. As shown in the note on 4 11, Sidney is indeed fond of playing upon words, and occasionally indulges in alliteration. The instances of the latter are but few, and would never be remarked were it not for the verbal jingles which fall under the former head. At times this vainly repetitious form of Arcadianism is nothing but Ciceronianism of a rather indefensible sort, and any censure passed upon Sidney for his transgression of good taste is but too apt to light upon the idol of the Renaissance humanists (cf. note on 54 32). It was hardly to be expected that this stumbling-block should be altogether avoided by men who thought it a venial fault to love language in some measure for its own sake, — so long at least as they were under the exclusive sway of the Latins. We must not forget that it was a besetting peccadillo of Shakespeare, and does it not too often excite the smile of pitying derision as we turn the majestic page of Milton? Nothing less than passionate reverence for the severe purity of the chastest Attic could avail to remove this blemish from modern writing. But at that time a familiarity with Greek models of composition naturally drew after it a practice scarcely less opposed to the more rigorous canons of artistic prose;—

The employment of such compound words as are fitted to heighten the style of dithyrambic and other elevated poetry, was interdicted to prose on the authority of Aristotle. The formation of these compounds is alien to the genius of certain modern tongues, such as French. Yet even this native lack of plasticity was vanquished, for a time at least, by the Hellenizing impulse which swept over the sixteenth century. The stubbornness of French was forced to yield to the pertinacity of Du Bartas, while the more pliable English, mindful of an earlier power which had been spell-bound into enacting the part of the Sleeping Beauty, responded quickly to the efforts made by Chapman and others to imitate in their own tongue the magnificent rhythmical combinations which constitute so material a part of the Homeric and Pindaric charm. The reward of Du Bartas was a doubtful and ephemeral success ; the fashion he set soon went the way of all attempts to set aside natural law. French poetry promptly discarded these compounds, and it may be said that French prose never accepted them. Not so in England. Here they were soon rendered popular in consequence of their adoption by the dramatists, and even earlier began to appear in prose fiction. These compounds form one feature of Arcadianism, and one which Sidney never wholly outgrew. Accordingly we find them scattered throughout the *Defense,* just as they occur in the more florid prose of our own day (cf. note on 55 25). Whatever may be urged against their employment, they are certainly an indication of formative energy, and the state-ment of a literary historian about Lucretius may be applied, with an obvious difference, to Sidney (Sellar, *Roman Poets of the Republic,* p. 382) : " His abundant use of compound words, . . . most of which fell into disuse in the Augus-tan age, [was a product] of the same creative force which enabled Plautus and Ennius to add largely to the resources of the Latin tongue. In him, more than in any Latin poet before or after him, we meet with phrases too full of imagi-native life to be in perfect keeping with the more sober tones and tamer spirit of the national literature."

It would be tedious to enumerate the specific marks of Sidney's prose as exhibited in his essay. This task may well be reserved for those who undertake a systematic study of his tractate with reference to the illustration of rhetorical principles or historical tendencies. The key to many of its peculiarities will, however, be found in one or two general considerations. First of all, Sidney's may be called an emotional prose. There is a prose of light only, and there is another of light and heat conjoined. That of Sidney belongs to the latter class. It seeks to persuade, and is in that sense oratorical; Hallam even calls it declamatory. Yet while in its argumentative sequences it falls under the head of oratory, in its procession from the emotions and frequent appeal to them, in its imagery and melodious rhythm, it has something in common with poetry. In this union of qualities will be found alike its merits and its defects.

There is a somewhat different point of view from which the whole may be regarded. Though the author of the *Defense* had before him the finished prose of other nations and languages, he stood at the formative period of an artistic prose in English, and the conditions under which all men work at such epochs are less materially affected by their acquaintance with existing models in other tongues than may at first thought be supposed. They know and perhaps approve the better, but instinctively or deliberately follow the worse; or, in the absence of approved precedent, they attempt to fashion an organ for the more purely intellectual faculties, and find themselves slipping back into the balanced constructions and regular cadences of verse. The era of the English Renaissance has in this respect many points of resemblance with the intellectual awakening of Greece after the Persian wars. The evolution of Greek prose finds its counterpart in the struggle to shape a literary medium in English for thought too purely rational and utilitarian in its character to be fitly couched in the ornate diction and measured rhythms of poetry. The description of the former by an accomplished living scholar will fairly characterize the stage through which the more ambitious English prose was at this time passing (Jebb, *Attic Orators* I. 18–21): "The outburst of intellectual life in Hellas

during the fifth century before Christ had for one of its
results the creation of Greek prose. Before that age no
Greek had conceived artistic composition except in the form
of poetry.... As the mental horizon of Greece was widened,
as subtler ideas and more various combinations began to ask
for closer and more flexible expression, the desire grew for
something more precise than poetry, firmer and more com-
pact than the idiom of conversation. Two special causes
aided this general tendency. The development of demo-
cratic life, making the faculty of speech before popular
assemblies and popular law-courts a necessity, hastened the
formation of an oratorical prose. The Persian wars, by
changing Hellenic unity from a sentiment into a fact, and
reminding men that there was a corporate life, higher and
grander than that of the individual city, of which the story
might be told, supplied a new motive to historical prose....
But the process of maturing the new kind of composition
was necessarily slow; for it required, as its first condition,
little less than the creation of a new language, of an idiom
neither poetical nor mean. Herodotos, at the middle point
of the fifth century, shows the poetical element still prepon-
derant.... The prose-writer of this epoch instinctively
compares himself with the poet.... He does not care to
be simply right and clear: rather he desires to have the
whole advantage which his skill gives him over ordinary
men; he is eager to bring his thoughts down upon them
with a splendid and irresistible force.... At the moment
when prose was striving to disengage itself from the diction
of poetry, Gorgias gave currency to the notion that poetical
ornament of the most florid type was its true charm. When,
indeed, he went further, and sought to imitate the rhythm
as well as the phrase of poetry, this very extravagance had
a useful result. Prose has a rhythm, though not of the kind
at which Gorgias aimed; and the mere fact of the Greek
ear becoming accustomed to look for a certain proportion

between the parts of a sentence hastened the transition from the old running style to the periodic."

Jebb still further characterizes the Gorgian manner in his Introduction, pp. cxxvi–cxxvii : "That which was to the Athenians . . . the element of distinction in the Sicilian's speaking was its poetical character ; and this depended on two things — the use of poetical words, and the use of symmetry or assonance between clauses in such a way as to give a strongly marked prose-rhythm and to reproduce, as far as possible, the metres of verse. . . . Gorgias was the first man who definitely conceived how literary prose might be artistic. That he should instinctively compare it with the only other form of literature which was already artistic, namely poetry, was inevitable. Early prose necessarily begins by comparing itself with poetry."

If the Euphuistic and Arcadian prose of the sixteenth century be read in the light of this account of the Gorgian writing, it will be impossible to overlook certain points of similarity, and equally impossible to ignore certain resemblances in the conditions under which the Greek and the English prose were respectively developed. But in instituting such a comparison, there are important differences which must not be disregarded, though there is no space to touch upon them here. And whatever conclusions are reached respecting Euphuism and Arcadianism must certainly undergo modification before proving applicable to the style of the *Defense*.

5. THEORY OF POETRY.

The theory of poetry advanced by Sidney is, in its essentials, the oldest of which we have any knowledge, so old, indeed, that by Sidney's time the world had well-nigh forgotten it, or had deliberately chosen to ignore it. This theory may be expressed in words borrowed from Shelley's *Defense of Poetry*, a work many of whose chief positions are almost precise counterparts of those assumed by Sidney: " A poet participates in the eternal, the infinite, and the one. . . . . Poetry in a more restricted sense expresses those arrangements of language, and especially metrical language, which are created by that imperial faculty whose throne is curtained within the invisible nature of man." Is it indeed true that these words represent Sidney's conception, and, if so, how is this conception related to the chief rival theories which have been, or were then, current? This is the question we have briefly to examine.

Sidney assumes that there is an architectonic science, in this following the lead of Aristotle, who in his *Ethics* (see the note on 12 32 of the *Defense*) demands this rank for what he calls Political Science, but what we are accustomed to term Moral Philosophy. Speaking as an ethnic, Aristotle had virtually said : " Above all other learnings stands moral philosophy, for it points out the goal of all wisely directed human effort." Speaking as a Christian, Sidney in effect exclaims : " Above all secular learnings stands poetry, for it appropriates the purest ethical teaching, and presents it in a form universally attractive and intensely stimulating." Even in making this statement Sidney is following the lead of Aristotle, who had thus exalted poetry : " Poetry is of a more philosophical and serious character than history " (see note on 18 25). Had Aristotle been asked to determine the relative values of ethics, poetry, and history in a descending scale, he would perhaps have hesitated before giving a categorical answer ; had he been urged, he would hardly have done otherwise than arrange them in the order named. Sidney's reply is different. He practically divides the whole of ethics into religion and natural ethics, the latter being understood as moral philosophy unattended with any diviner sanction than such as is derived from the evident nature of things and the purest intuitions of the human spirit. To the former he assigns an indisputable preëminence, but removes it from the province of discussion by asserting that he is concerned with secular learning only. The latter, or natural ethics, human philosophy as bearing upon the conduct of life, he makes distinctly inferior to poetry, because, unsupported by the sanctions of revealed religion, it is provided with no adequate motive force. Such a motive force may, however, be supplied by the imaginative presentation of the respective consequences of good and evil action, but, when thus supplied, it converts philosophy into something superior to philosophy : ethics has become poetry. Thus Homer had taught the whole Hellenic race ; thus Æschylus had taught the Athenian democracy. It follows that every creative poet — for it is of creative poets that Sidney is speaking — must be in a true sense a philosopher, though it is by no means true that every philosopher is necessarily a poet.

We may now return to our point of departure in Shelley's definition. "A poet," he says, "participates in the eternal, the infinite, and the one." But may we not with equal truth affirm that the philosopher participates in the eternal, the infinite, and the one? And indeed the statement thus far is true of both, — the philosopher and the creative poet. Both, under the veil of phenomena, through the dim glass of appearance, descry the pure and radiant form of truth. To the vision of both — this time employing the beautiful words of Shelley in the *Adonais* —

> The One remains, the Many change and pass;
> Heaven's light for ever shines, Earth's shadows fly;
> Life, like a dome of many-colored glass,
> Stains the white radiance of Eternity.

What, then, is the difference between them? It is this. When the philosopher has discovered the One in the Many, the principle of unity embracing the variety of phenomena, he must pause, or, if he seem to proceed, if he respond to the urgent desire of men that he shall furnish them with a guide to life, a clue through the tangled maze of earthly vicissitude, he is reduced to the presentation of cold analyses, or the bare enunciation of a moral dictum, a cate-\ gorical imperative. Not so the poet. He also affirms, but he likewise stirs the feelings. He also affirms, but the form of his affirmation, in its exquisite blending of truth with symbol, in its representation of the hidden verity by a cunning arrangement of the lovely shows of things, delights every sense and faculty of the whole being. Poetry thus actualizes what in philosophy is only potential. Philosophy is a Merlin, but a Merlin shut away from the world in a hollow oak, through some charm " of woven paces and of waving hands " which effectually debars it from exercising its natural prerogative, the ordering of human lives according to the eternal idea of the good, the necessary, and the true. But poetry is a Prospero whom the lightest airs of heaven obey, and whose empire is absolute over the hearts and consciences of men. The ugly and the vicious may grumble at its dominion, but are powerless, are even half-won to reverence for the viewless might by which they are fettered ; while all gentle spirits rejoice in being so sweetly attuned to the central harmonies of Order and Law, and in finding their heedless courses wrought, through a constraining magic, into patterns of an endless and most felicitous beauty.

We can thus understand how Sidney the Puritan was also Sidney the poet, and how religion and creative poetry were to him almost as sisters. Both assume this function of guidance, both exercise it to the noblest ends, and both achieve their purpose through the kindling of the imagination and an appeal to the emotional nature. The one, it is_ true, lays direct claim to a divine mission ; the other, though conscious of its divine origin, is often content to be regarded merely as the efflux of the exalted and enraptured

human soul. But is there not a point where the two coa-
lesce? Who, were he to encounter for the first time the
following passage from the *Phædrus* of Plato, dissociated
from its context, could tell whether the author was speaking
of poetry or religion — or perchance of philosophy tinged
with emotion? "And he who employs aright these memories
is ever being initiated into perfect mysteries and alone becomes truly perfect. But, as he forgets earthly interests
and is rapt in the divine, the vulgar deem him mad, and
rebuke him ; they do not see that he is inspired. Thus far
I have been speaking of the fourth and last kind of madness,
which is imputed to him who, when he sees the beauty of
earth, is transported with the recollection of the true beauty ;
he would like to fly away, but he cannot ; he is like a bird
fluttering and looking upward and careless of the world
below ; and he is therefore esteemed mad. And I have
shown this of all inspirations to be the noblest and highest
and the offspring of the highest " (Jowett's tr., 2. 126).
Or, suppose the word 'religion' to be substituted for
'poetry' in these sentences from Schiller's Essay on Pathos
(Hempel's tr., 2. 486), and note whether any susceptibility
is shocked, or any convictions antagonized, by the affirmations
thus made : " In the case of man poetry never executes a
special business, and no instrument is less fitted to perform
some special service. Her sphere of action is the totality
of human nature ; she can only affect single traits or acts
by affecting human character generally. Poetry may be to
man what love is to the hero. She can neither advise him,
nor fight his battles, nor perform any other work for him ;
but she may educate him to become a hero, she may call
him to perform deeds, she may arm him with strength."

Sidney's theory might be illustrated by the practice of the
more illustrious of Dante's contemporaries and thirteenth
century predecessors, especially by that of such poets as
Wolfram von Eschenbach and Guido Guinicelli. The tech-

nic invented or perfected by the troubadours, and which they had employed in amatory, satirical, or martial compositions, had become, in the course of time, the instrument of philosophy. A definite meaning was now embodied by the poet in his verse, and this meaning comprehended much more than the incidents of a tale, or the longing for a beloved one. It was not exhausted when considered as an attack upon a personal enemy, or as an exhortation to deeds of physical valor. Dante himself, alike in his theory and his practice, furnishes the most convenient exponent of this conception of poetry as the teacher and guide of men, full of significance when apparently most sensuous, intending the spiritual and transcendent when most occupied with colors, and odors, and sweet sounds. In both the *New Life* and the *Banquet* (*Convito*) Dante gives lengthy expositions of a few poems, revealing by analysis the fundamental truths which determined the structure and even the ornament of each. In the *New Life* (Rossetti's tr., p. 81) he protests against meaningless poetry : "Neither did these ancient poets speak thus without consideration, nor should they who are makers of rime in our day write after the same fashion, having no reason in what they write ; for it it were a shameful thing if one should rime under the semblance of metaphor or rhetorical similitude, and afterwards, being questioned thereof, should be able to rid his words of such semblance, unto their right understanding. Of whom (to wit, of such as rime thus foolishly) myself and the first among my friends do know many." And in his *Letter to Can Grande*, in which he explains the scope and purport of the *Divine Comedy*, he says (Hillard's tr., pp. 393, 396) : "There are six things, therefore, that must be sought out in beginning any instructive work ; that is to say, the *subject*, the *agent*, the *form*, the *end*, the *title of the book*, and the *nature of its philosophy*. . . . Setting aside all subtlety of investigation, we may say briefly that the end of both (the whole and the part) is to rescue those who live in this life from their state of misery, and to guide them to the state of blessedness. *The nature of the philosophy* governing both the whole and the part is moral action, or *ethics*, because the object of the whole work is not speculative, but practical. Therefore, even if certain places or passages are treated in a speculative manner, this is not for the sake of speculation, but of operation." The substantial identity of Dante's theory of poetry with that of Sidney, will, in the light of these and similar passages, scarcely be questioned (cf. 54 2 ff., 13 1 ff.).

But it is perhaps more obvious to compare Sidney, the Puritan and poet, with Milton, the Puritan and poet. Does not Milton seem to be reviving the memory of Sidney, as well as tracing an ideal for himself, in the well-known passage from the *Apology for Smectymnuus :* " I was confirmed in this opinion, that he who would not be frustrate of his hope to write well hereafter in laudable things ought himself to be a true poem, — that is, a composition of the best and honorablest things ; not presuming to sing high praises of heroic men or famous cities, unless he have in himself the experience and the practice of all that which is praiseworthy." When Sidney says of the poet, " For he doth not only show the way, but giveth so sweet a prospect into the way as will entice any man to enter into it " (see 23 15 ff.), are we not reminded of Milton's words in the *Reason of Church Government :* " Teaching over the whole book of sanctity and virtue through all the instances of example, with such delight — to those especially of soft and delicious temper, who will not so much as look upon truth herself unless they see her elegantly dressed — that, whereas the paths of honesty and good life appear now rugged and difficult though they be indeed easy and pleasant, they will then appear to all men both easy and pleasant though they were rugged and difficult indeed." Milton, like Sidney, had a keen æsthetic appreciation of the poetical parts of the Bible, as appears from his estimate of the Song of Solomon and the Book of Revelation, concluding with the following words (*Reason of Church Government*) : " But those frequent songs throughout the law and prophets beyond all these, not in their divine argument alone, but in the very critical art of composition, may be easily made appear over all the kinds of lyric poesy to be incomparable " (see 6 3 ff., 9 19 ff.). And Milton, like Sidney, inveighs against those who persist in writing verse while still ignorant of the first principles of poetry conceived as an ethical force, or rather while deliberately inculcating the negation of all principle, and abandonment to the seductions of vice. Thus again in the *Reason of Church Government*, Milton denounces " the writings and interludes of libidinous and ignorant poetasters, who, having scarce ever heard of that which is the main consistence of a true poem, the choice of such persons as they ought to introduce, and what is moral and decent to each one, do for the most part lay up vicious principles in sweet pills to be swallowed down, and make the taste of virtuous documents harsh and sour " (cf. 45 20 ff., 23 29 ff.).

These comparisons illustrate the consensus of opinion among men of different centuries, but substantially equal endowments, with respect to the ethical function of the highest creative poetry, and its kinship with religion. It can hardly be necessary to provide further proof that Sidney's position is not only defensible, but inexpugnable. As he himself says, poetry may be perverted and turned from its rightful use ; but this being true of every most excellent thing, we should not allow ourselves to be prejudiced by the fact of such abuse, otherwise, if we are logical, we shall approve of nothing, however blameless and salutary in its unpolluted state.

Sidney owes much to Plato, but still more to Aristotle. Plato, in his joy over the new-found virtues of philosophy, was scarcely capable of recognizing poetry as a coördinate, much less a superior, power. He demanded a purer ethics as the guide of life than any which he found in the poetry then extant. That it taught moral lessons he could not deny; but it was neither free from imperfections, nor did it contain, in his view, any sufficient self-regenerative or self-purifying principle. This must be supplied by philosophy. Failing to perceive that his own philosophy was merely a phase of poetry, dependent like poetry upon undemonstrable intuitions for its beauty and efficacy, he endeavored to sunder them by artificial distinctions, though such as must have had a certain validity to his own mind. But in the very act of dethroning poetry he gave it a new title to dominion. The spoils with which he endowed philosophy returned by inheritance to her elder sister and rival. Platonism became the intellectual ally of Christianity, and Christianity generated a new poetry. Nay, Platonism itself reappeared in the intellectual awakening of modern Europe as the quickening impulse, in some instances as the very soul, of Italian and English poetry. Who can measure Michael Angelo's debt to Plato, or Spenser's? In this debt Sidney shared, as his allusions clearly show. As Spenser would not have been the poet we know, had he been deprived of the influence of Plato, so neither would Sidney have been the essayist we know, had he not read and reread the burning pages where poetry strives to masquerade as philosophy, and betrays, by the very rhythm of her movements, her incapacity to keep the sober pace of reasoning prose. But as the framework of the *Fairy Queen* depends upon Aristotle's classification of the virtues, so the framework of the *Defense of Poetry*, or at least of its central and most important division, depends upon the opening paragraphs of Aristotle's *Ethics* and a few sentences from his *Poetics*.

That there is a branch of learning sovran over all the rest, that poetry is superior to history, and that poetry contains a philosophic element, — such were the cardinal truths which Sidney learned from Aristotle. From these premises Sidney deduced that, as poetry superadds a peculiar attractiveness to the philosophic element it embodies, it must in its effects be superior to philosophy, as it is, by the demonstration of Aristotle, to history, and that it must accordingly be entitled to the highest rank among secular learnings. This being granted, the further course of his main argument follows in natural sequence.

Sidney was not unacquainted with Dante, and there are even reasons for supposing that he may have perused one or more of Dante's prose treatises. If the evidence derived from the quotations from Dante on a preceding page is regarded as slight, this may be supplemented by other considerations. In his *Convito*, which is largely based upon Aristotle's *Ethics*, Dante, like Sidney, enters into a defense of his mother-tongue. Sidney, near the close of his argument, supplements this defense of English with a discussion of its prosody, apparently following the example of Dante in his *De Vulgari Eloquio*. Even more curious is the circumstance that Dante attributes the same two senses to the word 'rime' as does Sidney (see note on 56 17). In the *Convito* (Hillard's tr., p. 233), Dante thus distinguishes between these senses: "Strictly speaking, it [i.e. rime] means that correspondence of the ultimate and penultimate syllables which it is customary to use ; generally speaking, it means any speech which, regulated by number and time, falls into rhythmic consonance." These correspondences will hardly be thought accidental, and must incline us to the belief that Sidney had Dante's prose writing in mind in composing his own treatise. The improbability that two authors, one in Italian and the other in English, should independently arrive, in the treatment of themes then so novel in their respective tongues, at so similar a mode of introducing the same subsidiary topics, is too evident to require comment.

Grosart, in his edition of Spenser, suggests that Sidney may have utilized Spenser's unpublished treatise, *The English Poet.* Thus he says (1. 99) : " If not bodily, yet largely, I like to think that we have *The Englishe Poet* utilized at least in Sidney's *Apology* or *Defense of Poetry.* It is also to be remembered it was posthumously published." And again (1. 453-4) : "I may be wrong, but I have a *soupçon* of suspicion that if Sir Philip Sidney had lived to have published his *Defense of Poesy* himself, there would have been an acknowledgment of indebtedness to Spenser in its composition. Is it utterly improbable — as I ventured earlier to suggest — that Sir Philip should have incorporated or adapted the *English Poet* of Spenser in his *Defense?* I trow not. Only thus can I understand its suppression when ' finished ' and ready for the press." Since we know nothing of the contents of Spenser's work, this surmise is incapable of confirmation, and the question thus raised must for ever remain indeterminable.

To sum up our chief results, Sidney's fundamental doctrine is true of the highest creative poetry, and in general of the noblest literature produced by the creative imagination, whether executed in verse or prose. This doctrine is founded upon Aristotle's teaching, and leavened with the best of Plato's spirit, as interpreted and supplemented by Christianity and the literature produced under Christian influence. Of the latter Dante was probably recognized by Sidney as the foremost representative, and he may thus have come to be accepted as Sidney's guide in the conception and arrangement of some of the minor topics of the *Defense.* Finally, his threefold division of poetry is taken from Scaliger's *Poetics* (see note on 9 17). A reference to the Analysis (p. xli ff.) will suffice to show the nature and extent of Sidney's originality, after allowance has been made for his borrowings from predecessors.

6. FOLLOWERS AND IMITATORS.

Sidney's *Defense* must have been extensively circulated in manuscript before its publication in 1595. Extensive quotations from it are found in Puttenham's *Art of English Poesy*, published in 1589; in Harington's *Apology of Poetry*, prefixed to the first edition of his translation of the *Orlando Furioso*, and published in 1591; and in Meres' *Palladis Tamia*, 1598. These have all been reprinted in Haslewood's *Critical Essays upon English Poets and Poesy*, London, 2 vols., the first volume bearing date of 1811, the second of 1815. This edition is the one which has been cited in the notes to the present volume. Harington is outspoken with regard to his knowledge of Sidney (Haslewood, 2. 123): "For as for all, or the most part, of such questions, I will refer you to Sir Philip Sidney's *Apology*, who doth handle them right learnedly." The obligations of the others, however, are no less evident, and it is instructive to observe how Meres makes literal excerpts from Sidney, while Puttenham now adopts his method of treatment, and now employs his illustrations, or slightly varies his phraseology.

Among moderns it is difficult to believe that Shelley was ignorant of Sidney's tractate, though the similarities of opinion may be due to familiarity with common sources in Plato and Aristotle, or to the deeper insight of which genius alone is capable. As to modern imitations in general, it will suffice to quote from the essay on the *Defense* in Vol. 10 of the *Retrospective Review*, published in 1824: "Should it occur to the reader, in the midst of his admiration of these passages, that he has met with something like parts of them before, we can readily believe that he is not mistaken ; for the truth is, that the *Defense of Poesy* has formed the staple of all the ' thousand and one ' dissertations on that art, with which our magazines and reviews have teemed during the last twenty years."

THE DEFENSE OF POESY.

WHEN the right virtuous Edward Wotton and I were at the Emperor's court together, we gave ourselves to learn horsemanship of John Pietro Pugliano, one that with great commendation had the place of an esquire in his stable ; and he, according to the fertileness of the Italian wit, did not only afford us the demonstration of his practice, but sought to enrich our minds with the contemplations therein which he thought most precious. But with none I remember mine ears were at any time more loaden, than when — either angered with slow payment, or moved with our learner-like admiration — he exercised his speech in the praise of his faculty. He said soldiers were the noblest estate of mankind, and horsemen the noblest of soldiers. He said they were the masters of war and ornaments of peace, speedy goers and strong abiders, triumphers both in camps and courts. Nay, to so unbelieved a point he proceeded, as that no earthly thing bred such wonder to a prince as to be a good horseman ; skill of government was but a *pedanteria* in comparison. Then would he add certain praises, by telling what a peerless beast the horse was, the only serviceable courtier without flattery, the beast of most beauty, faithfulness, courage, and such more, that if I had not been a piece of a logician before I came to him, I think he would have persuaded me to have wished myself a horse. But thus much at least with his no few words he drave into me, that self-love is better than any gilding to make that seem gorgeous wherein ourselves be parties.

Wherein if Pugliano's strong affection and weak arguments will not satisfy you, I will give you a nearer example of myself, who, I know not by what mischance, in
these my not old years and idlest times, having slipped
5 into the title of a poet, am provoked to say something
unto you in the defense of that my unelected vocation,
which if I handle with more good will than good reasons,
bear with me, since the scholar is to be pardoned that
followeth the steps of his master. And yet I must say
10 that, as I have just cause to make a pitiful defense of
poor poetry, which from almost the highest estimation of
learning is fallen to be the laughing-stock of children,
so have I need to bring some more available proofs, since
the former is by no man barred of his deserved credit,
15 the silly latter hath had even the names of philosophers
used to the defacing of it, with great danger of civil war
among the Muses.

And first, truly, to all them that, professing learning,
inveigh against poetry, may justly be objected that they
20 go very near to ungratefulness, to seek to deface that
which, in the noblest nations and languages that are
known, hath been the first light-giver to ignorance, and
first nurse, whose milk by little and little enabled them
to feed afterwards of tougher knowledges. And will they
25 now play the hedgehog, that, being received into the
den, drave out his host? Or rather the vipers, that with
their birth kill their parents? Let learned Greece in any
of her manifold sciences be able to show me one book
before Musæus, Homer, and Hesiod, all three nothing
30 else but poets. Nay, let any history be brought that can
say any writers were there before them, if they were not
men of the same skill, as Orpheus, Linus, and some other
are named, who, having been the first of that country
that made pens deliverers of their knowledge to their
35 posterity, may justly challenge to be called their fathers

in learning. For not only in time they had this priority
— although in itself antiquity be venerable — but went
before them as causes, to draw with their charming sweetness the wild untamed wits to an admiration of knowledge. So as Amphion was said to move stones with his ₅
poetry to build Thebes, and Orpheus to be listened to by
beasts, — indeed stony and beastly people. So among
the Romans were Livius Andronicus and Ennius ; so in
the Italian language the first that made it aspire to be a
treasure-house of science were the poets Dante, Boccace, ₁₀
and Petrarch ; so in our English were Gower and
Chaucer, after whom, encouraged and delighted with
their excellent foregoing, others have followed to beautify
our mother-tongue, as well in the same kind as in other
arts.   ₁₅

This did so notably show itself, that the philosophers
of Greece durst not a long time appear to the world but
under the masks of poets. So Thales, Empedocles, and
Parmenides sang their natural philosophy in verses ; so
did Pythagoras and Phocylides their moral counsels ; so ₂₀
did Tyrtæus in war matters, and Solon in matters of
policy ; or rather they, being poets, did exercise their
delightful vein in those points of highest knowledge
which before them lay hidden to the world. For that
wise Solon was directly a poet it is manifest, having ₂₅
written in verse the notable fable of the Atlantic Island
which was continued by Plato. And truly even Plato
whosoever well considereth, shall find that in the body
of his work though the inside and strength were philosophy, the skin as it were and beauty depended most ₃₀
of poetry. For all standeth upon dialogues ; wherein he
feigneth many honest burgesses of Athens to speak of
such matters that, if they had been set on the rack, they
would never have confessed them ; besides his poetical
describing the circumstances of their meetings, as the ₃₅

well-ordering of a banquet, the delicacy of a walk, with
interlacing mere tales, as Gyges' Ring and others, which
who knoweth not to be flowers of poetry did never walk
into Apollo's garden.

5   And even historiographers, although their lips sound
of things done, and verity be written in their foreheads,
have been glad to borrow both fashion and perchance
weight of the poets. So Herodotus entituled his history
by the name of the nine Muses; and both he and all
10 the rest that followed him either stole or usurped of
poetry their passionate describing of passions, the many
particularities of battles which no man could affirm, or,
if that be denied me, long orations put in the mouths
of great kings and captains, which it is certain they
15 never pronounced.

So that truly neither philosopher nor historiographer
could at the first have entered into the gates of popular
judgments, if they had not taken a great passport of
poetry, which in all nations at this day, where learning
20 flourisheth not, is plain to be seen; in all which they
have some feeling of poetry. In Turkey, besides their
lawgiving divines they have no other writers but poets.
In our neighbor country Ireland, where truly learning
goeth very bare, yet are their poets held in a devout
25 reverence. Even among the most barbarous and simple
Indians, where no writing is, yet have they their poets,
who make and sing songs (which they call *areytos*), both
of their ancestors' deeds and praises of their gods, — a
sufficient probability that, if ever learning come among
30 them, it must be by having their hard dull wits softened
and sharpened with the sweet delights of poetry; for
until they find a pleasure in the exercise of the mind,
great promises of much knowledge will little persuade
them that know not the fruits of knowledge. In Wales,
35 the true remnant of the ancient Britons, as there are

good authorities to show the long time they had poets
which they called bards, so through all the conquests
of Romans, Saxons, Danes, and Normans, some of whom
did seek to ruin all memory of learning from among
them, yet do their poets even to this day last; so as it 5
is not more notable in soon beginning, than in long continuing.

But since the authors of most of our sciences were
the Romans, and before them the Greeks, let us a little
stand upon their authorities, but even so far as to see 10
what names they have given unto this now scorned skill.
Among the Romans a poet was called *vates*, which is as
much as a diviner, foreseer, or prophet, as by his conjoined words, *vaticinium* and *vaticinari*, is manifest;
so heavenly a title did that excellent people bestow upon 15
this heart-ravishing knowledge. And so far were they
carried into the admiration thereof, that they thought in
the chanceable hitting upon any such verses great fore-
tokens of their following fortunes were placed; whereupon grew the word of *Sortes Virgilianæ*, when by 20
sudden opening Virgil's book they lighted upon some
verse of his making. Whereof the Histories of the Emperors' Lives are full: as of Albinus, the governor of our
island, who in his childhood met with this verse,

Arma amens capio, nec sat rationis in armis, 25

and in his age performed it. Although it were a very
vain and godless superstition, as also it was to think that
spirits were commanded by such verses — whereupon
this word charms, derived of *carmina*, cometh — so yet
serveth it to show the great reverence those wits were 30
held in, and altogether not without ground, since both
the oracles of Delphos and Sibylla's prophecies were
wholly delivered in verses; for that same exquisite observing of number and measure in words, and that high-

flying liberty of conceit proper to the poet, did seem
to have some divine force in it.

And may not I presume a little further to show the
reasonableness of this word *vates*, and say that the holy
5 David's Psalms are a divine poem? If I do, I shall not
do it without the testimony of great learned men, both
ancient and modern. But even the name of Psalms will
speak for me, which, being interpreted, is nothing but
Songs; then, that it is fully written in metre, as all
10 learned Hebricians agree, although the rules be not yet
fully found; lastly and principally, his handling his proph-
ecy, which is merely poetical. For what else is the awaking his musical instruments, the often and free changing
of persons, his notable prosopopœias, when he maketh
15 you, as it were, see God coming in His majesty, his telling of the beasts' joyfulness and hills' leaping, but a
heavenly poesy, wherein almost he showeth himself a
passionate lover of that unspeakable and everlasting
beauty to be seen by the eyes of the mind, only cleared
20 by faith? But truly now having named him, I fear I
seem to profane that holy name, applying it to poetry,
which is among us thrown down to so ridiculous an estimation. But they that with quiet judgments will look
a little deeper into it, shall find the end and working of
25 it such as, being rightly applied, deserveth not to be
scourged out of the church of God.

But now let us see how the Greeks named it and how
they deemed of it. The Greeks called him ποιητήν,
which name hath, as the most excellent, gone through
30 other languages. It cometh of this word ποιεῖν, which
is "to make"; wherein I know not whether by luck or
wisdom we Englishmen have met with the Greeks in
calling him a maker. Which name how high and incomparable a title it is, I had rather were known by mark-
35 ing the scope of other sciences than by any partial

allegation. There is no art delivered unto mankind that
hath not the works of nature for his principal object,
without which they could not consist, and on which they
so depend as they become actors and players, as it were,
of what nature will have set forth. So doth the astron- 5
omer look upon the stars, and, by that he seeth, set down
what order nature hath taken therein. So do the geometrician and arithmetician in their divers sorts of quantities.
So doth the musician in times tell you which by nature
agree, which not. The natural philosopher thereon hath 10
his name, and the moral philosopher standeth upon the
natural virtues, vices, and passions of man ; and " follow
nature," saith he, "therein, and thou shalt not err."
The lawyer saith what men have determined, the historian what men have done. The grammarian speaketh 15
only of the rules of speech, and the rhetorician and logician, considering what in nature will soonest prove and
persuade, thereon give artificial rules, which still are compassed within the circle of a question, according to the
proposed matter. The physician weigheth the nature of 20
man's body, and the nature of things helpful or hurtful unto it. And the metaphysic, though it be in the
second and abstract notions, and therefore be counted
supernatural, yet doth he, indeed, build upon the depth
of nature. 25

Only the poet, disdaining to be tied to any such sub-
jection, lifted up with the vigor of his own invention,
doth grow, in effect, into another nature, in making
things either better than nature bringeth forth, or, quite
anew, forms such as never were in nature, as the heroes, 30
demi-gods, cyclops, chimeras, furies, and such like ; so
as he goeth hand in hand with nature, not enclosed
within the narrow warrant of her gifts, but freely ranging
within the zodiac of his own wit. Nature never set
forth the earth in so rich tapestry as divers poets have 35

done; neither with pleasant rivers, fruitful trees, sweet-smelling flowers, nor whatsoever else may make the too-much-loved earth more lovely; her world is brazen, the poets only deliver a golden.

5   But let those things alone, and go to man — for whom as the other things are, so it seemeth in him her utter-most cunning is employed — and know whether she have brought forth so true a lover as Theagenes; so constant a friend as Pylades; so valiant a man as Orlando; so 10 right a prince as Xenophon's Cyrus; so excellent a man every way as Virgil's Æneas? Neither let this be jestingly conceived, because the works of the one be essential, the other in imitation or fiction; for any understanding knoweth the skill of each artificer standeth 15 in that idea, or fore-conceit of the work, and not in the work itself. And that the poet hath that idea is mani-fest, by delivering them forth in such excellency as he hath imagined them. Which delivering forth, also, is not wholly imaginative, as we are wont to say by them 20 that build castles in the air; but so far substantially it worketh, not only to make a Cyrus, which had been but a particular excellency, as nature might have done, but to bestow a Cyrus upon the world to make many Cyruses, if they will learn aright why and how that maker made 25 him. Neither let it be deemed too saucy a comparison to balance the highest point of man's wit with the efficacy of nature; but rather give right honor to the Heavenly Maker of that maker, who, having made man to His own likeness, set him beyond and over all the works of that 30 second nature. Which in nothing he showeth so much as in poetry, when with the force of a divine breath he bringeth things forth far surpassing her doings, with no small argument to the incredulous of that first accursed fall of Adam, — since our erected wit maketh us know what 35 perfection is, and yet our infected will keepeth us from

reaching unto it. But these arguments will by few be understood, and by fewer granted; thus much I hope will be given me, that the Greeks with some probability of reason gave him the name above all names of learning. 5

Now let us go to a more ordinary opening of him, that the truth may be the more palpable; and so, I hope, though we get not so unmatched a praise as the etymology of his names will grant, yet his very description, which no man will deny, shall not justly be barred from 10 a principal commendation.

Poesy, therefore, is an art of imitation, for so Aristotle termeth it in his word μίμησις, that is to say, a representing, counterfeiting, or figuring forth; to speak metaphorically, a speaking picture, with this end, — to 15 teach and delight.

Of this have been three general kinds. The chief, both in antiquity and excellency, were they that did imitate the inconceivable excellencies of God. Such were David in his Psalms; Solomon in his Song of Songs, in his 20 Ecclesiastes and Proverbs; Moses and Deborah in their Hymns; and the writer of Job; which, beside other, the learned Emanuel Tremellius and Franciscus Junius do entitle the poetical part of the Scripture. Against these none will speak that hath the Holy Ghost in due holy 25 reverence. In this kind, though in a full wrong divinity, were Orpheus, Amphion, Homer in his Hymns, and many other, both Greeks and Romans. And this poesy must be used by whosoever will follow St. James' counsel in singing psalms when they are merry; and I know 30 is used with the fruit of comfort by some, when, in sorrowful pangs of their death-bringing sins, they find the consolation of the never-leaving goodness.

The second kind is of them that deal with matters philosophical: either moral, as Tyrtæus, Phocylides, and 35

Cato ; or natural, as Lucretius and Virgil's Georgics ; or astronomical, as Manilius and Pontanus ; or historical, as Lucan ; which who mislike, the fault is in their judgment quite out of taste, and not in the sweet food of
5 sweetly uttered knowledge.

But because this second sort is wrapped within the fold of the proposed subject, and takes not the free course of his own invention, whether they properly be poets or no let grammarians dispute, and go to the
10 third, indeed right poets, of whom chiefly this question ariseth. Betwixt whom and these second is such a kind of difference as betwixt the meaner sort of painters, who counterfeit only such faces as are set before them, and the more excellent, who having no law but wit,
15 bestow that in colors upon you which is fittest for the eye to see, — as the constant though lamenting look of Lucretia, when she punished in herself another's fault ; wherein he painteth not Lucretia, whom he never saw, but painteth the outward beauty of such a virtue. For
20 these third be they which most properly do imitate to teach and delight ; and to imitate borrow nothing of what is, hath been, or shall be ; but range, only reined with learned discretion, into the divine consideration of what may be and should be. These be they that, as
25 the first and most noble sort may justly be termed *vates,* so these are waited on in the excellentest languages and best understandings with the foredescribed name of poets. For these, indeed, do merely make to imitate, and imitate both to delight and teach, and delight
30 to move men to take that goodness in hand, which without delight they would fly as from a stranger ; and teach to make them know that goodness whereunto they are moved :—which being the noblest scope to which ever any learning was directed, yet want there not idle tongues
35 to bark at them.

' These be subdivided into sundry more special denomi-
nations. The most notable be the heroic, lyric, tragic,
comic, satiric, iambic, elegiac, pastoral, and certain
others, some of these being termed according to the
matter they deal with, some by the sort of verse they 5
liked best to write in, — for indeed the greatest part of
poets have apparelled their poetical inventions in that
numberous kind of writing which is called verse. Indeed
but apparelled, verse being but an ornament, and no
cause to poetry, since there have been many most excel- 10
lent poets that never versified, and now swarm many
versifiers that need never answer to the name of poets.
For Xenophon, who did imitate so excellently as to give
us *effigiem justi imperii* — the portraiture of a just empire
under the name of Cyrus (as Cicero saith of him) — made 15
therein an absolute heroical poem ; so did Heliodorus in
his sugared invention of that picture of love in Theagenes
and Chariclea ; and yet both these wrote in prose. Which
I speak to show that it is not riming and versing that
maketh a poet — no more than a long gown maketh an 20
advocate, who, though he pleaded in armor, should be
an advocate and no soldier — but it is that feigning
notable images of virtues, vices, or what else, with that
delightful teaching, which must be the right describing
note to know a poet by. Although indeed the senate of 25
poets hath chosen verse as their fittest raiment, meaning, as in matter they passed all in all, so in manner to
go beyond them ; not speaking, table-talk fashion, or like
men in a dream, words as they chanceably fall from the
mouth, but peizing each syllable of each word by just 30
proportion, according to the dignity of the subject.

Now therefore it shall not be amiss, first to weigh
this latter sort of poetry by his works, and then by his
parts ; and if in neither of these anatomies he be con-
demnable, I hope we shall obtain a more favorable sen- 35

tence. This purifying of wit, this enriching of memory,
enabling of judgment, and enlarging of conceit, which
commonly we call learning, under what name soever it
come forth or to what immediate end soever it be
5 directed, the final end is to lead and draw us to as high
a perfection as our degenerate souls, made worse by
their clay lodgings, can be capable of.   This, according
to the inclination of man, bred many-formed impressions.   For some that thought this felicity principally to
10 be gotten by knowledge, and no knowledge to be so
high or heavenly as acquaintance with the stars, gave
themselves to astronomy ; others, persuading themselves
to be demi-gods if they knew the causes of things,
became natural and supernatural philosophers.   Some
15 an admirable delight drew to music, and some the
certainty of demonstration to the mathematics ; but all,
one and other, having this scope : — to know, and by
knowledge to lift up the mind from the dungeon of the
body to the enjoying his own divine essence.   But when
20 by the balance of experience it was found that the
astronomer, looking to the stars, might fall into a ditch,
that the inquiring philosopher might be blind in himself,
and the mathematician might draw forth a straight line
with a crooked heart ; then lo ! did proof, the overruler
25 of opinions, make manifest, that all these are but serving sciences, which, as they have each a private end in
themselves, so yet are they all directed to the highest end
of the mistress-knowledge, by the Greeks called ἀρχιτεκτονική, which stands, as I think, in the knowledge of a
30 man's self, in the ethic and politic consideration, with
the end of well-doing, and not of well-knowing only : —
even as the saddler's next end is to make a good saddle,
but his further end to serve a nobler faculty, which is
horsemanship ; so the horseman's to soldiery ; and the
35 soldier not only to have the skill, but to perform the

practice of a soldier. So that the ending end of all earthly learning being virtuous action, those skills that most serve to bring forth that have a most just title to be princes over all the rest; wherein, if we can show, the poet is worthy to have it before any other competitors. 5

Among whom as principal challengers step forth the moral philosophers; whom, me thinketh, I see coming toward me with a sullen gravity, as though they could not abide vice by daylight; rudely clothed, for to witness outwardly their contempt of outward things; with books 10 in their hands against glory, whereto they set their names; sophistically speaking against subtility; and angry with any man in whom they see the foul fault of anger. These men, casting largess as they go of definitions, divisions, and distinctions, with a scornful interrogative 15 do soberly ask whether it be possible to find any path so ready to lead a man to virtue, as that which teacheth what virtue is, and teacheth it not only by delivering forth his very being, his causes and effects, but also by making known his enemy, vice, which must 20 be destroyed, and his cumbersome servant, passion, which must be mastered; by showing the generalities that contain it, and the specialities that are derived from it; lastly, by plain setting down how it extendeth itself out of the limits of a man's own little world, to the govern- 25 ment of families, and maintaining of public societies?

The historian scarcely giveth leisure to the moralist to say so much, but that he, loaden with old mouse-eaten records, authorizing himself for the most part upon other histories, whose greatest authorities are built upon 30 the notable foundation of hearsay; having much ado to accord differing writers, and to pick truth out of partiality; better acquainted with a thousand years ago than with the present age, and yet better knowing how this world goeth than how his own wit runneth; curious for 35

antiquities and inquisitive of novelties, a wonder to young folks and a tyrant in table-talk ; denieth, in a great chafe, that any man for teaching of virtue and virtuous actions is comparable to him. " I am *testis temporum, lux veri-*
5 *tatis, vita memoriæ, magistra vitæ, nuntia vetustatis.* The philosopher," saith he, " teacheth a disputative virtue, but I do an active. His virtue is excellent in the dangerless Academy of Plato, but mine showeth forth her honorable face in the battles of Marathon, Pharsalia,
10 Poitiers, and Agincourt. He teacheth virtue by certain abstract considerations, but I only bid you follow the footing of them that have gone before you. Old-aged experience goeth beyond the fine-witted philosopher ; but I give the experience of many ages. Lastly, if he
15 make the song-book, I put the learner's hand to the lute ; and if he be the guide, I am the light." Then would he allege you innumerable examples, confirming story by story, how much the wisest senators and princes have been directed by the credit of history, as
20 Brutus, Alphonsus of Aragon — and who not, if need be ? At length the long line of their disputation maketh a point in this, — that the one giveth the precept, and the other the example.

Now whom shall we find, since the question standeth
25 for the highest form in the school of learning, to be moderator ? Truly, as me seemeth, the poet ; and if not a moderator, even the man that ought to carry the title from them both, and much more from all other serving sciences. Therefore compare we the poet with
30 the historian and with the moral philosopher ; and if he go beyond them both, no other human skill can match him. For as for the divine, with all reverence it is ever to be excepted, not only for having his scope as far beyond any of these as eternity exceedeth a moment,
35 but even for passing each of these in themselves. And '

for the lawyer, though *Jus* be the daughter of Justice,
and Justice the chief of virtues, yet because he seeketh to
make men good rather *formidine pœnæ* than *virtutis*
amore; or, to say righter, doth not endeavor to make
men good, but that their evil hurt not others; having no 5
care, so he be a good citizen, how bad a man he be;
therefore, as our wickedness maketh him necessary, and
necessity maketh him honorable, so is he not in the
deepest truth to stand in rank with these, who all
endeavor to take naughtiness away, and plant goodness 10
even in the secretest cabinet of our souls. ' And these
four are all that any way deal in that consideration of
men's manners, which being the supreme knowledge,
they that best breed it deserve the best commendation.

  The philosopher therefore and the historian are they 15
which would win the goal, the one by precept, the other
by example; but both not having both, do both halt.
For the philosopher, setting down with thorny arguments the bare rule, is so hard of utterance and so
misty to be conceived, that one that hath no other guide 20
but him shall wade in him till he be old, before he
shall find sufficient cause to be honest. For his knowledge standeth so upon the abstract and general that
happy is that man who may understand him, and more
happy that can apply what he doth understand. On the 25
other side, the historian, wanting the precept, is so tied,
not to what should be but to what is, to the particular
truth of things and not to the general reason of things,
that his example draweth no necessary consequence, and
therefore a less fruitful doctrine.   30

  Now doth the peerless poet perform both; for whatsoever the philosopher saith should be done, he giveth a
perfect picture of it in some one by whom he presup-
poseth it was done, so as he coupleth the general notion
with the particular example. A perfect picture, I say; 35

for he yieldeth to the powers of the mind an image of
that whereof the philosopher bestoweth but a wordish
description, which doth neither strike, pierce, nor possess
the sight of the soul so much as that other doth. • For
5 as, in outward things, to a man that had never seen an
elephant or a rhinoceros, who should tell him most
exquisitely all their shapes, color, bigness, and particular
marks; or of a gorgeous palace, an architector, with
declaring the full beauties, might well make the hearer
10 able to repeat, as it were by rote, all he had heard, yet
should never satisfy his inward conceit with being witness to itself of a true lively knowledge; but the same
man, as soon as he might see those beasts well painted,
or that house well in model, should straightways grow,
15 without need of any description, to a judicial compre-
hending of them:• so no doubt the philosopher, with
his learned definitions, be it of virtues or vices, matters
of public policy or private government, replenisheth the
memory with many infallible grounds of wisdom, which
20 notwithstanding lie dark before the imaginative and
judging power, if they be not illuminated or figured forth
by the speaking picture of poesy.

Tully taketh much pains, and many times not without
poetical helps, to make us know the force love of our
25 country hath in us.   Let us but hear old Anchises speaking in the midst of Troy's flames, or see Ulysses, in the
fulness of all Calypso's delights, bewail his absence from
barren and beggarly Ithaca.   Anger, the Stoics said, was
a short madness.   Let but Sophocles bring you Ajax on a
30 stage, killing and whipping sheep and oxen, thinking them
the army of Greeks, with their chieftains Agamemnon
and Menelaus, and tell me if you have not a more
familiar insight into anger, than finding in the schoolmen
his genus and difference. • See whether wisdom and
35 temperance in Ulysses and Diomedes, valor in Achilles,

friendship in Nisus and Euryalus, even to an ignorant man carry not an apparent shining. ' And, contrarily, the remorse of conscience in Œdipus; the soon-repenting pride of Agamemnon; the self-devouring cruelty in his father Atreus; the violence of ambition in the two 5 Theban brothers; the sour sweetness of revenge in Medea; and, to fall lower, the Terentian Gnatho and our Chaucer's Pandar so expressed that we now use their names to signify their trades; and finally, all virtues, vices, and passions so in their own natural states laid to 10 the view, that we seem not to hear of them, but clearly to see through them.

But even in the most excellent determination of goodness, what philosopher's counsel can so readily direct a prince, as the feigned Cyrus in Xenophon? Or a virtuous 15 man in all fortunes, as Æneas in Virgil? Or a whole commonwealth, as the way of Sir Thomas More's Utopia? I say the way, because where Sir Thomas More erred, it was the fault of the man, and not of the poet; for that way of patterning a commonwealth was most 20 absolute, though he, perchance, hath not so absolutely performed it. For the question is, whether the feigned image of poesy, or the regular instruction of philosophy, hath the more force in teaching. Wherein if the philosophers have more rightly showed themselves philoso- 25 phers than the poets have attained to the high top of their profession, — as in truth,

> Mediocribus esse poetis
> Non Dii, non homines, non concessere columnæ, —

it is, I say again, not the fault of the art, but that by few 30 men that art can be accomplished.

Certainly, even our Saviour Christ could as well have given the moral commonplaces of uncharitableness and humbleness as the divine narration of Dives and Laz-

.arus; or of disobedience and mercy, as that heavenly
discourse of the lost child and the gracious father; but
that his through-searching wisdom knew the estate of
Dives burning in hell, and of Lazarus in Abraham's
5 bosom, would more constantly, as it were, inhabit both
the memory and judgment. Truly, for myself, me seems
I see before mine eyes the lost child's disdainful prodigality, turned to envy a swine's dinner; which by the
learned divines are thought not historical acts, but in-
10 structing parables.

For conclusion, I say the philosopher teacheth, but he
teacheth obscurely, so as the learned only can understand him; that is to say, he teacheth them that are
already taught. But the poet is the food for the ten-
15 derest stomachs; the poet is indeed the right popular
philosopher. Whereof Æsop's tales give good proof;
whose pretty allegories, stealing under the formal tales
of beasts, make many, more beastly than beasts, begin
to hear the sound of virtue from those dumb speakers.

20 But now may it be alleged that if this imagining of
matters be so fit for the imagination, then must the historian needs surpass, who bringeth you images of true
matters, such as indeed were done, and not such as
fantastically or falsely may be suggested to have been
25 done. Truly, Aristotle himself, in his Discourse of Poesy,
plainly determineth this question, saying that poetry is
φιλοσοφώτερον and σπουδαιότερον, that is to say, it is more
philosophical and more studiously serious than history.
His reason is, because poesy dealeth with καθόλου, that is
30 to say with the universal consideration, and the history
with καθ' ἕκαστον, the particular. "Now," saith he, "the
universal weighs what is fit to be said or done, either
in likelihood or necessity—which the poesy considereth
in his imposed names; and the particular only marketh
35 whether Alcibiades did, or suffered, this or that:" thus

far Aristotle. Which reason of his, as all his, is most full of reason.

For, indeed, if the question were whether it were better to have a particular act truly or falsely set down, there is no doubt which is to be chosen, no more than whether s you had rather have Vespasian's picture right as he was, or, at the painter's pleasure, nothing resembling. But if the question be for your own use and learning, whether it be better to have it set down as it should be or as it was, then certainly is more doctrinable the feigned Cyrus 10 in Xenophon than the true Cyrus in Justin; and the feigned Æneas in Virgil than the right Æneas in Dares Phrygius; as to a lady that desired to fashion her countenance to the best grace, a painter should more benefit her to portrait a most sweet face, writing Canidia upon 15 it, than to paint Canidia as she was, who, Horace sweareth, was foul and ill-favored.

If the poet do his part aright, he will show you in Tantalus, Atreus, and such like, nothing that is not to be shunned; in Cyrus, Æneas, Ulysses, each thing to be 20 followed. Where the historian, bound to tell things as things were, cannot be liberal — without he will be poetical — of a perfect pattern; but, as in Alexander, or Scipio himself, show doings, some to be liked, some to be misliked; and then how will you discern what to 25 follow but by your own discretion, which you had without reading Quintus Curtius? And whereas a man may say, though in universal consideration of doctrine the poet prevaileth, yet that the history, in his saying such a thing was done, doth warrant a man more in that he shall 30 follow,— the answer is manifest: that if he stand upon that *was*, as if he should argue, because it rained yesterday therefore it should rain to-day, then indeed it hath some advantage to a gross conceit. But if he know an example only informs a conjectured likelihood, and 35

so go by reason, the poet doth so far exceed him as he
is to frame his example to that which is most reasonable,
be it in warlike, politic, or private matters; where the
historian in his bare *was* hath many times that which we
5 call fortune to overrule the best wisdom. ' Many times
he must tell events whereof he can yield no cause; or
if he do, it must be poetically.

For, that a feigned example hath as much force to
teach as a true example — for as for to move, it is clear,
10 since the feigned may be tuned to the highest key of
passion — let us take one example wherein a poet and a
historian do concur.   Herodotus and Justin do both testify that Zopyrus, king Darius' faithful servant, seeing
his master long resisted by the rebellious Babylonians,
15 feigned himself in extreme disgrace of his king; for
verifying of which he caused his own nose and ears to
be cut off, and so flying to the Babylonians, was received,
and for his known valor so far credited, that he did
find means to deliver them over to Darius.   Much-like
20 matter doth Livy record of Tarquinius and his son.
Xenophon excellently feigneth such another stratagem,
performed by Abradatas in Cyrus' behalf.   Now would I
fain know, if occasion be presented unto you to serve
your prince by such an honest dissimulation, why do you
25 not as well learn it of Xenophon's fiction as of the
other's verity? and, truly, so much the better, as you
shall save your nose by the bargain; for Abradatas did
not counterfeit so far.

So, then, the best of the historian is subject to the
30 poet; for whatsoever action or faction, whatsoever counsel,
policy, or war-stratagem the historian is bound to recite,
that may the poet, if he list, with his imitation make his
own, beautifying it both for further teaching and more
delighting, as it pleaseth him; having all, from Dante's
35 Heaven to his Hell, under the authority of his pen.

Which if I be asked what poets have done? so as I
might well name some, yet say I, and say again, I speak
of the art, and not of the artificer.

Now, to that which commonly is attributed to the
praise of history, in respect of the notable learning 5
is gotten by marking the success, as though therein
a man should see virtue exalted and vice punished, —
truly that commendation is peculiar to poetry and far
off from history. For, indeed, poetry ever setteth virtue
so out in her best colors, making Fortune her well-waiting 10
handmaid, that one must needs be enamored of her.
Well may you see Ulysses in a storm, and in other hard
plights; but they are but exercises of patience and
magnanimity, to make them shine the more in the near
following prosperity.' And, of the contrary part, if evil 15
men come to the stage, they ever go out — as the tragedy
writer answered to one that misliked the show of such
persons — so manacled as they little animate folks to
follow them.' But the historian, being captived to the truth
of a foolish world, is many times a terror from well-doing, 20
and an encouragement to unbridled wickedness. For
see we not valiant Miltiades rot in his fetters? The just
Phocion and the accomplished Socrates put to death
like traitors? The cruel Severus live prosperously? The
excellent Severus miserably murdered? Sylla and Marius 25
dying in their beds? Pompey and Cicero slain then,
when they would have thought exile a happiness? See
we not virtuous Cato driven to kill himself, and rebel
Cæsar so advanced that his name yet, after sixteen hundred years, lasteth in the highest honor? And mark but 30
even Cæsar's own words of the forenamed Sylla — who
in that only did honestly, to put down his dishonest
tyranny — *literas nescivit:* as if want of learning caused
him to do well. He meant it not by poetry, which, not
content with earthly plagues, deviseth new punishments 35

in hell for tyrants; nor yet by philosophy, which teacheth *occidendos esse;* but, no doubt, by skill in history,
for that indeed can afford you Cypselus, Periander,
Phalaris, Dionysius, and I know not how many more of
5 the same kennel, that speed well enough in their abominable injustice or usurpation.

I conclude, therefore, that he excelleth history, not
only in furnishing the mind with knowledge, but in setting it forward to that which deserveth to be called and
10 accounted good; which setting forward, and moving to
well-doing, indeed setteth the laurel crown upon the
poet as victorious, not only of the historian, but over
the philosopher, howsoever in teaching it may be ques-
tionable. For suppose it be granted — that which I sup-
15 pose with great reason may be denied — that the philosopher, in respect of his methodical proceeding, teach
more perfectly than the poet, yet do I think that no
man is so much φιλοφιλόσοφος as to compare the philosopher in moving with the poet. And that moving is of a
20 higher degree than teaching, it may by this appear, that
it is well nigh both the cause and the effect of teaching;
for who will be taught, if he be not moved with desire to
be taught? And what so much good doth that teaching
bring forth — I speak still of moral doctrine — as that
25 it moveth one to do that which it doth teach? For, as
Aristotle saith, it is not γνῶσις but πρᾶξις must be the
fruit; and how πρᾶξις cannot be, without being moved to
practise, it is no hard matter to consider. The philosopher showeth you the way, he informeth you of the par-
30 ticularities, as well of the tediousness of the way, as of
the pleasant lodging you shall have when your journey is
ended, as of the many by-turnings that may divert you
from your way; but this is to no man but to him that
will read him, and read him with attentive, studious pain-
35 fulness; which constant desire whosoever hath in him,

hath already passed half the hardness of the way, and therefore is beholding to the philosopher but for the other half. ᐅNay, truly, learned men have learnedly thought, that where once reason hath so much overmastered passion as that the mind hath a free desire to do well, the inward light each mind hath in itself is as good as a philosopher's book; since in nature we know it is well to do well, and what is well and what is evil, although not in the words of art which philosophers bestow upon us ; for out of natural conceit the philosophers drew it.   But to be moved to do that which we know, or to be moved with desire to know, *hoc opus, hic labor est.*

Now therein of all sciences — I speak still of human, and according to the human conceit — is our poet the monarch.   For he doth not only show the way, but giveth so sweet a prospect into the way as will entice any man to enter into it.   Nay, he doth, as if your journey should lie through a fair vineyard, at the very first give you a cluster of grapes, that full of that taste you may long to pass further.   He beginneth not with obscure definitions, which must blur the margent with interpretations, and load the memory with doubtfulness.   But he cometh to you with words set in delightful proportion, either accompanied with, or prepared for, the well-enchanting skill of music; and with a tale, forsooth, he cometh unto you, with a tale which holdeth children from play, and old men from the chimney-corner, and, pretending no more, doth intend the winning of the mind from wickedness to virtue; even as the child is often brought to take most wholesome things, by hiding them in such other as have a pleasant taste, — which, if one should begin to tell them the nature of the aloes or rhubarb they should receive, would sooner take their physic at their ears than at their mouth.· So is it in men, most of which are childish in the best things, till they

be cradled in their graves, — glad they will be to hear
the tales of Hercules, Achilles, Cyrus, Æneas; and, hearing them, must needs hear the right description of
wisdom, valor, and justice ; which, if they had been
5 barely, that is to say philosophically, set out, they would
swear they be brought to school again.

⌐ That imitation whereof poetry is, hath the most conveniency to nature of all other ; insomuch that, as Aristotle
saith, those things which in themselves are horrible, as
10 cruel battles, unnatural monsters, are made in poetical
imitation delightful.   Truly, I have known men, that even
with reading Amadis de Gaule, which, God knoweth,
wanteth much of a perfect poesy, have found their hearts
moved to the exercise of courtesy, liberality, and espe-
15 cially courage.   Who readeth Æneas carrying old Anchises on his back, that wisheth not it were his fortune
to perform so excellent an act?   Whom do not those
words of Turnus move, the tale of Turnus having planted
his image in the imagination?

20   Fugientem hæc terra videbit?
              Usque adeone mori miserum est?

Where the philosophers, as they scorn to delight, so must
they be content little to move — saving wrangling whether
virtue be the chief or the only good, whether the con-
25 templative or the active life do excel — which Plato
and Boethius well knew, and therefore made Mistress
Philosophy very often borrow the masking raiment of
Poesy.   For even those hard-hearted evil men who
think virtue a school-name, and know no other good
30 but *indulgere genio*, and therefore despise the austere
admonitions of the philosopher, and feel not the inward
reason they stand upon, yet will be content to be delighted, which is all the good-fellow poet seemeth to
promise ; and so steal to see the form of goodness —

which seen, they cannot but love — ere themselves be
aware, as if they took a medicine of cherries.

Infinite proofs of the strange effects of this poetical
invention might be alleged; only two shall serve, which
are so often remembered as I think all men know them. 5
The one of Menenius Agrippa, who, when the whole
people of Rome had resolutely divided themselves from
the senate, with apparent show of utter ruin, though he
were, for that time, an excellent orator, came not among
them upon trust either of figurative speeches or cunning 10
insinuations, and much less with far-fet maxims of philosophy, which, especially if they were Platonic, they must
have learned geometry before they could well have conceived ; but, forsooth, he behaves himself like a homely
and familiar poet. He telleth them a tale, that there 15
was a time when all the parts of the body made a
mutinous conspiracy against the belly, which they thought
devoured the fruits of each other's labor ; they con-
cluded they would let so unprofitable a spender starve.
In the end, to be short — for the tale is notorious, and 20
as notorious that it was a tale — with punishing the belly
they plagued themselves. This, applied by him, wrought
such effect in the people, as I never read that ever words
brought forth but then so sudden and so good an altera-
tion ; for upon reasonable conditions a perfect reconcile- 25
ment ensued.

The other is of Nathan the prophet, who, when the
holy David had so far forsaken God as to confirm adul-
tery with murder, when he was to do the tenderest office
of a friend, in laying his own shame before his eyes, — 30
sent by God to call again so chosen a servant, how doth
he it but by telling of a man whose beloved lamb was
ungratefully taken from his bosom ? The application
most divinely true, but the discourse itself feigned ; which
made David (I speak of the second and instrumental 35

cause) as in a glass to see his own filthiness, as that
heavenly Psalm of Mercy well testifieth.

By these, therefore, examples and reasons, I think it
may be manifest that the poet, with that same hand of
5 delight, doth draw the mind more effectually than any
other art doth. And so a conclusion not unfitly ensueth :
that as virtue is the most excellent resting-place for all
worldly learning to make his end of, so poetry, being the
most familiar to teach it, and most princely to move
10 towards it, in the most excellent work is the most excellent workman.

But I am content not only to decipher him by his
works — although works in commendation or dispraise
must ever hold a high authority — but more narrowly will
15 examine his parts; so that, as in a man, though all
together may carry a presence full of majesty and beauty,
perchance in some one defectious piece we may find
a blemish.

Now in his parts, kinds, or species, as you list to term
20 them, it is to be noted that some poesies have coupled
together two or three kinds, — as tragical and comical,
whereupon is risen the tragi-comical; some, in the like
manner, have mingled prose and verse, as Sannazzaro and
Boethius; some have mingled matters heroical and pas-
25 toral; but that cometh all to one in this question, for,
if severed they be good, the conjunction cannot be hurtful. Therefore, perchance forgetting some, and leaving
some as needless to be remembered, it shall not be
amiss in a word to cite the special kinds, to see what
30 faults may be found in the right use of them.

Is it then the pastoral poem which is misliked? — for
perchance where the hedge is lowest they will soonest
leap over. Is the poor pipe disdained, which sometimes out of Meliboeus' mouth can show the misery of
35 people under hard lords and ravening soldiers, and

again, by Tityrus, what blessedness is derived to them
that lie lowest from the goodness of them that sit highest?
sometimes, under the pretty tales of wolves and sheep,
can include the whole considerations of wrong-doing and
patience ; sometimes show that contention for trifles can 5
get but a trifling victory ; where perchance a man may
see that even Alexander and Darius, when they strave
who should be cock of this world's dunghill, the benefit
they got was that the after-livers may say :

> Hæc memini et victum frustra contendere Thyrsim;   10
> Ex illo Corydon, Corydon est tempore nobis.

Or is it the lamenting elegiac, which in a kind heart
would move rather pity than blame ; who bewaileth, with
the great philosopher Heraclitus, the weakness of mankind and the wretchedness of the world ; who surely is 15
to be praised, either for compassionate accompanying
just causes of lamentation, or for rightly painting out
how weak be the passions of wofulness?

Is it the bitter but wholesome iambic, who rubs the
galled mind, in making shame the trumpet of villainy with 20
bold and open crying out against naughtiness?

Or the satiric? who

> Omne vafer vitium ridenti tangit amico;

who sportingly never leaveth till he make a man laugh
at folly, and at length ashamed to laugh at himself, which 25
he cannot avoid without avoiding the folly ; who, while
circum præcordia ludit, giveth us to feel how many head-
aches a passionate life bringeth us to, — how, when all
is done,

> Est Ulubris, animus si nos non deficit æquus.   30

No, perchance it is the comic ; whom naughty play-
makers and stage-keepers have justly made odious. To
the argument of abuse I will answer after. Only thus

much now is to be said, that the comedy is an imitation
of the common errors of our life, which he representeth
in the most ridiculous and scornful sort that may be, so
as it is impossible that any beholder can be content to
5 be such a one.   Now, as in geometry the oblique must
be known as well as the right, and in arithmetic the odd
as well as the even ; so in the actions of our life who
seeth not the filthiness of evil, wanteth a great foil to
perceive the beauty of virtue.   This doth the comedy
10 handle so, in our private and domestical matters, as with
hearing it we get, as it were, an experience what is
to be looked for of a niggardly Demea, of a crafty
Davus, of a flattering Gnatho, of a vain-glorious Thraso ;
and not only to know what effects are to be expected,
15 but to know who be such, by the signifying badge given
them by the comedian.   And little reason hath any man
to say that men learn evil by seeing it so set out ;
since, as I said before, there is no man living, but by the
force truth hath in nature, no sooner seeth these men
20 play their parts, but wisheth them *in* ━━ *tri* ━━ although
perchance the sack of his own faults lie so behind his
back, that he seeth not himself to dance the same measure, — whereto yet nothing can more open his eyes than
to find his own actions contemptibly set forth.
25   So that the right use of comedy will, I think, by nobody
be blamed, and much less of the high and excellent
tragedy, that openeth the greatest wounds, and showeth
forth the ulcers that are covered with tissue ; that maketh kings fear to be tyrants, and tyrants manifest their
30 tyrannical humors ; that with stirring the effects of admiration and commiseration teacheth the uncertainty of
this world, and upon how weak foundations gilden roofs
are builded ; that maketh us know :

        Qui sceptra sævus duro imperio regit,
35   Timet timentes, metus in auctorem redit.

But how much it can move, Plutarch yieldeth a notable
testimony of the abominable tyrant Alexander Pheræus;
from whose eyes a tragedy, well made and represented,
drew abundance of tears, who without all pity had murdered infinite numbers, and some of his own blood; so as 5
he that was not ashamed to make matters for tragedies, yet
could not resist the sweet violence of a tragedy. And if
it wrought no further good in him, it was that he, in despite of himself, withdrew himself from hearkening to that
which might mollify his hardened heart. But it is not 10
the tragedy they do mislike, for it were too absurd to
cast out so excellent a representation of whatsoever is
most worthy to be learned.

Is it the lyric that most displeaseth, who with his tuned
lyre and well-accorded voice, giveth praise, the reward of 15
virtue, to virtuous acts; who giveth moral precepts and
natural problems; who sometimes raiseth up his voice
to the height of the heavens, in singing the lauds of the
immortal God? Certainly I must confess mine own
barbarousness; I never heard the old song of Percy and 20
Douglas that I found not my heart moved more than
with a trumpet; and yet it is sung but by some blind
crowder, with no rougher voice than rude style; which
being so evil apparelled in the dust and cobwebs of that
uncivil age, what would it work, trimmed in the gorgeous 25
eloquence of Pindar? In Hungary I have seen it the
manner at all feasts, and other such meetings, to have
songs of their ancestors' valor, which that right soldier-
like nation think the chiefest kindlers of brave courage.
The incomparable Lacedæmonians did not only carry 30
that kind of music ever with them to the field, but even
at home, as such songs were made, so were they all
content to be singers of them; when the lusty men were
to tell what they did, the old men what they had done,
and the young men what they would do. And where a 35

man may say that Pindar many times praiseth highly
victories of small moment, matters rather of sport than
virtue; as it may be answered, it was the fault of the
poet, and not of the poetry, so indeed the chief fault
5 was in the time and custom of the Greeks, who set
those toys at so high a price that Philip of Macedon
reckoned a horserace won at Olympus among his three
fearful felicities.   But as the unimitable Pindar often did,
so is that kind most capable and most fit to awake the
10 thoughts from the sleep of idleness, to embrace honorable enterprises.

There rests the heroical, whose very name, I think,
should daunt all backbiters.   For by what conceit can a
tongue be directed to speak evil of that which draweth
15 with it no less champions than Achilles, Cyrus, Æneas,
Turnus, Tydeus, Rinaldo? who doth not only teach and
move to a truth, but teacheth and moveth to the most
high and excellent truth; who maketh magnanimity and
justice shine through all misty fearfulness and foggy
20 desires; who, if the saying of Plato and Tully be true,
that who could see virtue would be wonderfully ravished
with the love of her beauty, this man setteth her out to
make her more lovely, in her holiday apparel, to the eye
of any that will deign not to disdain until they under-
25 stand.   But if anything be already said in the defense of
sweet poetry, all concurreth to the maintaining the heroical, which is not only a kind, but the best and most
accomplished kind of poetry.   For, as the image of each
action stirreth and instructeth the mind, so the lofty
30 image of such worthies most inflameth the mind with
desire to be worthy, and informs with counsel how to be
worthy.   Only let Æneas be worn in the tablet of your
memory, how he governeth himself in the ruin of his
country; in the preserving his old father, and carrying
35 away his religious ceremonies; in obeying the god's com-

mandment to leave Dido, though not only all passionate kindness, but even the human consideration of virtuous gratefulness, would have craved other of him ; how
in storms, how in sports, how in war, how in peace, how
a fugitive, how victorious, how besieged, how besieging, 5
how to strangers, how to allies, how to enemies, how to
his own ; lastly, how in his inward self, and how in his
outward government ; and I think, in a mind most prejudiced with a prejudicating humor, he will be found in
excellency fruitful, — yea, even as Horace saith, *melius* 10
Chrysippo et Crantore. But truly I imagine it falleth out
with these poet-whippers as with some good women who
often are sick, but in faith they cannot tell where. So
the name of poetry is odious to them, but neither his
cause nor effects, neither the sum that contains him nor 15
the particularities descending from him, give any fast
handle to their carping dispraise.

Since, then, poetry is of all human learnings the most
ancient and of most fatherly antiquity, as from whence
other learnings have taken their beginnings ; since it is so 20
universal that no learned nation doth despise it, nor barbarous
nation is without it ; since both Roman and Greek gave
divine names unto it, the one of "prophesying," the other
of "making," and that indeed that name of "making" is fit
for him, considering that whereas other arts retain them- 25
selves within their subject, and receive, as it were, their
being from it, the poet only bringeth his own stuff, and doth
not learn a conceit out of a matter, but maketh matter for
a conceit ; since neither his description nor his end containeth
any evil, the thing described cannot be evil ; since his effects 30
be so good as to teach goodness, and delight the learners of
it ; since therein — namely in moral doctrine, the chief of
all knowledges — he doth not only far pass the historian,
but for instructing is well nigh comparable to the philosopher, and for moving leaveth him behind him ; since the 35

Holy Scripture, wherein there is no uncleanness, hath whole parts in it poetical, and that even our Saviour Christ vouchsafed to use the flowers of it; since all his kinds are not only in their united forms, but in their several dissections
5 fully commendable; I think, and think I think rightly, the laurel crown appointed for triumphant captains doth worthily, of all other learnings, honor the poet's triumph.

But because we have ears as well as tongues, and that the lightest reasons that may be will seem to weigh
10 greatly, if nothing be put in the counter-balance, let us hear, and, as well as we can, ponder, what objections be made against this art, which may be worthy either of yielding or answering.

First, truly, I note. not only in these μισομοῦσοι, poet-
15 haters, but in all that kind of people who seek a praise by dispraising others, that they do prodigally spend a great many wandering words in quips and scoffs, carping and taunting at each thing which, by stirring the spleen, may stay the brain from a through-beholding the worthi-
20 ness of the subject. Those kind of objections, as they are full of a very idle easiness — since there is nothing of so sacred a majesty but that an itching tongue may rub itself upon it — so deserve they no other answer, but, instead of laughing at the jest, to laugh at the jester.
25 We know a playing wit can praise the discretion of an ass, the comfortableness of being in debt, and the jolly commodity of being sick of the plague. So of the contrary side, if we will turn Ovid's verse,

Ut lateat virtus proximitate mali,

30 "that good lie hid in nearness of the evil," Agrippa will be as merry in showing the vanity of science, as Erasmus was in commending of folly; neither shall any man or matter escape some touch of these smiling railers. But for Erasmus and Agrippa, they had another foundation

than the superficial part would promise. Marry, these
other pleasant fault-finders, who will correct the verb
before they understand the noun, and confute others'
knowledge before they confirm their own, I would have
them only remember that scoffing cometh not of wisdom ; 5
so as the best title in true English they get with their
merriments is to be called good fools, — for so have our
grave forefathers ever termed that humorous kind of
jesters.

But that which giveth greatest scope to their scorning 10
humor is riming and versing.   It is already said, and
as I think truly said, it is not riming and versing that
maketh poesy.   One may be a poet without versing, and
a versifier without poetry.   But yet presuppose it were
inseparable — as indeed it seemeth Scaliger judgeth — 15
truly it were an inseparable commendation.   For if *oratio*
next to *ratio*, speech next to reason, be the greatest
gift bestowed upon mortality, that cannot be praiseless
which doth most polish that blessing of speech ; which
considereth each word, not only as a man may say by 20
his forcible quality, but by his best-measured quantity ;
carrying even in themselves a harmony, — without, perchance, number, measure, order, proportion be in our
time grown odious.

But lay aside the just praise it hath by being the only 25
fit speech for music — music, I say, the most divine
striker of the senses — thus much is undoubtedly true,
that if reading be foolish without remembering, memory
being the only treasurer of knowledge, those words which
are fittest for memory are likewise most convenient for 30
knowledge.   Now that verse far exceedeth prose in the
knitting up of the memory, the reason is manifest ; the
words, besides their delight, which hath a great affinity
to memory, being so set, as one cannot be lost but
the whole work fails ; which, accusing itself, calleth the 35

remembrance back to itself, and so most strongly con-
firmeth it. Besides, one word so, as it were, begetting
another, as, be it in rime or measured verse, by the
former a man shall have a near guess to the follower.
5 Lastly, even they that have taught the art of memory
have showed nothing so apt for it as a certain room
divided into many places, well and throughly known;
now that hath the verse in effect perfectly, every word
having his natural seat, which seat must needs make the
10 word remembered. But what needeth more in a thing so
known to all men? Who is it that ever was a scholar
that doth not carry away some verses of Virgil, Horace,
or Cato, which in his youth he learned, and even to his
old age serve him for hourly lessons? as :

15   Percontatorem fugito, nam garrulus idem est.
       Dum sibi quisque placet, credula turba sumus.

But the fitness it hath for memory is notably proved by
all delivery of arts, wherein, for the most part, from
grammar to logic, mathematic, physic, and the rest, the
20 rules chiefly necessary to be borne away are compiled in
verses. So that verse being in itself sweet and orderly,
and being best for memory, the only handle of knowledge, it must be in jest that any man can speak against it.
| Now then go we to the most important imputations
25 laid to the poor poets; for aught I can yet learn they
are these.

First, that there being many other more fruitful knowledges, a man might better spend his time in them than
in this.

30   Secondly, that it is the mother of lies.
   Thirdly, that it is the nurse of abuse, infecting us with
many pestilent desires, with a siren's sweetness drawing
the mind to the serpent's tail of sinful fancies, — and
herein especially comedies give the largest field to ear,

as Chaucer saith ; how, both in other nations and in ours, before poets did soften us, we were full of courage, given to martial exercises, the pillars of manlike liberty, and not lulled asleep in shady idleness with poets' pastimes.

And, lastly and chiefly, they cry out with an open mouth, 5 as if they had overshot Robin Hood, that Plato banished them out of his Commonwealth. Truly this is much, if there be much truth in it.

First, to the first, that a man might better spend his time is a reason indeed ; but it doth, as they say, but 10 *petere principium.* For if it be, as I affirm, that no learning is so good as that which teacheth and moveth to virtue, and that none can both teach and move thereto so much as poesy, then is the conclusion manifest that ink and paper cannot be to a more profitable purpose 15 employed. And certainly, though a man should grant their first assumption, it should follow, me thinks, very unwillingly, that good is not good because better is better. But I still and utterly deny that there is sprung out of earth a more fruitful knowledge. 20

To the second therefore, that they should be the principal liars, I answer paradoxically, but truly, I think truly, that of all writers under the sun the poet is the least liar ; and though he would, as a poet can scarcely be a liar. The astronomer, with his cousin the geometri- 25 cian, can hardly escape when they take upon them to measure the height of the stars. How often, think you, do the physicians lie, when they aver things good for sicknesses, which afterwards send Charon a great number of souls drowned in a potion before they come to his 30 ferry? And no less of the rest which take upon them to affirm. Now for the poet, he nothing affirmeth, and therefore never lieth. For, as I take it, to lie is to affirm that to be true which is false ; so as the other artists, and especially the historian, affirming many things, can, in 35

the cloudy knowledge of mankind, hardly escape from
many lies.' But the poet, as I said before, never affirmeth
The poet never maketh any circles about your imagination, to conjure you to believe for true what he writeth.
5 He citeth not authorities of other histories, but even for
his entry calleth the sweet Muses to inspire into him a
good invention; in troth, not laboring to tell you what
is or is not, but what should or should not be. And
therefore though he recount things not true, yet because
10 he telleth them not for true he lieth not; without we
will say that Nathan lied in his speech, before alleged,
to David; which, as a wicked man durst scarce say, so
think I none so simple would say that Æsop lied in the
tales of his beasts; for who thinketh that Æsop wrote it
15 for actually true, were well worthy to have his name
chronicled among the beasts he writeth of. What child
is there that, coming to a play, and seeing Thebes written in great letters upon an old door, doth believe that
it is Thebes? If then a man can arrive at that child's-
20 age, to know that the poet's persons and doings are but
pictures what should be, and not stories what have been,
they will never give the lie to things not affirmatively but
allegorically and figuratively written. And therefore, as in
history looking for truth, they may go away full-fraught
25 with falsehood, so in poesy looking but for fiction, they
shall use the narration but as an imaginative ground-plot
of a profitable invention. But hereto is replied that
the poets give names to men they write of, which argueth
a conceit of an actual truth, and so, not being true,
30 proveth a falsehood. And doth the lawyer lie then,
when, under the names of John of the Stile, and John
of the Nokes, he putteth his case? But that is easily
answered: their naming of men is but to make their
picture the more lively, and not to build any history.
35 Painting men, they cannot leave men nameless. We see

we cannot play at chess but that we must give names to
our chess-men; and yet, me thinks, he were a very partial champion of truth that would say we lied for giving
a piece of wood the reverend title of a bishop. The
poet nameth Cyrus and Æneas no other way than to 5
show what men of their fames, fortunes, and estates
should do.

Their third is, how much it abuseth men's wit, training
it to wanton sinfulness and lustful love. For indeed that
is the principal, if not the only, abuse I can hear alleged. 10
They say the comedies rather teach than reprehend
amorous conceits. They say the lyric is larded with passionate sonnets, the elegiac weeps the want of his
mistress, and that even to the heroical Cupid hath
ambitiously climbed. Alas! Love, I would thou couldst 15
as well defend thyself as thou canst offend others! I
would those on whom thou dost attend could either put
thee away, or yield good reason why they keep thee!
But grant love of beauty to be a beastly fault, although
it be very hard, since only man, and no beast, hath that 20
gift to discern beauty; grant that lovely name of Love
to deserve all hateful reproaches, although even some of
my masters the philosophers spent a good deal of their
lamp-oil in setting forth the excellency of it; grant, I
say, whatsoever they will have granted, — that not only 25
love, but lust, but vanity, but, if they list, scurrility, pos-
sesseth many leaves of the poets' books; yet think I when
this is granted, they will find their sentence may with
good manners put the last words foremost, and not say
that poetry abuseth man's wit, but that man's wit abuseth 30
poetry. For I will not deny, but that man's wit may
make poesy, which should be εἰκαστική, which some
learned have defined, figuring forth good things, to be
φανταστική, which doth contrariwise infect the fancy with
unworthy objects; as the painter that should give to 35

the eye either some excellent perspective, or some fine
picture fit for building or fortification, or containing in it
some notable example, as Abraham sacrificing his son
Isaac, Judith killing Holofernes, David fighting with
5 Goliath, may leave those, and please an ill-pleased eye
with wanton shows of better-hidden matters. But what !
shall the abuse of a thing make the right use odious?
Nay, truly, though I yield that poesy may not only be
abused, but that being abused, by the reason of his sweet
10 charming force, it can do more hurt than any other army
of words, yet shall it be so far from concluding that the
abuse should give reproach to the abused, that contrariwise it is a good reason, that whatsoever, being abused,
doth most harm, being rightly used — and upon the right
15 use each thing receiveth his title — doth most good.   Do
we not see the skill of physic, the best rampire to our
often-assaulted bodies, being abused, teach poison, the
most violent destroyer?   Doth not knowledge of law,
whose end is to even and right all things, being abused,
20 grow the crooked fosterer of horrible injuries ? Doth not,
to go in the highest, God's word abused breed heresy, and
his name abused become blasphemy?   Truly a needle
cannot do much hurt, and as truly — with leave of ladies
be it spoken — it cannot do much good. | With a sword
25 thou mayst kill thy father, and with a sword thou mayst
defend thy prince and country.   So that, as in their calling poets the fathers of lies they say nothing, so in this
their argument of abuse they prove the commendation.
They allege herewith, that before poets began to be
30 in price our nation hath set their hearts' delight upon
action, and not upon imagination ; rather doing things
worthy to be written, than writing things fit to be done.
What that before-time was, I think scarcely Sphinx can
tell ; since no memory is so ancient that hath the prece-
35 dence of poetry.   And certain it is that, in our plainest

homeliness, yet never was the Albion nation without
poetry. Marry, this argument, though it be levelled
against poetry, yet is it indeed a chain-shot against all
learning, — or bookishness, as they commonly term it. Of
such mind were certain Goths, of whom it is written 5
that, having in the spoil of a famous city taken a fair
library, one hangman — belike fit to execute the fruits of
their wits — who had murdered a great number of bodies,
would have set fire in it. "No," said another very
gravely, "take heed what you do; for while they are 10
busy about these toys, we shall with more leisure conquer their countries." This, indeed, is the ordinary
doctrine of ignorance, and many words sometimes I
have heard spent in it; but because this reason is generally against all learning, as well as poetry, or rather all 15
learning but poetry; because it were too large a digression to handle, or at least too superfluous, since it is
manifest that all government of action is to be gotten
by knowledge, and knowledge best by gathering many
knowledges, which is reading; I only, with Horace, to 20
him that is of that opinion

Jubeo stultum esse libenter;

for as for poetry itself, it is the freest from this objec-
tion, for poetry is the companion of the camps. I dare
undertake, Orlando Furioso or honest King Arthur will 25
never displease a soldier; but the quiddity of *ens*, and
prima materia, will hardly agree with a corselet. And
therefore, as I said in the beginning, even Turks and
Tartars are delighted with poets. /Homer, a Greek,
flourished before Greece flourished; and if to a slight 30
conjecture a conjecture may be opposed, truly it may
seem, that as by him their learned men took almost their
first light of knowledge, so their active men received
their first motions of courage. Only Alexander's example

may serve, who by Plutarch is accounted of such virtue,
that Fortune was not his guide but his footstool; whose
acts speak for him, though Plutarch did not; indeed the
phœnix of warlike princes. This Alexander left his
5 schoolmaster, living Aristotle, behind him, but took dead
Homer with him. He put the philosopher Callisthenes
to death, for his seeming philosophical, indeed mutinous,
stubbornness; but the chief thing he was ever heard to
wish for was that Homer had been alive. He well
10 found he received more bravery of mind by the pattern
of Achilles, than by hearing the definition of fortitude.
And therefore if Cato misliked Fulvius for carrying
Ennius with him to the field, it may be answered that if
Cato misliked it, the noble Fulvius liked it, or else he
15 had not done it. For it was not the excellent Cato Uticensis, whose authority I would much more have rev-
erenced; but it was the former, in truth a bitter punisher
of faults, but else a man that had never sacrificed to the
Graces. He misliked and cried out upon all Greek
20 learning; and yet, being fourscore years old, began to
learn it, belike fearing that Pluto understood not Latin.
Indeed, the Roman laws allowed no person to be carried
to the wars but he that was in the soldiers' roll. And
therefore though Cato misliked his unmustered person,
25 he misliked not his work. And if he had, Scipio Nasica,
judged by common consent the best Roman, loved
him. Both the other Scipio brothers, who had by their
virtues no less surnames than of Asia and Afric, so loved
him that they caused his body to be buried in their
30 sepulchre. So as Cato's authority being but against his
person, and that answered with so far greater than himself, is herein of no validity.

But now, indeed, my burthen is great, that Plato's
name is laid upon me, whom, I must confess, of all philoso-
35 phers I have ever esteemed most worthy of reverence;

and with great reason, since of all philosophers he is the most poetical; yet if he will defile the fountain out of which his flowing streams have proceeded, let us boldly examine with what reasons he did it.

First, truly, a man might maliciously object that Plato, being a philosopher, was a natural enemy of poets. For, indeed, after the philosophers had picked out of the sweet mysteries of poetry the right discerning true points of knowledge, they forthwith, putting it in method, and making a school-art of that which the poets did only teach by a divine delightfulness, beginning to spurn at their guides, like ungrateful prentices were not content to set up shops for themselves, but sought by all means to discredit their masters; which by the force of delight being barred them, the less they could overthrow them the more they hated them. For, indeed, they found for Homer seven cities strave who should have him for their citizen; where many cities banished philosophers, as not fit members to live among them. For only repeating certain of Euripides' verses, many Athenians had their lives saved of the Syracusans, where the Athenians themselves thought many philosophers unworthy to live. Certain poets as Simonides and Pindar, had so prevailed with Hiero the First, that of a tyrant they made him a just king; where Plato could do so little with Dionysius, that he himself of a philosopher was made a slave. But who should do thus, I confess, should requite the objections made against poets with like cavillations against philosophers; as likewise one should do that should bid one read Phædrus or Symposium in Plato, or the Discourse of Love in Plutarch, and see whether any poet do authorize abominable filthiness, as they do.

Again, a man might ask out of what commonwealth Plato doth banish them. In sooth, thence where he himself alloweth community of women. So as belike this

banishment grew not for effeminate wantonness, since
little should poetical sonnets be hurtful when a man
might have what woman he listed.   But I honor philosophical instructions, and bless the wits which bred them,
5 so as they be not abused, which is likewise stretched to
poetry.   Saint Paul himself, who yet, for the credit of
poets, allegeth twice two poets, and one of them by the
name of a prophet, setteth a watchword upon philosophy, — indeed upon the abuse. So doth Plato upon
10 the abuse, not upon poetry.   Plato found fault that the
poets of his time filled the world with wrong opinions of
the gods, making light tales of that unspotted essence,
and therefore would not have the youth depraved with
such opinions.   Herein may much be said ; let this suf-
15 fice : the poets did not induce such opinions, but did
imitate those opinions already induced.   For all the
Greek stories can well testify that the very religion of
that time stood upon many and many-fashioned gods ;
not taught so by the poets, but followed according to their
20 nature of imitation.   Who list may read in Plutarch
the discourses of Isis and Osiris, of the Cause why
Oracles ceased, of the Divine Providence, and see
whether the theology of that nation stood not upon such
dreams, — which the poets indeed superstitiously ob-
25 served ; and truly, since they had not the light of Christ,
did much better in it than the philosophers, who, shaking
off superstition, brought in atheism.
    Plato therefore, whose authority I had much rather
justly construe than unjustly resist, meant not in general
30 of poets, in those words of which Julius Scaliger saith,
*Qua authoritate barbari quidam atque hispidi abuti
velint ad poetas e republica exigendos ;* but only meant
to drive out those wrong opinions of the Deity, whereof
now, without further law, Christianity hath taken away
35 all the hurtful belief, perchance, as he thought, nourished

by the then esteemed poets. And a man need go no further
than to Plato himself to know his meaning; who, in his
dialogue called Ion, giveth high and rightly divine commendation unto poetry. So as Plato, banishing the abuse,
not the thing, not banishing it, but giving due honor unto 5
it, shall be our patron and not our adversary. For,
indeed, I had much rather, since truly I may do it, show
their mistaking of Plato, under whose lion's skin they
would make an ass-like braying against poesy, than go
about to overthrow his authority; whom, the wiser a 10
man is, the more just cause he shall find to have in
admiration; especially since he attributeth unto poesy
more than myself do, namely to be a very inspiring of a
divine force, far above man's wit, as in the forenamed
dialogue is apparent. 15

Of the other side, who would show the honors have
been by the best sort of judgments granted them, a
whole sea of examples would present themselves : Alexanders, Cæsars, Scipios, all favorers of poets; Lælius,
called the Roman Socrates, himself a poet, so as part of 20
Heautontimoroumenos in Terence was supposed to be
made by him. And even the Greek Socrates, whom
Apollo confirmed to be the only wise man, is said to
have spent part of his old time in putting Æsop's Fables
into verses ; and therefore full evil should it become his 25
scholar, Plato, to put such words in his master's mouth
against poets. But what needs more? Aristotle writes
the Art of Poesy ; and why, if it should not be written?
Plutarch teacheth the use to be gathered of them ; and
how, if they should not be read? And who reads Plu- 30
tarch's either history or philosophy, shall find he trim-
meth both their garments with guards of poesy. But I
list not to defend poesy with the help of his underling
historiography. Let it suffice that it is a fit soil for
praise to dwell upon ; and what dispraise may set upon 35

it, is either easily overcome, or transformed into just commendation.

So that since the excellencies of it may be so easily and so justly confirmed, and the low-creeping objections so soon
5 trodden down : it not being an art of lies, but of true doctrine ; not of effeminateness, but of notable stirring of courage ; not of abusing man's wit, but of strengthening man's wit ; not banished, but honored by Plato ; let us rather plant more laurels for to engarland our poets' heads — which honor
10 of being laureate, as besides them only triumphant captains were, is a sufficient authority to show the price they ought to be held in — than suffer the ill-savored breath of such wrong speakers once to blow upon the clear springs of poesy. |

But since I have run so long a career in this matter,
15 me thinks, before I give my pen a full stop, it shall be but a little more lost time to inquire why England, the mother of excellent minds, should be grown so hard a stepmother to poets ; who certainly in wit ought to pass all others, since all only proceedeth from their wit, being
20 indeed makers of themselves, not takers of others.   How can I but exclaim,

> Musa, mihi causas memora, quo numine læso?

Sweet poesy ! that hath anciently had kings, emperors, senators, great captains, such as, besides a thousand
25 others, David, Adrian, Sophocles, Germanicus, not only to favor poets, but to be poets ; and of our nearer times can present for her patrons a Robert, King of Sicily ; the great King Francis of France ; King James of Scotland ; such cardinals as Bembus and Bibbiena ; such
30 famous preachers and teachers as Beza and Melancthon ; so learned philosophers as Fracastorius and Scaliger ; so great orators as Pontanus and Muretus ; so piercing wits as George Buchanan ; so grave counsellors as — besides many, but before all — that Hospital of France, than

whom, I think, that realm never brought forth a more accomplished judgment more firmly builded upon virtue ; I say these, with numbers of others, not only to read others' poesies but to poetize for others' reading. That poesy, thus embraced in all other places, should only find in our time a hard welcome in England, I think the very earth lamenteth it, and therefore decketh our soil with fewer laurels than it was accustomed. For heretofore poets have in England also flourished ; and, which is to be noted, even in those times when the trumpet of Mars did sound loudest. And now that an over-faint quietness should seem to strew the house for poets, they are almost in as good reputation as the mountebanks at Venice. Truly even that, as of the one side it giveth great praise to poesy, which, like Venus — but to better purpose — hath rather be troubled in the net with Mars, than enjoy the homely quiet of Vulcan ; so serves it for a piece of a reason why they are less grateful to idle England, which now can scarce endure the pain of a pen. Upon this necessarily followeth, that base men with servile wits undertake it, who think it enough if they can be rewarded of the printer. And so as Epaminondas is said, with the honor of his virtue to have made an office, by his exercising it, which before was contemptible, to become highly respected ; so these men, no more but setting their names to it, by their own disgracefulness disgrace the most graceful poesy. For now, as if all the Muses were got with child to bring forth bastard poets, without any commission they do post over the banks of Helicon, till they make their readers more weary than post-horses ; while, in the mean time, they,

Queis meliore luto finxit præcordia Titan,

are better content to suppress the outflowings of their

wit, than by publishing them to be accounted knights of the same order.

But I that, before ever I durst aspire unto the dignity, am admitted into the company of the paper-blurrers, do find the very true cause of our wanting estimation is want of desert, taking upon us to be poets in despite of Pallas. Now wherein we want desert were a thank-worthy labor to express; but if I knew, I should have mended myself. But as I never desired the title, so have I neglected the means to come by it; only, overmastered by some thoughts, I yielded an inky tribute unto them. Marry, they that delight in poesy itself should seek to know what they do and how they do; and especially look themselves in an unflattering glass of reason, if they be inclinable unto it. For poesy must not be drawn by the ears, it must be gently led, or rather it must lead; which was partly the cause that made the ancient learned affirm it was a divine gift, and no human skill, since all other knowledges lie ready for any that hath strength of wit, a poet no industry can make if his own genius be not carried into it. And therefore is it an old proverb: *Orator fit, poeta nascitur.* · Yet confess I always that, as the fertilest ground must be manured, so must the highest-flying wit have a Dædalus to guide him. That Dædalus, they say, both in this and in other, hath three wings to bear itself up into the air of due commenda-tion: that is, art, imitation, and exercise. But these neither artificial rules nor imitative patterns, we much cumber ourselves withal. Exercise indeed we do, but that very fore-backwardly, for where we should exercise to know, we exercise as having known; and so is our brain delivered of much matter which never was begot-ten by knowledge. For there being two principal parts, matter to be expressed by words, and words to express the matter, in neither we use art or imitation rightly.

Our matter is *quodlibet* indeed, though wrongly perform-
ing Ovid's verse,

Quicquid conabar dicere, versus erat;

never marshalling it into any assured rank, that almost
the readers cannot tell where to find themselves.   5

Chaucer, undoubtedly, did excellently in his Troilus
and Cressida ; of whom, truly, I know not whether to
marvel more, either that he in that misty time could see
so clearly, or that we in this clear age walk so stumblingly
after him.   Yet had he great wants, fit to be forgiven in 10
so reverend antiquity.   I account the Mirror of Magistrates meetly furnished of beautiful parts ; and in the
Earl of Surrey's lyrics many things tasting of a noble
birth, and worthy of a noble mind.   The Shepherd's
Calendar hath much poetry in his eclogues, indeed worthy 15
the reading, if I be not deceived.   That same framing
of his style to an old rustic language I dare not allow,
since neither Theocritus in Greek, Virgil in Latin, nor
Sannazzaro in Italian did affect it.   Besides these, I do
not remember to have seen but few (to speak boldly) 20
printed, that have poetical sinews in them.   For proof
whereof, let but most of the verses be put in prose, and
then ask the meaning, and it will be found that one verse
did but beget another, without ordering at the first
what should be at the last ; which becomes a confused 25
mass of words, with a tinkling sound of rime, barely
accompanied with reason.

Our tragedies and comedies not without cause cried
out against, observing rules neither of honest civility nor
of skilful poetry, excepting Gorboduc, — again I say of 30
those that I have seen.   Which notwithstanding as it
is full of stately speeches and well-sounding phrases,
climbing to the height of Seneca's style, and as full of
notable morality, which it doth most delightfully teach,

and so obtain the very end of poesy; yet in truth it is
very defectious in the circumstances, which grieveth me,
because it might not remain as an exact model of all
tragedies. ; For it is faulty both in place and time, the
5 two necessary companions of all corporal actions.   For
where the stage should always represent but one place,
and the uttermost time presupposed in it should be, both
by Aristotle's precept and common reason, but one day;
there is both many days and many places inartificially
10 imagined.

But if it be so in Gorboduc, how much more in all
the rest? where you shall have Asia of the one side, and
Afric of the other, and so many other under-kingdoms,
that the player, when he cometh in, must ever begin with
15 telling where he is, or else the tale will not be conceived.
Now ye shall have three ladies walk to gather flowers,
and then we must believe the stage to be a garden.   By
and by we hear news of shipwreck in the same place,
and then we are to blame if we accept it not for a rock.
20 Upon the back of that comes out a hideous monster
with fire and smoke, and then the miserable beholders
are bound to take it for a cave.   While in the mean time
two armies fly in, represented with four swords and
bucklers, and then what hard heart will not receive it
25 for a pitched field?

Now of time they are much more liberal. For ordinary
it is that two young princes fall in love; after many
traverses she is got with child, delivered of a fair boy,
he is lost, groweth a man, falleth in love, and is ready to
30 get another child, — and all this in two hours' space;
which how absurd it is in sense even sense may imagine, and art hath taught, and all ancient examples justi-
fied, and at this day the ordinary players in Italy will not
err in. . Yet will some bring in an example of Eunuchus
35 in Terence, that containeth matter of two days, yet far

short of twenty years. True it is, and so was it to be
played in two days, and so fitted to the time it set forth.
And though Plautus have in one place done amiss, let us
hit with him, and not miss with him. But they will
say, How then shall we set forth a story which containeth 5
both many places and many times? And do they not
know that a tragedy is tied to the laws of poesy, and not
of history; not bound to follow the story, but having
liberty either to feign a quite new matter, or to frame
the history to the most tragical conveniency? Again, 10
many things may be told which cannot be showed, — if
they know the difference betwixt reporting and representing. As for example I may speak, though I am here, of
Peru, and in speech digress from that to the description
of Calicut; but in action I cannot represent it without 15
Pacolet's horse. And so was the manner the ancients
took, by some *Nuntius* to recount things done in former
time or other place.   —

Lastly, if they will represent a history, they must not,
as Horace saith, begin *ab ovo*, but they must come to 20
the principal point of that one action which they will
represent. · By example this will be best expressed. I
have a story of young Polydorus, delivered for safety's
sake, with great riches, by his father Priamus to Polym-
nestor, King of Thrace, in the Trojan war time. He, 25
after some years, hearing the overthrow of Priamus,
for to make the treasure his own murdereth the child;
the body of the child is taken up by Hecuba; she, the
same day, findeth a sleight to be revenged most cruelly
of the tyrant. Where now would one of our tragedy- 30
writers begin, but with the delivery of the child? Then
should he sail over into Thrace, and so spend I know
not how many years, and travel numbers of places. But
where doth Euripides? Even with the finding of the
body, leaving the rest to be told by the spirit of Poly 35

dorus. This needs no further to be enlarged ; the dullest wit may conceive it.

But, besides these gross absurdities, how all their plays be neither right tragedies nor right comedies, mingling 5 kings and clowns, not because the matter so carrieth it, but thrust in the clown by head and shoulders to play a part in majestical matters, with neither decency nor discretion ; so as neither the admiration and commisera-tion, nor the right sportfulness, is by their mongrel tragi-10 comedy obtained. I know Apuleius did somewhat so, but that is a thing recounted with space of time, not represented in one moment ; and I know the ancients have one or two examples of tragi-comedies, as Plautus hath Amphytrio. But, if we mark them well, we shall 15 find that they never, or very daintily, match hornpipes and funerals. ' So falleth it out that, having indeed no right comedy in that comical part of our tragedy, we have nothing but scurrility, unworthy of any chaste ears, or some extreme show of doltishness, indeed fit to lift 20 up a loud laughter, and nothing else ; where the whole tract of a comedy should be full of delight, as the tragedy should be still maintained in a well-raised admiration. |

| But our comedians think there is no delight without laughter, which is very wrong ; for though laughter may 25 come with delight, yet cometh it not of delight, as though delight should be the cause of laughter ; but well may one thing breed both together. Nay, rather in them-selves they have, as it were, a kind of contrariety. For delight we scarcely do, but in things that have a con-30 veniency to ourselves, or to the general nature ; laughter almost ever cometh of things most disproportioned to ourselves and nature. Delight hath a joy in it either permanent or present ; laughter hath only a scornful tickling. For example, we are ravished with delight to 35 see a fair woman, and yet are far from being moved to—

laughter. We laugh at deformed creatures, wherein certainly we cannot delight. We delight in good chances,
we laugh at mischances. We delight to hear the happiness of our friends and country, at which he were worthy
to be laughed at that would laugh. We shall, contrarily,
laugh sometimes to find a matter quite mistaken and go
down the hill against the bias, in the mouth of some such
men, as for the respect of them one shall be heartily
sorry he cannot choose but laugh, and so is rather pained
than delighted with laughter. Yet deny I not but that
they may go well together. For as in Alexander's picture
well set out we delight without laughter, and in twenty
mad antics we laugh without delight; so in Hercules,
painted, with his great beard and furious countenance, in
woman's attire, spinning at Omphale's commandment,
it breedeth both delight and laughter; for the representing
of so strange a power in love, procureth delight, and the
scornfulness of the action stirreth laughter.

But I speak to this purpose, that all the end of the
comical part be not upon such scornful matters as stir
laughter only, but mixed with it that delightful teaching
which is the end of poesy. And the great fault, even in
that point of laughter, and forbidden plainly by Aristotle,
is that they stir laughter in sinful things, which are rather
execrable than ridiculous; or in miserable, which are
rather to be pitied than scorned. For what is it to make
folks gape at a wretched beggar or a beggarly clown,
or, against law of hospitality, to jest at strangers because
they speak not English so well as we do? what do we
learn? since it is certain:

> Nil habet infelix paupertas durius in se,
> Quam quod ridiculos homines facit.

But rather a busy loving courtier; a heartless threatening
Thraso; a self-wise-seeming schoolmaster; a wry-trans-

formed traveller : these if we saw walk in stage-names,
which we play naturally, therein were delightful laughter and teaching delightfulness, — as in the other, the tragedies of Buchanan do justly bring forth a divine admiration.
5   But I have lavished out too many words of this play-
matter.   I do it, because as they are excelling parts of
poesy, so is there none so much used in England, and
none can be more pitifully abused ; which, like an unman-
nerly daughter, showing a bad education, causeth her
10 mother Poesy's honesty to be called in question.
Other sorts of poetry almost have we none, but that
lyrical kind of songs and sonnets, which, Lord if he
gave us so good minds, how well it might be employed,
and with how heavenly fruits both private and public, in
15 singing the praises of the immortal beauty, the immortal
goodness of that God who giveth us hands to write, and
wits to conceive ! — of which we might well want words,
but never matter ; of which we could turn our eyes to
nothing, but we should ever have new-budding occasions.
20   But truly, many of such writings as come under the
banner of unresistible love, if I were a mistress would
never persuade me they were in love ; so coldly they
apply fiery speeches, as men that had rather read lovers'
writings, and so caught up certain swelling phrases — which
25 hang together like a man which once told me the wind
was at north-west and by south, because he would be
sure to name winds enough — than that in truth they
feel those passions, which easily, as I think, may be
bewrayed by that same forcibleness, or *energia* (as the
30 Greeks call it) of the writer.   But let this be a sufficient,
though short note, that we miss the right use of the
material point of poesy.
Now for the outside of it, which is words, or (as I may
term it) diction, it is even well worse, so is that honey-
35 flowing matron eloquence apparelled, or rather disguised,

in a courtesan-like painted affectation : one time with so
far-fet words, that many seem monsters — but must seem
strangers — to any poor Englishman ; another time with
coursing of a letter, as if they were bound to follow the
method of a dictionary ; another time with figures and 5
flowers extremely winter-starved.

But I would this fault were only peculiar to versifiers,
and had not as large possession among prose-printers,
and, which is to be marvelled, among many scholars,
and, which is to be pitied, among some preachers. Truly 10
I could wish — if at least I might be so bold to wish in
a thing beyond the reach of my capacity — the diligent
imitators of Tully and Demosthenes (most worthy to be
imitated) did not so much keep Nizolian paper-books of
their figures and phrases, as by attentive translation, as 15
it were devour them whole, and make them wholly theirs.
For now they cast sugar and spice upon every dish that
is served to the table ; like those Indians, not content to
wear ear-rings at the fit and natural place of the ears,
but they will thrust jewels through their nose and lips, 20
because they will be sure to be fine.' Tully, when he
was to drive out Catiline as it were with a thunderbolt
of eloquence, often used that figure of repetition, as
Vivit. Vivit? Immo vero etiam in senatum venit, etc.
Indeed, inflamed with a well-grounded rage, he would 25
have his words, as it were, double out of his mouth ;
and so do that artificially, which we see men in choler
do naturally. And we, having noted the grace of those
words, hale them in sometime to a familiar epistle, when
it were too much choler to be choleric. How well 30
store of *similiter cadences* doth sound with the gravity
of the pulpit, I would but invoke Demosthenes' soul to
tell, who with a rare daintiness useth them. Truly they
have made me think of the sophister that with too much
subtility would prove two eggs three, and though he 35

might be counted a sophister, had none for his labor. So these men bringing in such a kind of eloquence, well may they obtain an opinion of a seeming fineness, but persuade few, — which should be the end of their fineness.

5 Now for similitudes in certain printed discourses, I think all herbarists, all stories of beasts, fowls, and fishes are rifled up, that they may come in multitudes to wait upon any of our conceits, which certainly is as absurd a surfeit to the ears as is possible. For the force of a 10 similitude not being to prove any thing to a contrary disputer, but only to explain to a willing hearer; when that is done, the rest is a most tedious prattling, rather overswaying the memory from the purpose whereto they were applied, than any whit informing the judgment, already 15 either satisfied or by similitudes not to be satisfied.

For my part, I do not doubt, when Antonius and Crassus, the great forefathers of Cicero in eloquence, the one (as Cicero testifieth of them) pretended not to know art, the other not to set by it, because with a plain 20 sensibleness they might win credit of popular ears, which credit is the nearest step to persuasion, which persuasion is the chief mark of oratory, — I do not doubt, I say, but that they used these knacks very sparingly; which who doth generally use any man may see doth 25 dance to his own music, and so be noted by the audience more careful to speak curiously than truly. Undoubtedly (at least to my opinion undoubtedly) I have found in divers small-learned courtiers a more sound style than in some professors of learning; of which I 30 can guess no other cause, but that the courtier following that which by practice he findeth fittest to nature, therein, though he know it not, doth according to art, though not by art; where the other, using art to show art and not to hide art — as in these cases he should do — flieth 35 from nature, and indeed abuseth art.

But what ! me thinks I deserve to be pounded for stray-
ing from poetry to oratory.   But both have such an affinity
in the wordish consideration, that I think this digression
will make my meaning receive the fuller understanding : —
which is not to take upon me to teach poets how they 5
should do, but only, finding myself sick among the rest,
to show some one or two spots of the common infection
grown among the most part of writers ; that, acknowl-
edging ourselves somewhat awry, we may bend to the
right use both of matter and manner : whereto our lan- 10
guage giveth us great occasion, being, indeed, capable of
any excellent exercising of it.

I know some will say it is a mingled language.   And
why not so much the better, taking the best of both
the other?   Another will say it wanteth grammar.   Nay, 15
truly, it hath that praise that it wanteth not grammar.
For grammar it might have, but it needs it not ; being
so easy in itself, and so void of those cumbersome differences of cases, genders, moods, and tenses, which, I
think, was a piece of the Tower of Babylon's curse, that 20
a man should be put to school to learn his mother-
tongue. · But for the uttering sweetly and properly the
conceits of the mind, which is the end of speech, that
hath it equally with any other tongue in the world ; and
is particularly happy in compositions of two or three words 25
together, near the Greek, far beyond the Latin, — which
is one of the greatest beauties can be in a language.

Now of versifying there are two sorts, the one ancient,
the other modern. / The ancient marked the quantity of
each syllable, and according to that framed his verse ; 30
the modern observing only number, with some regard of
the accent, the chief life of it standeth in that like sounding of the words, which we call rime. · Whether of
these be the more excellent would bear many speeches ;
the ancient no doubt more fit for music, both words 35

and tune observing quantity; and more fit lively to express divers passions, by the low or lofty sound of the
well-weighed syllable. The latter likewise with his rime
striketh a certain music to the ear; and, in fine, since
5 it doth delight, though by another way, it obtaineth the
same purpose; there being in either, sweetness, and
wanting in neither, majesty. Truly the English, before
any other vulgar language I know, is fit for both sorts.
For, for the ancient, the Italian is so full of vowels that
10 it must ever be cumbered with elisions; the Dutch so,
of the other side, with consonants, that they cannot yield
the sweet sliding fit for a verse. The French in his
whole language hath not one word that hath his accent in
the last syllable saving two, called antepenultima, and little
15 more hath the Spanish; and therefore very gracelessly
may they use dactyls. The English is subject to none
of these defects. Now for rime, though we do not observe quantity, yet we observe the accent very precisely,
which other languages either cannot do, or will not do
20 so absolutely. That cæsura, or breathing-place in the
midst of the verse, neither Italian nor Spanish have, the
French and we never almost fail of.

Lastly, even the very rime itself the Italian cannot
put in the last syllable, by the French named the mas-
25 culine rime, but still in the next to the last, which the
French call the female, or the next before that, which
the Italians term *sdrucciola*. The example of the former
is *buono : suono;* of the *sdrucciola* is *femina : semina.*
The French, of the other side, hath both the male, as
30 *bon : son,* and the female, as *plaise : taise;* but the
sdrucciola he hath not. Where the English hath all
three, as *due : true, father : rather, motion : potion;*
with much more which might be said, but that already I
find the triflingness of this discourse is much too much
35 enlarged.

So that since the ever praiseworthy poesy is full of virtue-breeding delightfulness, and void of no gift that ought to be in the noble name of learning; since the blames laid against it are either false or feeble; since the cause why it is not esteemed in England is the fault of poet-apes, not poets; 5 since, lastly, our tongue is most fit to honor poesy, and to be honored by poesy; I conjure you all that have had the evil luck to read this ink-wasting toy of mine, even in the name of the Nine Muses, no more to scorn the sacred mysteries of poesy; no more to laugh at the name of poets, as though 10 they were next inheritors to fools; no more to jest at the reverend title of "a rimer"; but to believe, with Aristotle, that they were the ancient treasurers of the Grecians' divinity; to believe, with Bembus, that they were first bringers-in of all civility; to believe, with Scaliger, that no philoso-15 pher's precepts can sooner make you an honest man than the reading of Virgil; to believe, with Clauserus, the translator of Cornutus, that it pleased the Heavenly Deity by Hesiod and Homer, under the veil of fables, to give us all knowledge, logic, rhetoric, philosophy natural and moral, and 20 *quid non?* to believe, with me, that there are many mysteries contained in poetry which of purpose were written darkly, lest by profane wits it should be abused; to believe, with Landino, that they are so beloved of the gods, that whatsoever they write proceeds of a divine fury; lastly, 25 to believe themselves, when they tell you they will make you immortal by their verses.

Thus doing, your name shall flourish in the printers' shops. Thus doing, you shall be of kin to many a poetical preface. Thus doing, you shall be most fair, most rich, 30 most wise, most all; you shall dwell upon superlatives. Thus doing, though you be *libertino patre natus,* you shall suddenly grow *Herculea proles,*

Si quid mea carmina possunt.

Thus doing, your soul shall be placed with Dante's Bea-trice or Virgil's Anchises.

But if — fie of such a but ! — you be born so near the dull-making cataract of Nilus, that you cannot hear the planet-like music of poetry; if you have so earth-creeping a mind that it cannot lift itself up to look to the sky of poetry, or rather, by a certain rustical disdain, will become such a mome as to be a Momus of poetry; then, though I will not wish unto you the ass's ears of Midas, nor to be driven by a poet's verses, as Bubonax was, to hang himself; nor to be rimed to death, as is said to be done in Ireland; yet thus much curse I must send you in the behalf of all poets : — that while you live you live in love, and never get favor for lacking skill of a sonnet; and when you die, your memory die from the earth for want of an epitaph.

NOTES.

1 1. *Edward Wotton.* One of Sidney's dearest friends, whom he remembered in the will made on his death-bed, and who was one of the four pall-bearers at his funeral.

1 2. *Emperor's.* Maximilian II. (1527–1576).

1 3. *Horsemanship.* This was in the winter of 1574–75, when Sidney had just arrived at the age of 20. That Sidney profited by these lessons in horsemanship is apparent from his own statement in the 41st sonnet of *Astrophel and Stella*, written, as Pollard, one of his latest editors, thinks, in April or May, 1581 :

> Having this day my horse, my hand, my lance
> Guided so well that I obtained the prize,
> Both by the judgment of the English eyes
> And of some sent from that sweet enemy France,
> Horsemen my skill in horsemanship advance,
> Town-folks my strength.

The year before he had given this advice to his brother Robert : "At horsemanship, when you exercise it, read Crison Claudio, and a book that is called *La Gloria del Cavallo* withal, that you may join the thorough contemplation of it with the exercise; and so shall you profit more in a month than others in a year, and mark the bitting, saddling and curing of horses " (Fox Bourne, *Memoir*, p. 278). Cf. also Sonnets 49 and 53 of *Astrophel and Stella*.

1 6. *Wit.* A favorite word with Sidney. Used in the singular, 7 34, 8 26, 8 34, 10 14, 12 1, 13 35, 32 25, 37 8, 30, 31, 43 14, 44 7, 8, 18, 19, 46 1, 24, 50 2; in the plural, 3 4, 4 30, 5 31, 39 8, 42 4, 44 32, 52 17. Cf. also *fine-witted*, 14 13.

1 10. *Loaden.* Cf. 13 28. Dr. J. A. H. Murray kindly informs me that this form of the past participle is found as early as 1545, in Brinklow's *Lamentacyon* (E. E. T. S. Extra Ser. No. 22), p. 82, in the translation of Matt. 11. 28. From this time onward, for a hundred years, it is common, being found several times in Shakespeare and Milton, as well

as in more obscure authors. It is still in use at the close of the eighteenth century, as, for example, in Ann Radcliffe's *Journey made in the Summer of 1794.* Sterne (*Sentimental Journey, Amiens*) even treats it as the infinitive of a weak verb: "he had loaden'd himself." Perhaps it is at present restricted to the Scotch dialect. The Scotch steward in Robert Louis Stevenson's *Master of Ballantrae* speaks of a ship as being "too deeply loaden." The last three references I owe to Mr. Ralph O. Williams of New Haven.

1 12. *He said soldiers*, etc. *That* is frequently omitted at the beginning of object clauses. Cf. 1 14, 8 14, 9 7, 15 34, 32 5, 37 3, 11, 12, 40 10, 41 16, 43 31, 50 10, 12, 23, 53 7, 11, 54 6, 55 3, 13, 15.

1 19. *Pedanteria.* Piece of pedantry.

1 24. *A piece.* Or, as we say colloquially, "a bit." Cf. 45 18.

Logician. See the *Retr. Review*, 10. 45: "Sir Philip Sidney, in the opening paragraph of his essay, gives himself out as 'a piece of a logician'; and, in fact, the *Defense of Poesy* may be regarded as a logical discourse from beginning to end, interspersed here and there with a few of the more flowery parts of eloquence, but everywhere keeping in view the main objects of all logic and of all eloquence, — namely, proof and persuasion. It is, in fact, — contrary to the general notion that prevails concerning it in the minds of those who do not take the trouble of judging for themselves, — a sober and serious disquisition, almost entirely rejecting the 'foreign aid of ornament,' and equally free from dogmatism and declamation."

1 25. *To have wished.* A construction no longer favored.

1 26. *A horse.* Sidney's humor is quiet, but unmistakable. Other instances may be found in 20 26–8, 31 11 –13, 35 29–31, 38 23, 48 11 ff., 58 3 16.

1 27. *Drave.* Cf. 2 25, stale, 4 10 (Ponsonby's ed.), strave, 27 7, 41 17.

2 6. *Unelected.* Sidney, like Milton in his prose, is partial to adjectives (past participles), with the negative prefix *un.* See 30 8, 52 21. *Unelected vocation.* Cf. Sonnet 74 of *Astrophel and Stella :*

> I never drank of Aganippe well,
> Nor ever did in shade of Tempe sit,
> And Muses scorn with vulgar brains to dwell;
> Poor layman I, for sacred rites unfit,
> Some do I hear of poets' fury tell,
> But, God wot, wot not what they mean by it.

See also 46 3 ff.

2 10–13. *As . . . so.* For this construction, cf. 4 35, 15 7–8, 16 5–16, 24 22–23, 28 5–7, 29 32, 30 3–4, 8–9, 32 20–23, 36 12, 38 26–7, 39 32–3, 45 14–17, 46 9, 23, 52 6–7.

2 15. *Silly.* Nearly = poor, as used in 2 11. Cf. Shak., *2 Hen. VI.* I 1. 225–6:

> While as the silly owner of the goods
> Weeps over them and wrings his hapless hands.

Names of philosophers. Meaning Plato : 35 6, 40 33.

2 16. *The defacing of it.* Sidney sometimes construes the verbal noun with a following *of,* as here, and sometimes directly with the object, the preposition being omitted. Examples of the former are : 4 1, 4 11, 5 34–5, 6 13–14, 12 1, 13 26, 16 15–16, 32 32, 33 32, 44 6, 47 16–17, 49 34. For the latter, see 3 35, 4 2, 5 21, 6 12–13, 11 22–23, 12 19, 27 16–17, 30 26, 30 34–35, 32 19, 55 22–23.

2 18. *And first,* etc. Puttenham's *Art of English Poesy* follows, for its first five chapters, with the exception of the second, much the same lines as Sidney in his opening.

2 23. *First nurse.* So Harington (Haslewood, 2. 121) : "The very first nurse and ancient grandmother of all learning."

2 24–27. Sidney elsewhere condemns such similitudes (54 5 ff.), and is perhaps only employing them here for an humorous purpose, and in allusion to the excessive use of them by Gosson, who, in fact, introduces the adder in his *School of Abuse* (p. 46) : "The adder's death is her own brood."

2 25. *Hedgehog.* Prof. T. F. Crane of Cornell University refers me to Kirchhof's *Wendunmuth,* a German collection of fables (*Bibl. des litt. Vereins in Stuttgart,* Bd. 98), where the story is given (7. 74). It is also said to be found in Camerarius' edition of Æsop, Leipsic, 1564, and elsewhere (cf. Regnier's *La Fontaine,* 1. 146, in Hachette's *Les Grands Écrivains de la France*). I have also found it in a school edition (p. 90) of *Æsop's Fables,* published by Ginn & Co. in their "Classics for Children."

2 26. *Vipers.* Referring to Pliny's *Natural History,* 10. 82. 2 : "On the third day it hatches its young in the uterus, and then excludes them, one every day, and generally twenty in number. The last ones become so impatient of their confinement that they force a passage through the sides of their parent, and so kill her." Again used by Daniel, *Apology for Rime* (Haslewood, 2. 209) : " But this innovation, like a viper, must ever make way into the world's opinion through the bowels of her own breeding." Cf. *Englische Studien* 14. 195–6.

2 29. *Musæus, Homer, and Hesiod.* Plato thus groups these names near the close of his *Apology* (41; Jowett 1. 374) : "What would not a man give if he might converse with Orpheus and Musæus and Hesiod and Homer?"

For Musæus, see Mahaffy, *Hist. Grk. Lit.* 1. 14: "This Musæus was supposed to have been a pupil or successor to Orpheus." On Hesiod, cf. Mahaffy, 1. 98–99: "It is an admitted fact that, about the beginning of the seventh century B.C., the heroic epics of the Greeks were being supplanted by the poetry of real life — iambic satire, elegiac confessions, gnomic wisdom, and proverbial philosophy. The Greeks grew tired of all the praise of courts and ladies and bygone wars, and turned to a sober — nay even exaggerated — realism, by way of reaction from the worship of Homeric rhapsody. The father and forerunner of all this school is clearly Hesiod."

2 30. *That can say*, etc. Thus Shelley, in his *Defense of Poetry :* "In the infancy of society every author is necessarily a poet, because language itself is poetry." And again: "They are the institutors of laws and the founders of civil society, and the inventors of the arts of life, and the teachers, who draw into a certain propinquity with the beautiful and the true that partial apprehension of the agencies of the invisible world which is called religion."

2 32. *Orpheus, Linus.* These, like Musæus, and perhaps Hesiod and Homer, are semi-mythical personages. In discussing the legends concerning them Mahaffy says (*Hist. Grk. Lit.* 1. 10) : "But the very fact of the forging of the name of Orpheus, Musæus, and others proves clearly the antiquity of these names, and that the poetry ascribed to them was of a character quite different from that of the Epos. The very frequent allusions of Plato, on the other hand, who even in three places quotes the words of Orpheus, show clearly that he accepted Orpheus and Musæus, whom he usually co-ordinates, as ancient masters of religious song, and on a par with Homer and Hesiod. This general acceptance of Orpheus as a real personage, with no less frequent suspicions as to the genuineness of the current Orphic books, appears in other Greek writers; e.g. Aristotle cites the so-called Orphic poems, just as he cites the so-called Pythagorean books. Apart from these casual allusions, our really explicit authorities are the antiquaries of later days, to whom we owe almost all the definite knowledge we possess. Pausanias, in particular, not only speaks constantly of these poets, but refers to some of their hymns which he had heard, and it is he and Strabo who afford us the materials for constructing a general theory about them."

Of Linus, Mahaffy says (1. 14) : "There are other names which Pausanias considers still older — Linus, the personification of the Linus song mentioned by Homer, and from early times identified more or less with the Adonis song of the Phœnicians and the Maneros of the Egyptians."

3 1-2. *Not only . . . but.* Cf. 8 21-2, 26 12-14, 32 14-15, 33 20-21.

3 5. *Amphion.* Cf. Horace, *Art of Poetry* 391-6: " Once in the woods men lived ; then holy Orpheus, heaven's interpreter, turned them from slaughter and their foul manner of life; hence he was said to have soothed tigers and ravening lions; hence too it was said that Amphion, founder of the Theban citadel, moved rocks to the strains of his lyre, and led them by alluring persuasion whithersoever he listed."

Addressing Stella, in Sonnet 68 of *Astrophel and Stella*, Sidney writes:

> Why dost thou spend the treasure of thy sprite
> With voice more fit to wed Amphion's lyre?

In the third of his *Sonnets of Variable Verse*, Sidney again couples Orpheus and Amphion :

> If Orpheus' voice had force to breathe such music's love
> Through pores of senseless trees, as it could make them move;
> If stones good measure danced the Theban walls to build,
> To cadence of the tunes which Amphion's lyre did yield,
>> More cause a like effect at leastwise bringeth.
>> O stones, O trees, learn hearing, Stella singeth.

3 7. *Beasts.* Cf. 18 18, 37 19.

3 8. *Livius Andronicus.* About 284-204 B.C. Cf. Simcox, *Hist. Lat. Lit.* I. 19: "The first Latin playwright, the first schoolmaster who taught Greek literature. . . . Perhaps his most considerable work was a school-book, an abridgment of the *Odyssey* in the saturnian metre." *Ennius.* 239-169 B.C. Cf. Simcox, I. 22: "Throughout the republican period he was recognized as the great Roman poet. Cicero appeals to him as *summus poeta*. Lucretius speaks of the doctrines of the world to come which he had enshrined in everlasting verse."

3 8 ff. Cf. Shelley, *Defense of Poetry:* "The age immediately succeeding to that of Dante, Petrarch, and Boccaccio was characterized by a revival of painting, sculpture, and architecture. Chaucer caught the sacred inspiration, and the superstructure of English literature is based upon the materials of Italian invention."

3 13. *Others.* Cf. 47 6 ff.

3 18. *Masks of poets.* Cf. Mahaffy, *Hist. Grk. Lit.* I. 186-7: " While education and consequently literature were being more and more disseminated, prose had not yet been adopted as a vehicle of thought, and thus the whole intellectual outcome of the nation took the form of verse. Much of what remains is indeed prosaic in idea. . . . The wisdom of Phokylides and of Theognis is not half so poetical as Plato's

prose. But the Greeks awoke very slowly, as is well known, to the necessity of laying aside metre in writing for the public, and even when they did, we shall find their prose never shaking off a painful attention to rhythm." So likewise Moulton, *Ancient Classical Drama*, p. 121 : " In all literatures poetry is at the outset the sole medium of expression; with the advance of scientific thought a second medium is elaborated, but the transference of topics from poetry to prose is only gradual."

3 18. *Thales.* See Mahaffy, *Hist. Grk. Lit.* 2. 7 : " Neither Thales nor Pythagoras left anything written, and it is remarkable that Xenophanes, though he was a great adversary of the poets and of public opinion in general, and led the conflict between philosophy and poetry, nevertheless employed, not only the poetic form, but even the poetic habit of public recitation, to disseminate his views."

Empedocles. Cf. Mahaffy, 1. 125 : " Mr. Symonds, in his essay on the poet, goes so far as to call him the Greek Shelley, and gives some striking grounds for this singular judgment. As a poet, therefore, Empedocles must be ranked very high, and Cicero expressly tells us that his verses were far superior to those of Xenophanes and Parmenides, themselves no mean artists on similar subjects." See also Matthew Arnold's poem, *Empedocles on Etna*.

3 19. *Parmenides.* Cf. Mahaffy, 1. 123 : " It seems more likely that Parmenides came earlier, perhaps about the opening of the fifth century, and he still adhered in philosophy to the old didactic epic, which had been consecrated to serious teaching by Hesiod and his school."

3 20. *Pythagoras.* Cf. 3 18, above.

Phocylides. Of him Mahaffy says, *Hist. Grk. Lit.* 1. 188: " He imitates Simonides in satirising women by comparing them to domestic animals, he speaks of Nineveh familiarly as a great city, he wishes to be of the middle class, and even ridicules the advantages of high birth, so that he can in no wise be regarded as an instance of the common statement, that all the poets of the lyric age were aristocrats."

3 21. *Tyrtæus.* See Mahaffy, 1. 162–3: " When the famous Leonidas was asked what he thought of Tyrtæus, he answered that he was . . . good for stimulating the soul of youth, and the extant fragments confirm this judgment. We have several long exhortations to valor (about 120 lines), with pictures of the advantages of this virtue and the disgrace and loss attending on cowardice."

Solon. Cf. Mahaffy, 1. 175 · " He is remarkable in having written poetry, not as a profession, nor as his main occupation, but as a relaxation from graver cares. He was first a merchant, then a general, then a lawgiver, and, at last, a philosophic traveller; and all these conditions of life, except the first, are reflected in his extant fragments."

Spurious remains of some of the above poets were accepted as genuine in Sidney's time, so that the Elizabethans had more confidence in
their knowledge of them than the critical historians of this century are
willing to profess.

3 24. *Hidden to.* Note the idiom.

3 26. *Atlantic Island.* With respect to Solon's authorship of the
story related by Plato in the *Critias,* Jowett says (*Plato* 3. 679): " We
may safely conclude that the entire narrative is due to the imagination
of Plato, . . . who has used the name of Solon (of whose poem there
is no trace in antiquity) . . . to give verisimilitude to his story."

3 27. *Plato.* Cf. the first quotation under 3 18, 11 19 note, and Mahaffy,
Hist. Grk. Lit. 2. 207–8: " In his style he is as modern as in his thinking. He employed that mixture of sober prose argument and of poetical metaphor which is usual in the ornate prose of modern Europe, but
foreign to the character and stricter art of the Greeks. This style,
which is freely censured by Greek critics as a hybrid or bastard prose,
was admirably suited to a lively conversation, where a sustained and
equable tone would have been a mistake. . . . Yet his appreciation
of the great poets, though his criticisms of them are always moral, and
never æsthetic, was certainly thorough, and told upon his style. Above
all, he shows a stronger Homeric flavor than all those who professed to
worship the epics which he censured. His language everywhere bears
the influence of Homer, just as some of our greatest and purest writer ṣ
and speakers use unconsciously Biblical phrases and metaphors." See
also 24 26–7, 41 1.

4 2. *Gyges' Ring.* The story is told in the *Republic,* 359–360 (Jowett's translation, 3. 229–230): " According to the tradition, Gyges was
a shepherd in the service of the king of Lydia, and, while he was in the
field, there was a storm and earthquake which made an opening in the
earth at the place where he was feeding his flock. Amazed at the sight,
he descended into the opening, where, among other marvels, he beheld
a hollow brazen horse, having doors, at which he, stooping and looking
in, saw a dead body, of stature, as appeared to him, more than human,
and having nothing on but a gold ring; this he took from the finger
of the dead and reascended. Now the shepherds met together, according to custom, that they might send their monthly report concerning
the flock to the king; and into their assembly he came having the ring
on his finger; and as he was sitting among them he chanced to turn
the collet of the ring towards the inner side of his hand, when instantly
he became invisible, and the others began to speak of him as if he were
no longer there. He was astonished at this, and again touching the

ring he turned the collet outwards and reappeared ; thereupon he
made trials of the ring, and always with the same result: when he
turned the collet inwards he became invisible, when outwards he reappeared.   Perceiving this, he immediately contrived to be chosen one of
the messengers sent to the court, where he no sooner arrived than he
seduced the queen, and with her help conspired against the king and
slew him, and took the kingdom."

4 8.   *Herodotus.*   "The history of Herodotus is half a poem; it was
written while the whole field of literature yet belonged to the Muses,
and the nine books of which it was composed were therefore of right,
as well as of courtesy, superinscribed with their nine names."   T. L.
Peacock, *The Four Ages of Poetry.*

4 10.   *Stole or usurped of poetry.*   So in Sidney's letter to his brother
Robert, quoted in Fox Bourne, *Memoir of Sidney,* p. 276: "Besides
this, the historian makes himself a discourser for profit, and an orator,
yea, a poet sometimes, for ornament; . . . a poet in painting forth the
effects, the motions, the whisperings of the people, which though in
disputation one might say were true, yet who will mark them well
shall find them taste of a poetical vein."

4 11.   *Their passionate describing of passions.*   Sidney is fond of
these verbal jingles, produced by the repetition of the same word or
root-syllable.   Cf. 8 27–28, 34–35, 9 14–15, 10 4–5, 11 27, 13 10–13, 18 18,
18 20–21, 19 1–2, 23 3, 28, 25 20–21, 23, 26 10–11, 28 1–2, 30 24, 31 8–9, 32 5,
33 15–16, 35 7–8, 22–23, 37 21, 38 5, 45 27, 48 31, 51 5, 53 16, 53 30, 54 32–35,
56 35, 58 8.   Specimens of rime are: 20 30.   44 20.   Of assonance:
45 19–20, 54 8–9.   Of alliteration: 16 28, 32 17, 32–33, 34 32–33, 39 24, 41 11.
Cf. also 33 34.   Many of the above repetitions fall under the head
of allowable rhetorical figures, and some of them would scarcely be
remarked on a first reading; but there can be no question that Sidney's
prose would be improved by a retrenchment of the more conspicuous
examples.

4 23.   *Ireland.*   Cf. 58 11–12, and see Spenser, *State of Ireland* (Hales'
edition, p. 626): "For where you say that the Irish have always been
without letters, you are therein much deceived, for it is certain that
Ireland hath had the use of letters very anciently, and long before
England. . . . For the Saxons of England are said to have their letters
and learning and learned men from the Irish, and that also appeareth
by the likeness of the characters, for the Saxons' character is the same
with the Irish. . . . It is to be gathered that that nation which came
out of Spain into Ireland were anciently Gauls, and that they brought
with them those letters which they had learned in Spain, first into
Ireland."

4 27. *Areytos.* Prof. Daniel G. Brinton, of the University of Penn-sylvania, kindly gives me the following information: "This was the name applied by the Spaniards to the combination of song and dancing which was the usual ritual of the native tribes. They picked up the word on the Great Antilles, and it is derived from the Arawack *aririn,* ' to rehearse, repeat.' See Oviedo, *Hist. Gen. de las Indias,* Lib. V. cap. 1 (Madrid edition)."

A fuller account, probably from Oviedo, but not a mere transcript, is given by Purchas, *Pilgrims,* Lib. V. ch. 3 (edition of 1625; 3. 994): "When their Caciques are dead they lay them on a piece of wood or stone, and make a fire about the same which may not burne them, but by degrees draw forth all the moysture in sweat, leaving only the skin and bones, and then in a place separate repose the same with the Ancestors which before had beene so dealt with; this being their best Booke of Heraldrie to recount the Names and severall Descents in that Pedegree. If any die in battell, or so that they cannot recover his body, they compose Songs which the Children learne touching him, and the manner of his death, to supply that memoriall. These Songs they call Areytos. As for Letters they were so ignorant, that seeing the intercourse of Spaniards by Letters, they thought that Letters could speake, and were very cautelous in their carriage of them, lest the Letters might accuse them of ill demeanor by the way. When they will disport themselves, the Men and Women meet and take each other by the hand, and one goeth before which is called Tequina or their Master, with certaine paces measured to his singing in a low voice what commeth in his minde, and after him all the multitude answereth in a higher voice with like measures proportioned to the tune, and so continue they three or foure houres, with *Chicha* or Mayz-wine among; sometimes also changing the Tequina and taking another with a new tune and song."

The passage from Oviedo is as follows: "In this island, as far as I have been able to learn, their songs, which they call *areytos,* constitute the only book or memorial which in these various tribes remains from father to son, and from the present to future times, as shall here be related" (p. 125). "These people have a good and courteous man-ner of communicating things past and ancient; this they do by means of their songs and dances, which they call *areyto,* and which is the same that is known among us as carol (ring-dance or chain-dance) . . . This *areyto* they perform in the following manner: When they desire recreation, as at the celebration of some notable festival, or merely for pastime on other occasions, they hold an assembly of many Indians of both sexes (now and then of men only, and again of women by themselves); and so likewise at the public festivals, as for a victory over their enemies, or at the marriage of their cacique or provincial king, or other case in which there is universal rejoicing, so that men and women mingle freely together. In order to the increase of their joy and hilarity, they take one another by the hand, or link themselves arm in arm, or seat themselves in a line or ring. The office of leader is then assumed by some one, either man or woman, who proceeds to take certain steps backwards and forwards, after the manner of a well-ordered *contrapas.* Immediately they all repeat it after him, and thus they go about, singing in that key, whether low or high, that the leader sounds for them, and imitating him in all that he does and says, the number of the steps keeping measure and harmony with the verses or words that they sing. And according to his direction, they all respond with the same steps, and words, and order; and while they are responding the guide keeps silence, but never ceases to indicate the dancing step. The response having been finished, that is, the repetition of what the leader has prescribed, he at once proceeds to another verse and other words, which the whole company repeat in turn; and so they continue without ceasing for three or four hours or more, until the master or leader of the dance finishes his story, and sometimes they even adjourn from one day to the next. . . . And thus with this rude instrument (i.e. a kind of drum), or without it, they rehearse in song their memoirs and past histories, and tell of the caciques who are no more, how they died, who and how great they were, and other things which they do not wish to have forgotten" (pp. 127–28). Cf. also Puttenham, Bk. I. ch. 5.

5 10. *Even.* Merely.

5 13. *Prophet.* Cf. Shelley, *Defense of Poetry:* "Poets, according to the circumstances of the age and nation in which they appeared, were called, in the earlier epochs of the world, legislators or prophets. A poet essentially comprises and unites both these characters. For he not only beholds intensely the present as it is, and discovers those laws according to which present things ought to be ordered, but he beholds the future in the present, and his thoughts are the germs of the flower and the fruit of latest time."

5 20. *Sortes Virgilianæ.* Cf. the General Introduction to Lonsdale and Lee's translation of Virgil, p. 4: "As the Sibylline books were consulted for the indications of the divine will, so the poems of Virgil, even in early times, were opened at random to obtain directions from them. It is said that the emperor Alexander Severus was encouraged

by lighting upon the passage in the sixth book of the *Æneid* which
bids the Roman 'rule mankind and make the world obey.' . . . Perhaps the most famous instance is that of the passage in the fourth book
of the *Æneid*, which it is said King Charles I. opened, and which runs
as follows:

> And when at length the cruel war shall cease,
> On hard conditions may he buy the peace;
> Nor let him then enjoy supreme command,
> But fall untimely by some hostile hand."

§ 22. *Histories of the Emperors' Lives.* The so-called *Augustan
Histories.* The six authors represented are Ælius Spartianus, Vulcacius
Gallicanus, Trebellius Pollio, Julius Capitolinus, Flavius Vopiscus, and
Ælius Lampridius. The collection includes the lives of the Roman
emperors from 117 to 284 A.D., but the authorship of the various
biographies cannot always be made out with certainty. Simcox, *Hist.
Lat. Lit.*, says (2. 314–15): "In general the majority of the writers
of Augustan history huddle notes from different sources together without criticism. The only point they endeavor to form a real judgment
on is the moral and political worth of the different emperors, and here
they are not without insight." The life of Albinus is probably by
Spartianus (Teuffel, *Gesch. röm. Lit.* § 392).

§ 23. *Albinus.* For Albinus in general, see Gibbon, ch. 5. The
anecdote referred to by Sidney is related in the *Augustan History*,
ch. 5 of the *Life of Albinus:* "He passed the whole of his boyhood
in Africa, where he obtained such a tincture of Greek and Latin literature as might be expected of a mind which had already begun to manifest a martial and haughty temper. As a proof of this disposition it
is related that he used frequently to sing among his playmates,

> Arma amens capio, nec sat rationis in armis,

afterward repeating 'Arma amens capio' as a kind of refrain." The
line is from the *Æneid*, 2. 314: "To arms I rush in frenzy — not that
good cause is shown for arms." Albinus, who was governor of Britain,
led an army over to Lyons against his rival, Septimius Severus, and
was there slain. "The head of Albinus," says Gibbon, "accompanied
with a menacing letter, announced to the Romans that he (i.e. Severus)
was resolved to spare none of the adherents of his unfortunate competitors."

§ 29. *Carmina.* The true etymology.

§ 31. *Altogether not.* Not altogether.

§ 32. *Delphos.* Instead of Delphi. Occasionally found in Latin writers, and common among the Elizabethans. Florio uses it in his translation of Montaigne, Shakespeare in the *Winter's Tale*, and Greene in his *Pandosto*, or *History of Dorastus and Fawnia* (1588), on which the *Winter's Tale* is founded.

Sibylla's prophecies. See Fisher, *Hist. Christian Church*, pp. 73-4: "The 'Sibylline Oracles' is a collection of prophecies, partly Jewish, and antedating the birth of Jesus, and partly Christian. They relate to the Messiah and his work, and were invented with a pious intent to disseminate what their authors considered important religious truths. They are frequently quoted by early ecclesiastical writers." The best edition is that by Alexandre, Paris, 1869.

5 34. *Number and measure.* Cf. 11 30-31, 23 23, 33 22-24, 34 21.

High-flying. Cf. highest-flying, 46 24.

6 1. *Conceit.* Invention, imagination. So 12 2. Sometimes = conception, idea: 31 28, 29, 36 29, 54 8, 55 23; cf. fore-conceit, 8 15. Sometimes = apprehension, understanding: 16 11, 19 34, 23 10, 14, 30 13 (?).

6 2. *In it.* Sidney does not often end a sentence with small and insignificant words. Other examples are 6 28, 11 25, 12 7, etc.

6 6. *Great learned men.* Cf. 9 22-24.

6 9. *Metre.* Cf. Harington (Haslewood, 2. 132): "Some part of the Scripture was written in verse, as the Psalms of David, and certain other songs of Deborah, of Solomon, and others, which the learnedest divines do affirm to be verse, and find that they are in metre, though the rule of the Hebrew verse they agree not on." See also Puttenham, Bk. I. ch. 4: "King David also, and Solomon his son, and many other of the holy prophets, wrate in metres, and used to sing them to the harp, although to many of us, ignorant of the Hebrew language and phrase, and not observing it, the same seem but a prose."

6 12-13. *Awaking his musical instruments.* Ps. 57. 8, 108. 2: "Awake, psaltery and harp."

6 15. *Majesty.* Cf. Ps. 45. 4, "And in thy majesty ride on prosperously because of truth and meekness and righteousness." Also, and especially, Ps. 18. 7-15; 97. 2-5; 104. 3; 144. 5-6.

6 16. *Beasts' joyfulness and hills' leaping.* Ps. 114. 4, "The mountains skipped like rams and the little hills like young sheep."

6 17. *Almost.* Pleonastic, or nearly so. See under *almost*, in the Phil. Society's Dictionary. Cf. 47 4.

6 19. *Beauty.* From Plato, *Symposium* 211 (Jowett's tr. 2. 62): "But what if man had eyes to see the true beauty — the divine beauty, I mean, pure and clear and unalloyed, not clogged with the pollutions of mortality, and all the colors and vanities of human life — thither

looking, and holding converse with the true beauty divine and simple?"

6 19–20. *Only cleared by faith.* Perhaps with allusion to such passages as 2 Cor. 3. 18, " But we all, with unveiled face reflecting as a mirror the glory of the Lord, are transformed into the same image from glory to glory." Or Heb. 11. 1, " Now faith is the assurance of things hoped for, the proving of things not seen." Or Heb. 12. 27, " He endured, as seeing him who is invisible." Or Isa. 33. 17, " Thine eyes shall see the king in his beauty."

6 22–23. *Ridiculous an estimation.* Cf. 2 12, 44 16–18, 45 4–6.

6 24. *Deeper.* Note the form of the adverb, and cf. 15 4.

6 25. *Deserveth.* Plural subject with force of singular. Cf. 11 19–20.

6 28. Ποιητήν. Poiëtēn. Cf. the Variants.

6 30. Ποιεῖν. Cf. the Variants.

6 33. *Maker.* This word was especially used in Scotland to designate a poet.

7 4. *Actors and players.* Cf. Emerson, *Uses of Great Men :* " As plants convert the minerals into food for animals, so each man converts some raw material in nature to human use. . . . Each man is, by secret liking, connected with some district of nature, whose agent and interpreter he is."

7 5. *Astronomer.* Cf. 12 9–12, 35 25.

7 7. *Geometrician.* Cf. 12 16, 28 5, 35 25.

7 8. *Arithmetician.* Cf. 28 6.

7 10. *Natural philosopher.* Cf. 12 14.

7 11. *Moral philosopher.* Cf. 13 7.

7 12. *Virtues, vices, and passions.* Cf. 11 23, 16 17, but especially 17 9–10. See also Sidney's letter to his brother Robert, quoted in Fox Bourne, *Memoir,* p. 277 : " A moral philosopher, either in the epic part when he sets forth virtues or vices, and the natures of passions, or in the politic, when he doth (as he often doth) meddle sententiously with matters of estate."

Follow nature. Cf., for example, Marcus Aurelius, *Thoughts* 7. 55 : " Do not look around thee to discover other men's ruling principles, but look straight to this, to what nature leads thee, both the universal nature through the things which happen to thee, and thy own nature through the things which must be done by thee."

7 18–19. *Compassed within the circle of a question.* Cf. Sidney's letter to his brother Robert, quoted in Fox Bourne, *Memoir,* p. 276 : " We leave all these discourses to the confused trust of our memory, because they, being not tied to the tenor of a question . . ."

7 20. *Physician.* Cf. 35 28.

7 22. *Metaphysic.* Metaphysician (?). Cf. 12 14, and Bacon's use of *politic* for *politician*, *Adv. Learning* 1. 1. 1, 1. 2. 1, etc.

7 22–24. *Though . . . yet.* Cf. 9 8–9, 15 1–2, 38 8–11, 39 2–3, 50 24–25.

7 30. *The.* Superfluous according to present usage. Cf. 28 2.

7 35. *So rich.* Cf. 5 15, 6 22, 8 8–10, 32 22, 44 31–33, 52 13, but *such famous*, 44 29–30.

8 2. *Too-much-loved.* Cf. 55 25, and Warton, *Hist. Eng. Poetry* 4. 394: "Compound epithets, which Sir Philip Sidney had imported from France, and first used in his *Arcadia.*"

8 5. *Go to man.* Cf. Everett, *Poetry, Comedy, and Duty*, p. 312: "Poetry produces its creations to supplement the world. Art rears temples, which, in the words of Emerson already quoted, nature adopts into her race. Shakespeare creates a world of characters and events which takes its place by the side of the world of actual persons and events."

8 6. *It seemeth in him.* For the omission of *that* before a subject clause cf. 18 7.

8 8. *Theagenes.* Cf. 11 16–18.

8 9. *Pylades.* See Euripides' drama, *Iphigenia among the Tauri* (Morley's Universal Library, No. 54).

Orlando. The hero of Ariosto's poem, the *Orlando Furioso* (English translation by Rose, in Bohn's Illustrated Library).

8 10. *Xenophon's Cyrus.* The hero of Xenophon's *Cyropædia*, a historical romance (translation in Bohn's Classical Library).

8 15. *Idea, or fore-conceit.* Cf. 10 14.

8 19. *By.* Concerning. Cf. 21 34, 22 1, 2.

8 25. *Neither let it*, etc. Cf. Shelley, *Defense of Poetry:* "It (i.e. poetry) creates anew the universe, after it has been annihilated in our minds by the recurrence of impressions blunted by reiteration. It justifies the bold and true word of Tasso, 'Non merita nome di creatore, se non Iddio ed il Poeta' (None merits the name of creator except God and the poet)."

8 29. *Over all the works.* Alluding to Heb. 2. 7, "And didst set him over the works of thy hands." Cf. Coleridge, *Biog. Lit.* ch. 13: "The primary imagination I hold to be the living power and prime agent of all human perception, and as a repetition in the finite mind of the eternal act of creation in the infinite I AM."

8 31. *Force of a divine breath.* Cf. 43 14, 57 25.

9 4. *Name above all names.* Philippians 2. 9.

9 12. *Art of imitation.* Cf. 24 10, 42 16, 42 20, and Aristotle, *Poetics,*

1. 2: "Not only the epic and tragedy, but comedy, dithyrambic poetry, and all such as is to be accompanied by the flute and the lyre — all these are (μιμήσεις) representations by means of imitation."

9 15. *Speaking picture.* Cf. 16 22; also 15 35.

9 16. *Teach and delight.* So 10 21, 10 29. Cf. 11 24, 20 8–9, 50 21, 52 3, and *Don Quixote*, Bk. I. ch. 47: "The better end of all writing, which is to instruct and delight together."

9 17. *Three general kinds.* This division is taken from Scaliger, *Poetics*, 5. d. 1, which I thus translate: "The kinds of poets may be reduced to three principal orders. The first is that of religious poets, such as Orpheus and Amphion, whose art was so divine that they are believed to have imparted a soul to inanimate things. The second is that of the philosophical poets, who are again of two sorts — natural, such as Empedocles, Nicander, Aratus, Lucretius, and moral, which is again divided into several species, such as political, represented by Solon and Tyrtæus, economical by Hesiod, and general by Phocylides, Theognis, and Pythagoras. The third are those of whom we shall presently speak."

9 22. *Hymns.* By the hymns of Moses Sidney probably means the Song of Deliverance after the passage of the Red Sea, Exod. 15. 1–19; his Song of God's Guidance, uttered just before his death, Deut. 32. 1–43; and perhaps the Ninetieth Psalm, usually ascribed to Moses. By that of Deborah he means the fifth chapter of Judges.

9 23. *Emanuel Tremellius.* A Biblical scholar (1510–1580 A.D.). Born a Jew, he was converted to Protestantism, and came to England, where he was settled for a time at Oxford. At the accession of Mary Tudor, in 1553, he left England.

Franciscus Junius. Francis Junius, or Du Jon, or Dujon, the Elder (1545–1602), not to be confounded with his famous son Francis, the Germanist and Old English scholar (1589–1677). He was associated with Tremellius in editing the Bible. The Third Part, which Sidney quotes, was issued in 1579.

9 24. *Poetical part of the Scripture.* In Part III. of their edition of the Bible, these scholars include among the poetical books Job, Psalms, Proverbs, Ecclesiastes, and Song of Solomon.

9 27. *Orpheus, Amphion.* Cf. note on 9 17 above, and the index of proper names.

Hymns. See Mahaffy, *Hist. Grk. Lit.* 1. 129: "There are transmitted to us, under the title of *Homeric Hymns*, a collection of five longer and twenty-nine shorter poems in epic dialect and metre, each inscribed to some particular god, and narrating some legend connected

with him, but in no sense religious hymns, as were those of Pamphus
or the hymns of the choral lyric poets. The Homeric Hymns are
essentially secular and not religious; they seem distinctly intended to
be recited in competitions of rhapsodes, and in some cases even for
direct pay." An English translation was made by George Chapman,
and may be found in his works, of which a convenient edition was
published in London in 1875.

9 29. *St. James'*. James 5. 13. In the Ponsonby edition of the
Defense this counsel is attributed to St. Paul. The Olney edition has
it correctly. The words are the well-known ones of the King James
version, " Is any merry? let him sing psalms."

9 30–31. *And I know is used.* Sidney himself translated the first
forty-three Psalms, leaving his sister,

> Sidney's sister, Pembroke's mother,

as Ben Jonson called her, to complete the Psalter. A selection from
the work of both is contained in Ruskin's *Rock Honeycomb*, Sidney's
work in Grosart's *Complete Poems of Sir Philip Sidney* (Fuller Worthies'
Library, 1873), Vol. II., and the whole Psalter in the Chiswick Press
edition of 1823. I subjoin the twenty-third Psalm in Sidney's version,
and two specimens of his sister's rendering (Psalms 119 B and 150):

PSALM 23.

The Lord, the Lord my shepherd is,
    And so can never I
    Taste misery.
He rests me in green pastures His;
    By waters still and sweet
    He guides my feet.

He me revives; leads me the way
    Which righteousness doth take,
    For His name's sake;
Yea, though I should through valleys stray
    Of death's dark shade, I will
    No whit fear ill.

For Thou, dear Lord, Thou me besett'st;
    Thy rod and Thy staff be
    To comfort me;
Before me Thou a table sett'st
    Even when foes' envious eye
    Doth it espy.

Thou oil'st my head, Thou fill'st my cup,
 Nay more, Thou, Endless Good,
  Shalt give me food ;
To Thee, I say, ascended up,
 Where Thou, the Lord of all,
  Dost hold Thy hall.

PSALM 119 B (9–16).

 By what correcting line
May a young man make straight his crooked way ?
 By level of Thy lore divine.
 Sith then with so good cause
My heart Thee seeks, O Lord, I seeking pray :
 Let me not wander from Thy laws.

 Thy speeches have I hid
Close lockèd up in casket of my heart,
 Fearing to do what they forbid.
 But this can not suffice ;
Thou wisest Lord, who ever-blessed art,
 Yet make me in Thy statutes wise.

 Then shall my lips declare
The sacred laws that from Thy mouth proceed,
 And teach all nations what they are ;
 For what Thou dost decree
To my conceit far more delight doth breed
 Than worlds of wealth, if worlds might be.

 Thy precepts, therefore, I
Will my continual meditation make,
 And to Thy paths will have good eye ;
 The orders by Thee set
Shall cause me in them greatest pleasure take,
 Nor once will I Thy words forget.

PSALM 150.

O laud the Lord, the God of Hosts commend,
 Exalt His power, advance His holiness,
 With all your might lift His almightiness ;
Your greatest praise upon His greatness spend.
Make trumpet's noise in shrillest notes ascend,
 Make lute and lyre His loved fame express,
 Him let the pipe, Him let the tabret bless,
Him organ's breath, that winds or waters lend.

> Let ringing timbrels so His honor sound,
> Let sounding cymbals so His glory ring,
> That in their tunes such melody be found
> As fits the pomp of most triumphant king;
> Conclude by all that air or life enfold,
> Let high Jehovah highly be extolled.

10 1. *Cato.* The aphorisms bearing his name are now thought to belong to the third century A.D. Cf. Simcox, *Hist. Lat. Lit.* 2. 302: "Another work of the same period, which had an enormous success in the Middle Ages, was the four books of moral aphorisms of Dionysius Cato, who has been, apparently, extensively edited by Christian copyists, who have left out and inserted as suited them. Still the old foundation is visible."

Lucretius. About 98–55 B.C. The work to which reference is made is entitled *On the Nature of Things.*

10 2. *Manilius.* A Roman poet who lived in the reigns of Augustus and Tiberius, concerning whom little else is known. Even his name is uncertain. He is an imitator of Lucretius, whose theories he opposes. Cf. Cruttwell, *Hist. Rom. Lit.* p. 315: "The subject is called *Astronomy,* but should rather be called *Astrology,* for more than half the space is taken up with those baseless theories of sidereal influence which belong to the imaginary side of the science. But in the exordia and perorations of the book, as well as in sundry digressions, may be found matter of greater value, embodying the poet's views on the great questions of philosophy."

Pontanus. An Italian scholar of the Renaissance (1426–1503). His poems were published at Venice in two volumes, 1505–8. He is said, on good authority, to have coined the word *alliteration,* in the sense now assigned to it. Cf. Symonds, *Renaissance in Italy* 2. 466: "It was not, however, by his lighter verses so much as by the five books called *De Stellis,* or *Urania,* that Pontanus won the admiration of Italian scholars. In this long series of hexameters he contrived to set forth the whole astronomical science of his age, touching upon the mythology of the celestial signs, describing the zodiac, discussing the motion of the heavens, raising the question of planetary influences, and characterizing the different regions of the globe by their relation to the sun's path across the sky."

10 3. *Lucan.* The author (39–65 A.D.) of the unfinished epic *Pharsalia.* Quintilian says of him (10. 1. 90): "Lucan is ardent, earnest, and full of admirably expressed sentiments, and, to give my real opinion, should be classed with orators rather than poets." Cf. also Servius, in his commentary on the *Æneid*, 1. 382 : "Lucan does not deserve to be included among the poets, because he appears rather to have composed a history than a poem." Cruttwell, *Hist. Rom. Lit.* p. 371 : "A strong depreciation of Lucan's genius has been for some time the rule of criticism. . . . Yet throughout the Middle Ages, and during more than one great epoch in French history, he was ranked among the highest epic poets." One of his greatest admirers was Dante (*Inf.* 4. 90), and one of his severest critics is Nisard, *Poètes latins de la décadence.*

10 7. *Fold of the proposed subject.* Cf. 7 19.

10 8. *Whether they*, etc. Cf. Ruskin's *Rock Honeycomb*, Preface, p. 4, note : "Satirical primarily, or philosophical, verses, as of Juvenal, Lucretius, or Pope's *Essay on Criticism*, are merely measured prose, — the grander for being measured, but not, because of their bonds, becoming poetry."

10 14. *Who having no law but wit.* Such was Cicero's notion of art, *Orator*, 2. 9 : "Nor did that artist (i.e. Phidias), in forming the statue of Jupiter or Minerva, have in mind some individual whom he imitated; rather was his soul haunted by a certain glorious beauty, upon which he gazed intently, and by this means directed his art and his hand to achieve the perfect resemblance." Cicero was probably dependent for his opinion upon Plato, as, for example, in *Timæus* 28 (Jowett 3. 612) : "The work of the artificer who looks always to the abiding and the unchangeable, and who designs and fashions his work after an unchangeable pattern, must of necessity be made fair and perfect; but that of an artificer who looks to the created only, and fashions his work after a created pattern, is not fair or perfect."

Cf. also Shakespeare's words, *M. N. D.* 5. 14–17 :

> And as imagination bodies forth
> The forms of things unknown, the poet's pen
> Turns them to shapes and gives to airy nothing
> A local habitation and a name.

10 17. *Lucretia.* The story is told in Livy 1. 58.

10 24. *May be and should be.* Cf. note on 18 25.

10 26. *Excellentest.* For other polysyllabic superlatives, cf. 15 11, 46 23.

10 30. *To move men*, etc. Cf. 23 15 ff., 24 28 ff.

10 33. *Noblest scope.* Cf. 13 1, 15 13.

10 34. *Idle tongues.* Cf. 32 14 ff.

11 2–3. *Heroic . . . pastoral.* By a sort of rhetorical device, Sidney.

when he again introduces these species of poetry, does so in an order the reverse of this. Cf. 26 31, 27 12, 27 19, 27 22, 27 31, 28 27, 29 14, 30 12.

11 7. *Apparelled.* Not merely ' dressed,' but ' showily dressed.' Cf. 29 24, 30 23, but especially 52 35. Shakespeare has a similar use of the word, as in *Err.* 3. 2. 12: " Apparel vice like virtue's harbinger."

11 8. *Numberous.* Note the form.

11 9. *But an ornament.* Cf. 33 11 ff. See also Harington (Haslewood, 2. 131) : " The other part of poetry, which is verse, as it were the clothing or ornament of it."

11 11. *Many versifiers.* Cf. 46 6.

11 13–16. *Xenophon . . . heroical poem.* Literally excerpted by Meres, *Palladis Tamia* (Haslewood, 2. 150).

11 15. *Cicero.* See his letter to his brother Quintus, 1. 1. 8. 23: " This Cyrus is not portrayed by Xenophon with historical accuracy, but in the likeness of just rule."

11 16. *Heliodorus.* Fox Bourne says of Sidney (*Memoir*, p. 324) : " In his youth he had read diligently the Ethiopic History of Heliodorus, lately translated out of the Greek by Thomas Underdown." Cf. also Warton, *Hist. Eng. Poetry* 4. 299, and see Dunlop, *History of Fiction*, ch. 1. The tale is found in *Greek Romances*, Bohn's Classical Library. Meres thus imitates Sidney (Haslewood, 2. 150) : " And as Heliodorus writ in prose his sugared invention of that picture of love in *Theagenes and Chariclea*, . . . so Sir Philip Sidney writ his immortal poem *The Countess of Pembroke's Arcadia* in prose, and yet our rarest poet." Cf. Vauquelin, *Art Poétique* (1605) 2. 261–6.

11 17. *Sugared.* A word much used by the Elizabethans, in the sense of ' charming,' ' delightful.'

11 19. *It is not riming and versing that maketh a poet.* Cf. Shelley, *Defense of Poetry :* " An observation of the regular mode of the recurrence of harmony in the language of poetical minds, together with its relation to music, produced metre, or a certain system of traditional forms of harmony and language. Yet it is by no means essential that a poet should accommodate his language to this traditional form, so that the harmony, which is its spirit, be observed. The practice is indeed convenient and popular, and to be preferred especially in such composition as includes much action; but every great poet must inevitably innovate upon the example of his predecessors in the exact structure of his peculiar versification. The distinction between poets and prose writers is a vulgar error. . . . Plato was essentially a poet — the truth and splendor of his imagery, and the melody of his language,

are the most intense that it is possible to conceive. . . . Lord Bacon was a poet. His language has a sweet and majestic rhythm, which satisfies the sense no less than the almost superhuman wisdom of his philosophy satisfies the intellect. . . . All the authors of revolutions in opinion are not only necessarily poets as they are inventors, nor even as their words unveil the permanent analogy of things by images which participate in the life of truth; but as their periods are harmonious and rhythmical, and contain in themselves the elements of verse; being the echo of the eternal music." See also Abbott, Introduction to *Bacon's Essays*, pp. 23–4: "But Bacon was a poet, the poet of Science. His eye, like the poet's —

> in a fine frenzy rolling,
> Doth glance from heaven to earth, from earth to heaven

— catching at similarities and analogies invisible to uninspired eyes, giving them names and shapes, investing them with substantial reality, and mapping out the whole realm of knowledge in ordered beauty." Cervantes says, *Don Quixote*, Bk. I. ch. 47: "An epic may also be as well written in prose as in verse." Cf. Vauquelin, *L'Art Poét*. 2. 261–6.

11 23. *Notable images.* Sidney, like Aristotle in his *Poetics*, is fond of using the language of the sister art of painting when discoursing of poetry. Cf. 9 15, 10 12 ff., 15 33, 16 13, 22, 19 6, 14, 36 21, 34–5, 37 35 ff.

11 26. *Fittest raiment*, etc. Cf. 33 16–24.

11 27. *Matter . . . manner.* Cf. 46 34.

11 29. *Chanceably.* Cf. 5 18.

11 30. *Peizing.* Poising, weighing. Used by Shakespeare.

11 34. *Parts.* Cf. 26 12 ff. *Anatomies.* Dissections.

12 15. *Music.* Cf. 23 25, 33 26, and see 20 10.

12 18. *Dungeon.* Cf. Plato, *Phædo* 82–3 (Jowett 1. 460): "The soul is able to view real existence only through the bars of a prison, and not of herself unhindered; she is wallowing in the mire of all ignorance; and philosophy, beholding the terrible nature of her confinement, inasmuch as the captive through lust becomes a chief accomplice in her own captivity . . . philosophy, I say, shows her that all this is visible and tangible, but that what she sees in her own nature is intellectual and invisible."

12 21. *Ditch.* See Plato, *Theætetus* 174 (Jowett 4. 324): "I will illustrate my meaning, Theodorus, by the jest which the clever witty Thracian handmaid made about Thales, when he fell into a well as he was looking up at the stars. She said that he was so eager to know what was going on in heaven, that he could not see what was before

his feet. This is a jest which is equally applicable to all philosophers."
Cf. Sonnet 19 of *Astrophel and Stella :*

> . . . Unto me, who fare like him that both
> Looks to the skies, and in a ditch doth fall ?

12 25. *Serving sciences.* Cf. 14 29.

12 28. *Mistress-knowledge.* Florio, in his translation of Montaigne,
uses *mistress* as a quasi-adjective: "The mistress and worthiest part"
(2. 13); "this sovran and mistress amity" (2. 19).

'Αρχιτεκτονική. For the English form of the adjective, see Fulke
Greville, *Life of Sidney* (*Works* 4. 21): "But the truth is, his end
was not writing, even while he wrote, nor his knowledge moulded for
tables or schools; but both his wit and understanding bent upon his
heart, to make himself and others, not in words or opinion but in life
and action, good and great. In which architectonical art he was such
a master, with so commanding and yet equal ways amongst men, that
wheresoever he went he was beloved and obeyed."

12 30. *Ethic and politic.* Cf. 13 24–26, 16 18, 20 3.

12 31. *Well-doing.* Cf. 15 13, 22 26.

12 32. *Saddler's,* etc. Cf. Aristotle, *Ethics* 1. 1: "All moral action,
that is to say all purpose, no less than all art and all science, would
seem to aim at some good result. Hence has come a not inapt
definition of the chief good as that one end at which all human actions
aim. Now ends clearly differ from one another. For, firstly, in some
cases the end is an act, while in others it is a material result beyond
and beside that act. And, where the action involves any such end
beyond itself, this end is of necessity better than is the act by which
it was produced. And, secondly, since there are many kinds of moral
action, and many arts, and many sciences, their ends are also many;
medicine, for example, giving us health, boat-building a boat, tactics
victory, and economics wealth. And, where many such arts are subordinated to some one, — as to riding is subordinated bridle-making, and
all other arts concerned with the production of accoutrements for
horses, while riding itself, and with it all other martial service, is subordinated to the science of military tactics, and in many other arts the
same scale of subordination is to be found, — in all such cases the end
of the supreme art or science is higher than are the ends of the arts
subordinate to it; for it is only for the sake of the former that the
latter are sought."

13 1. *So that,* etc. Cf. 26 7–8.

13 4. *Princes.* Cf. 26 9, and *Don Quixote*, Part II. ch. 16 (Duf-

field's translation): " Poetry, noble sir, to my seeming, is like unto a gentle maiden, young in years, and of extreme beauty, whom to enrich, beautify, and adorn, is the care of the many maidens who attend her — which be the other sciences, — and she must be served of all, while to all these she must lend her lustre. But this same maiden will brook no handling, nor be haled through the streets."

13 9. *For to.* Cf. 44 9, 49 27.

13 11. *Set their names.* Drawn from Cicero, *Archias* 11. 26 (cf. *Tusc. Disp.* 1. 15. 34) : "Those very philosophers even in the books which they write about despising glory, put their own names on the title-page. In the very act of recording their contempt for renown and notoriety, they desire to have their own names known and talked of."

13 12. *Subtility.* Cf. 53 35. *Angry.* See Trench's *Plutarch*, p. 132.

13 14. *Definitions.* Cf. 16 17, 23 21.

13 15. *Distinctions.* Cf. 16 34.

13 29. *Authorizing himself*, etc. Cf. 35 35, 36 5.

14 2. *In a great chafe.* The phrase is found again in Sidney's masque, *The Lady of the May.*

14 4. *Testis temporum.* From Cicero, *On Oratory* 2. 9. 36: " History, the evidence of time, the light of truth, the life of memory, the directress of life, the herald of antiquity."

14 11. *Abstract.* Cf. 15 23.

14 16. *Guide . . . light.* The antithesis will here be more striking if we substitute the Latin words, *dux, lux.*

14 20. *Brutus.* 85–42 B.C. The Brutus of Shakespeare's *Julius Cæsar.* Cf. Plutarch, *Brutus* 4 : " During the time that he was in camp, those hours that he did not spend with Pompey he employed in reading and study; and thus he passed the day before the battle of Pharsalia. It was the middle of summer, the heats were intense, the marshy situation of the camp disagreeable, and his tent-bearers were long in coming. Nevertheless, though extremely harassed and fatigued, he did not anoint himself till noon; and then, taking a morsel of bread, while others were at rest, or musing on the event of the ensuing day, he employed himself till the evening in writing an epitome of Polybius."

Alphonsus. 1385–1454. Ticknor, *Hist. Span. Lit.* 1. 317 (3d Amer. ed.) : " Alphonso the Fifth of Aragon, a prince of rare wisdom and much literary cultivation." Cf. Symonds, *Renaissance in Italy* 2. 252–3: "In the second age of humanism . . . Alfonso of Aragon deserved the praise bestowed on him by Vespasiano of being, next to Nicholas V., the most munificent promoter of learning. His love of letters was genuine. . . . Vespasiano relates that Beccadelli's daily readings to his master were not interrupted during the campaign of 1443, when Alfonso took the field. . . . The Neapolitan captains might be seen gathered round their monarch, listening to the scholar's exposition of Livy, instead of wasting their leisure in games of hazard. Beccadelli himself professes to have cured an illness of Alfonso's in three days by reading aloud to him Curtius's *Life of Alexander*. . . . When the Venetians sent him one of the recently discovered bones of Livy, he received it like the relic of a saint, nor could the fears of his physicians prevent him from opening and reading the MS. of Livy forwarded from Florence by Cosimo de' Medici, who was then suspected of wishing to poison him."

14 21. *Maketh a point.* Cometh to an end or focus.

14 29. *Compare we*, etc. Bacon follows Sidney in regarding this classification as exhaustive in respect to human learning. Cf. *De Augmentis* 2. 1 (*Works* 4. 293): "Wherefore from these three fountains, Memory, Imagination, and Reason, flow these three emanations, History, Poesy, and Philosophy; and there can be no others. For I consider history and experience to be the same thing, as also philosophy and the sciences."

14 32. *The divine.* Cf. 23 13–14.

15 3. *Formidine*, etc. From Horace, *Epist.* 1. 16. 52–3: "Through love of virtue good men shrink from sin: you commit no crime, because you fear punishment."

15 4. *Doth not endeavor.* Cf. 38 18.

15 10. *Naughtiness.* Wickedness. Cf. 27 21, 31.

15 13. *Manners.* With the sense of the Latin *mores*, including morals as well as manners. Cf. his letter to his brother Robert, quoted in Fox Bourne, *Memoir*, p. 223: "For he (i.e. Homer) doth not mean by *mores* how to look or put off one's cap with a new-found grace, although true behavior is not to be despised. . . . But *mores* he takes for that from whence moral philosophy is so called."

15 19. *Bare.* Cf. 24 5.

15 20. *Misty.* Cf. 30 19, 36 1, 47 8.

15 24. *Happy is that man*, etc. Cf. 18 12–13, 25 11–14.

15 27. *Particular truth*, etc. Cf. 15 34–35, 18 29–35.

15 34. *So as.* So that. Cf. 5 5, 7 31–32, 18 12, 28 3–4, 29 5, 33 6, 35 34, 40 30, 43 4, 20, 50 8, and 20 1, note.

16 2. *Wordish.* Cf. 55 3.

16 6. *Who.* Cf. 42 20, 43 30; and see 43 16.

16 8. *Gorgeous palace.* Cf. Shak. *Rom.* 3. 2. 85; *Rich. II.* 3. 3. 148; *Temp.* 4. 152. *Architector.* Architect.

16 12. *Lively.* Living. Cf. 36 34 (= lifelike), and its use as an adverb, 56 1.

16 21. *If they be not illuminated*, etc. Cf. Shelley, *Defense of Poetry* : " Ethical science arranges the elements which poetry has created, and propounds schemes and proposes examples of civil and domestic life : nor is it for want of admirable doctrines that men hate, and despise, and censure, and deceive, and subjugate one another. But poetry acts in another and diviner manner. . . . The great instrument of moral good is the imagination; and poetry administers to the effect by acting upon the cause." And see also Emerson, *Essay on Books :* " The imagination infuses a certain volatility and intoxication. It has a flute which sets the atoms of our frame in a dance, like planets; and, once so liberated, the whole man reeling drunk to the music, they never quite subside to their old stony state. But what is the imagination? Only an arm or weapon of the interior energy; only the precursor of the reason."

16 25. *Anchises.* Cf. *Æneid* 2. 634–650.

16 26. *Ulysses.* Cf. *Odyssey* 5. 149–158 : " But the lady nymph went on her way to the great-hearted Odysseus, when she had heard the message of Zeus. And there she found him sitting on the shore, and his eyes were never dry of tears, and his sweet life was ebbing away as he mourned for his return; for the nymph no more found favor in his sight. . . . And in the day-time he would sit on the rocks and on the beach, straining his soul with tears, and groans, and griefs, and through his tears he would look wistfully over the unharvested deep."

16 28. *Barren and beggarly.* Homer frequently calls Ithaca ' rocky ' and ' rugged.' Cf. *Odyssey* 1. 247. Modern writers confirm this description.

16 29. *Short madness.* The current form of the proverb is found in Horace, *Ep.* 1. 2. 62, but Sidney refers to Seneca, *On Anger* 1. 1. *Ajax.* In Sophocles' drama of that name.

16 35. *Ulysses.* Cf. Shelley, *Defense of Poetry :* " Homer embodied the ideal perfection of his age in human character; nor can we doubt that those who read his verses were awakened to an ambition of becoming like to Achilles, Hector, and Ulysses."

17 1. *Nisus and Euryalus.* Cf. Virgil, *Æneid* 9. 176–182, 433– 445 : " Nisus was guard of the gate, right valiant in arms, son of Hyrtacus; whom Ida, the hunter's hill, had sent to follow Æneas; quick was Nisus with the dart and flying arrows; by his side was his companion Euryalus; there was not a fairer than he among all the men of Æneas, who had put on Trojan arms; the unshorn cheeks of

the boy were just streaked with the early down of youth. One love
the two did feel, together to the wars they rushed. . . . Euryalus
falls and writhes in death, and the blood gushes o'er his lovely limbs,
and his neck sinking down reclines on his shoulder. Even as when a
bright flower cut down by the plough languishes in death, or when
poppies droop their heads with weary neck, if perchance they are
burdened with a weight of rain. But Nisus rushes into the midst;
among them all he makes for Volscens alone, on Volscens alone are
his efforts bent. Around him the foes collect, they close in fight, they
push him back on either side. He presses on with no less zeal, he
whirls his flashing sword, until he has buried it full in the shouting
Rutulian's mouth, and in the act of death he takes his enemy's life.
Then he threw himself on his lifeless friend, pierced with many a
wound, and there at last reposed in tranquil death."

17 3. *Œdipus.* In Sophocles' play of *Œdipus King.*

17 4. *Agamemnon.* In Æschylus' play of that name.

17 5. *Atreus.* Cf. Æschylus' *Agamemnon,* 1555–1580.

17 6. *Theban brothers.* Eteocles and Polynices. See Æschylus'
Seven against Thebes. Sour sweetness. Cf. Shak. *Rich. II.* 5. 5. 42.

17 7. *Medea.* See the *Medea* of Euripides. *Gnatho.* A parasite in
Terence's comedy, *The Eunuch;* cf. the English adjective *gnathonic.*

17 8. *Pandar.* In Chaucer's *Troilus and Cressida;* cf. the English
noun *pander.*

17 12. *See through them.* Cf. the compounds in 18 3, 32 19.

17 15. *Feigned Cyrus in Xenophon.* Cf. 19 10–11.

17 16. *Æneas.* Cf. 30 32 ff.

17 17. *Utopia.* Cf. Jowett's remarks in his translation of Plato,
3. 186–8: "The 'Utopia' of Sir Thomas More is a surprising monu-
ment of his genius, and shows a reach of thought far beyond his contemporaries. The book was written by him at the age of about 34,
and is full of the generous sentiments of youth. He brings the light
of Plato to bear upon the miserable state of his own country. . . . He
is gifted with far greater dramatic invention than any one who suc-
ceeded him, with the exception of Swift. . . . More is as free as Plato
from the prejudices of his age, and far more tolerant."

17 28. *Mediocribus,* etc. From Horace, *Art of Poetry* 372–3:
"Mediocrity in poets is condemned by gods and men, aye, and book-
sellers too."

17 32. *Our Saviour,* etc. Cf. Harington (Haslewood, 2. 131):
"But, to go higher, did not our Saviour himself speak in parables? —
as that divine parable of the Sower, that comfortable parable of the

Prodigal Son, that dreadful parable of Dives and Lazarus, though I know of this last, many of the Fathers hold that it is a story indeed, and no parable."

17 34. *Dives.* Luke 16. 19-31.

18 1. *That.* Like the Latin emphatic *ille.* Cf. 53 18, 53 23.

18 2. *Lost child.* The parable of the Prodigal Son, Luke 15. 11-32.

18 10. *Parables.* Bacon, *Adv. Learning* 2. 1. 1 : " Parables, which is divine poesy."

18 15. *Popular.* Cf. 25 14-15, and Harington (Haslewood, 2. 125) : " Such are the pleasant writings of learned poets, that are the popular philosophers and the popular divines."

18 24. *Fantastically.* Fancifully, imaginatively. Cf. note on 37 34, and Shak. *Macb.* 1. 3. 53, 139.

18 25. *Discourse of Poesy.* Cf. 43 28. The passage referred to is from the beginning of the ninth chapter (9. 1-3), which I thus translate : " From the foregoing remarks it must also be clear that the task of the poet as such is not to relate actual occurrences exactly as they took place, but rather to give an air of verisimilitude to what might happen, and to depict the possible in such a way as to make it seem either probable or necessary. The real distinction between the poet and the historian is not found in the employment of verse by the former, and of prose by the latter, for, if we suppose the history of Herodotus to be versified, it would be nothing but history still, only now in a metrical form. The true ground of difference is that the historian relates what has taken place, the poet how certain things might have taken place. Hence poetry is of a more philosophical and serious character than history; it is, we might say, more universal and more ideal. Poetry deals with the general, history with the particular. Now the general shows how certain typical characters will speak and act, according to the law of probability or of necessity, as poetry indicates by bestowing certain names upon these characters, but the particular merely relates what Alcibiades, a historic individual, actually did or suffered." See also 10 24, 49 6 ff.

18 34. *The particular only marketh,* etc. Cf. Shelley, *Defense of Poetry :* " There is this difference between a story and a poem, that a story is a catalogue of detached facts, which have no other connexion than time, place, circumstances, cause, and effect; the other is the creation of actions according to the unchangeable forms of human nature, as existing in the mind of the creator, which is itself the image of all other minds. . . . Time, which destroys the beauty and the use of the story of particular facts, stripped of the poetry which should

invest them, augments that of poetry, and for ever developes new and wonderful applications of the eternal truth which it contains."

19 1. *Which reason*, etc.   Cf. note on 54 32.

19 10. *Was.*   Cf. 19 32.   *Doctrinable.*   Instructive.

19 11. *Justin.*   A writer of the second century A.D., author of an abridgment of the older history of Pompeius Trogus, who was nearly contemporary with Livy.   The account of Cyrus is in Justin 1. 4–8, and is probably based upon that in Herodotus.

19 12. *Dares Phrygius.*   An apocryphal history of the Trojan war passed current in the Middle Ages under this name, and was regarded as the authentic account of an eye-witness and participant, since Homer actually mentions a certain Dares, *Iliad* 5. 9: "Now there was amid the Trojans one Dares, rich and noble, priest of Hephaistos."   Scaliger, in his *Poetics*, still assumes that the history is true, and Sidney apparently follows him.

19 16. *Horace.*   In his Fifth Epode, and again in the Eighth Satire of the First Book, Horace describes the witch Canidia.   Both descriptions recall the witch scenes in Macbeth.   The beginning of the description in the Eighth Satire is as follows, 23–28: "I myself saw Canidia stalking along with her sable robe tucked up, naked were her feet, dishevelled her hair, she howled in company with the elder Sagana; their ghastly color made them both horrible to look on.   Then they began to scrape the earth with their nails, and to tear with their teeth a black lamb."

19 19. *Tantalus.*   Cf. Euripides, *Orestes* 5–10:

> E'en Tantalus, the son of Jove the blest
> (Not to malign his fate), hangs in the air,
> And trembles at the rock which o'er his head
> Projects its threatening mass; a punishment
> They say, for that, to heaven's high feast admitted,
> A mortal equal with the immortals graced,
> He curbed not the intemperance of his tongue.

And Cicero, *Tusc. Disp.* 4. 16. 35 : "The poets, to express the greatness of this evil, imagine a stone to hang over the head of Tantalus, as a punishment for his wickedness, his pride, and his boasting.   And this is the common punishment of folly; for there hangs over the head of every one whose mind revolts from reason some similar fear."

19 21. *Where.*   Whereas.   So in 19 3, 24 22, 29 35, 41 18, 21, 25, 50 20; but *whereas*, 19 27.

19 22. *Without.*   Unless.   Cf. 33 22, 36 10.

19 25. *Misliked.* Disliked. Cf. 21 17, 24, 25, 40 19.

19 27. *Quintus Curtius.* A Latin writer who probably lived in the time of the Emperor Claudius, and who wrote a history of Alexander the Great in ten books, eight of which have been preserved.

20 1. *So . . . as.* So . . . that. Cf. 21 18, 25 5, 28 10, 33 34, 34 2-3.

20 13. *Zopyrus.* The story is related by Herodotus, 3. 153–160, and by Justin in 1. 10. Cervantes refers to it, *Don Quixote,* Bk. 1. ch. 47.

20 20. *Tarquinius.* Related by Livy, 1. 53–54.

20 22. *Abradatas.* Sidney means either Gadatas or Araspes; cf. the *Cyropædia,* Bk. 5. ch. 3; Bk. 6. ch. 1.

21 4. *To.* As to.

21 5. *Learning is gotten.* Omission of the relative, as in 43 16.

21 7. *Virtue exalted and vice punished.* Cf. Bacon, *Adv. Learning* 2. 4. 1–2: "In the latter it is (i.e. in respect of matter poesy is) . . . one of the principal portions of learning, and is nothing else but feigned history, which may be styled as well in prose as in verse. The use of this feigned history hath been to give some shadow of satisfaction to the mind of man in those points wherein the nature of things doth deny it, the world being in proportion inferior to the soul; by reason whereof there is, agreeable to the spirit of man, a more ample greatness, a more exact goodness, and a more absolute variety, than can be found in the nature of things. Therefore, because the acts or events of true history have not that magnitude which satisfieth the mind of man, poesy feigneth acts and events greater and more heroical. Because true history propoundeth the successes and issues of actions not so agreeable to the merits of virtue and vice, therefore poesy feigns them more just in retribution, and more according to revealed providence. Because true history representeth actions and events more ordinary and less interchanged, therefore poesy endueth them with more rareness, and more unexpected and alternative variations. So as it appeareth that poesy serveth and conferreth to magnanimity, morality, and to delectation. And therefore it was ever thought to have some participation of divineness, because it doth raise and erect the mind, by submitting the shows of things to the desires of the mind; whereas reason doth buckle and bow the mind unto the nature of things. And we see that by these insinuations and congruities with man's nature and pleasure, joined also with the agreement and consort it hath with music, it hath had access and estimation in rude times and barbarous regions, where other learning stood excluded."

21 11. *Handmaid.* Cf. 40 2.

21 12. *Storm. Odyssey,* Book V.

21 16. *As the tragedy-writer answered.* Cf. Plutarch, *On Listening to Poetry* (*Morals* 2. 54): "As Euripides is reported, when some blamed him for bringing such an impious and flagitious villain as Ixion upon the stage, to have given this answer: But yet I brought him not off till I had fastened him to a torturing wheel."

21 22. *Miltiades.* Cf. Cicero, *Republic* 1. 3. 5: "They tell us that Miltiades, the vanquisher and conqueror of the Persians, before even those wounds were healed which he had received in that most glorious victory, wasted away in the chains of his fellow-citizens that life which had been preserved from the weapons of the enemy."

21 23. *Phocion.* Cf. Plutarch, *Phocion* 38: "The proceedings against Phocion put the Greeks in mind of those against Socrates. The treatment of both was equally unjust, and the calamities thence entailed upon Athens were perfectly similar."

21 24. *Cruel Severus.* Septimius Severus.

21 25. *Excellent Severus.* Alexander Severus. For an account of both these emperors see Gibbon, *Decline and Fall*, chs. 5, 6, and 7.

Sylla. Cf. Mommsen, *Hist. Rome* (English tr.) 3. 469: "Little more than a year after his retirement, in the sixtieth year of his life, while yet vigorous in body and mind, he was overtaken by death; . . . the rupture of a blood-vessel carried him off."

Marius. Cf. Mommsen, 3. 391: "A burning fever seized him; after being stretched for seven days on a sick bed, in the wild fancies of which he was fighting on the fields of Asia Minor the battles whose laurels were destined for Sulla, he expired on the 13th Jan. 668 (i.e. 86 B.C.). He died, more than seventy years old, in full possession of what he called power and honor, and in his bed; but Nemesis assumes various shapes, and does not always expiate blood with blood."

21 26. *Pompey.* Cf. Mommsen, *Hist. Rome* 4. 508: "As he was stepping ashore, the military tribune Lucius Septimius stabbed him from behind, under the eyes of his wife and son, who were compelled to be spectators of the murder from the deck of their vessel, without being able to rescue or revenge. On the same day, on which thirteen years before he had entered the capital in triumph over Mithridates, the man, who for a generation had been called the Great and for years had ruled Rome, died on the desert sands of the inhospitable Casian shore by the hand of one of his soldiers."

Cicero. Cf. Plutarch, *Cicero* 48: "The tribune, taking a few soldiers with him, ran to the end of the walk where he was to come out. But Cicero perceiving that Herennius was hastening after him, ordered his servants to set the litter down; and putting his left hand to his chin, as it was his custom to do, he looked steadfastly upon his murderers Such an appearance of misery in his face, overgrown with hair, and wasted with anxiety, so much affected the servants of Herennius that they covered their faces during the melancholy scene. That officer despatched him, while he stretched his neck out of the litter to receive the blow. Thus fell Cicero, in the sixty-fourth year of his age."

21 28. *Virtuous Cato.* Cato of Utica.

21 31. *Cæsar's own words.* Reported by Suetonius, *Julius Cæsar* 77: "Sullam nescisse literas, qui dictaturam deposuerit." This, which would naturally be translated, "Sylla was an ignorant fellow to abdicate the dictatorship," might also be rendered, "Sylla was an ignorant fellow to abdicate the office of dictating to pupils." This, as my friend Professor Bernadotte Perrin, of Adelbert University, to whom I am indebted for this reference, says, is "an etymological joke, and a poor one." Sidney evidently gathers from it some such meaning as this: "Sylla was without learning (a man of untutored nobleness), and for this reason laid down the dictatorship." Cf. Bacon, *Adv. L.* 1. 7. 29.

Who. Cæsar. His whole later career was an undoing of Sylla's work. The beginning of it is marked by Suetonius, *Julius Cæsar* 5: "Having been elected military tribune, the first honor he received from the suffrages of the people after his return to Rome, he zealously assisted those who took measures for restoring the tribunitian authority, which had been greatly diminished during the usurpation of Sylla."

22 1. *In hell.* So by Virgil in the Sixth Book of the *Æneid*, and by Homer in the Eleventh Book of the *Odyssey*.

22 2. *Occidendos esse.* That they are to be slain. Cf. the note on Phalaris below.

22 3. *Cypselus, Periander.* Cf. Herodotus 5. 92: "And Cypselus, having obtained the tyranny, behaved himself thus: he banished many of the Corinthians, deprived many of their property, and many more of their life. When he had reigned thirty years, and ended his life happily, his son Periander became his successor in the tyranny. Now Periander at first was more mild than his father; but when he had communicated by embassadors with Thrasybulus, tyrant of Miletus, he became far more cruel than Cypselus; . . . whatever Cypselus had left undone, by killing and banishing, Periander completed."

22 4. *Phalaris.* Cf. Cicero, *On Duties* 2. 632: "Now, as to what relates to Phalaris, the decision is very easy; for we have no society with tyrants, but rather the widest separation from them; nor is it contrary to nature to despoil, if you can, him whom it is a virtue to slay -- and this pestilential and impious class ought to be entirely exterminated from the community of mankind."

Dionysius. Dionysius the Elder, tyrant of Syracuse. Cf. Cicero, *Tusc. Disp.* 5. 20–22, 57–63.

22 11. *Laurel crown.* Cf. 32 6, 44 9, 45 8.

22 12. *Victorious.* Note the double construction, with *of* and with *over.*

22 14. *For suppose,* etc. Cf. 35 12–14.

22 18. Φιλοφιλόσοφος. A friend to the philosopher. Apparently coined by Sidney.

22 26. Γνῶσις. Knowledge. Πρᾶξις. Practice. Cf. Aristotle, *Ethics* 1. 3: "For the true object of ethical study is not merely the knowledge of what is good, but the application of that knowledge."

22 30–32. *As well . . . as . . . as.* Note the peculiar structure.

23 2. *Beholding.* Beholden. Now obsolete in this sense.

23 12. *Hoc opus, hic labor est.* This is the task, this the struggle. Virgil, *Æneid* 6. 129.

23 21. *Margent.* This, and not *margin,* is the regular Shakespearian form.

23 25. *Forsooth.* Cf. 25 14.

23 26. *A tale,* etc. Cf. Harington (Haslewood, 2. 133): "They present unto us a pretty tale, able to keep a child from play, and an old man from the chimney corner."

23 31. *Pleasant taste.* Cf. 23 19, 25 2. A striking parallel to this is found in a book which we know Sidney had consulted (cf. 9 24 note), the edition of the Bible by Tremellius and Junius. I translate from the Preface to Part III.: "For when the Holy Spirit saw that mankind could scarcely be persuaded to the practice of virtue, and that we, being inclined by the wickedness of our nature to sensual delights, neglected the rule of right living, what did He do? In the midst of His graver instructions He scattered the alluring harmonies of song, that while our ears were attuned to their sweetness and grace, we might imperceptibly descry the lessons which the words convey, just as experienced physicians do, who, when they would administer unpleasant medicines to the sick, are wont to smear the mouth of the cup with honey, lest the bitterness of the drug cause the patient to refuse its virtue." He may also have seen the same idea expressed in Tasso 1. 3, here given in Fairfax's translation:

> Thither, thou know'st, the world is best inclined
> Where luring Parnass most his sweet imparts,
> And truth conveyed in verse of gentle kind,
> To read perhaps will move the dullest hearts;

So we, if children young diseased we find,
Anoint with sweets the vessel's foremost parts,
To make them taste the potions sharp we give ;
They drink deceived, and so deceived they live.

Cf. also Gosson, *School of Abuse*, p. 20: "The deceitful physician giveth sweet syrups, to make his poison go down the smoother." All of these go back to Lucretius, 1. 936–950: " But even as physicians when they purpose to give nauseous wormwood to children, first smear the rim round the bowl with the sweet yellow juice of honey, that the unthinking age of children may be fooled as far as the lips, and meanwhile drink up the bitter draught of wormwood and though beguiled yet not be betrayed, but rather by such means recover health and strength; so I now, since this doctrine seems generally somewhat bitter to those by whom it has not been handled, and the multitude shrinks back from it in dismay, I have resolved to set forth to you our doctrine in sweet-toned Pierian verse and o'erlay it as it were with the pleasant honey of the Muses, if haply by such means I might engage your mind on my verses, till such time as you clearly perceive with what shape the whole nature of things has been put together."

23 31. *Which.* Referring to persons. Cf. 23 35.

24 1. *Cradled in their graves.* Note this highly poetical expression.

24 8. *As Aristotle saith.* I translate from *Poetics* 4. 2. 3: "For imitation is inbred in men from childhood. And they differ in this respect from other living beings that they are the most imitative, and acquire their first learning through imitation, and that they all take pleasure in the products of the mimetic art. This is proved by experience. The pictures of those very things which in themselves are disagreeable to look on, these pictures, though painted with the utmost accuracy, we are delighted to gaze at, such, for example, as those of the vilest animals or of dead bodies."

24 12. *Amadis de Gaule.* A contemporary French critic, Baret, in a learned monograph on the *Amadis de Gaule* (Paris, 1873), says (p. 143): " In every other respect the Amadis is an exact reproduction of antique chivalric sentiments. Martial enthusiasm linked with the adoration of woman; religious faith; the inviolability of a promise once given; the constant endeavor to maintain the right of the weak by reason or by arms; honor and loyalty regarded as dearer than life itself; all these noble and useful virtues are to be found in the knights gathered round King Lisuarte, no less than in those who adorned the court of King Arthur."

24 15. *Courage.* Cf. 29 20–35, 35 2, 38 29–32, 39 24.

24 15. *Carrying old Anchises.* *Æneid* 2. 705-804.

24 20. *Fugientem,* etc. *Æneid* 12. 645-6: "Shall this land see Turnus a fugitive? Is it so passing hard to die?"

24 26. *Plato and Boethius.* Plato frequently quotes from Homer. For Boethius cf. 26 24.

24 30. *Indulgere genio.* Referring to Persius, *Sat.* 5. 151: "Give your genius play; let us take pleasure as it comes; life is ours and it is all we have."

25 6. *Menenius Agrippa.* The story is told by Livy, 2. 32. Cf. also Shak. *Cor.* 1. 1. 99-158.

25 11. *Far-fet.* Far-fetched. Cf. 53 2.

25 23. *As.* That.

25 27. *Nathan.* See 2 Sam. 12, and cf. 36 11, below. Sidney's words are echoed by Harington (Haslewood, 2. 131).

26 1. *In a glass.* Cf. 28 24, 46 14. *Filthiness.* Cf. the use of the same word in the rendering of this very Psalm of Mercy by Sidney's sister:

> For I, alas, acknowledging do know
> My filthy fault; my faulty filthiness
> To my soul's eye uncessantly doth show,
> Which done to thee, to thee I do confess,
> Just judge, true witness; that for righteousness
> Thy doom may pass against my guilt awarded,
> Thy evidence for truth may be regarded.

26 8. *So poetry,* etc. Cf. 30 28 ff.

26 17. *Defectious.* Cf. 48 2.

26 22. *Tragi-comical.* Cf. 50 10-14.

26 23. *Sannazzaro.* A Neapolitan scholar and poet (1458-1530) the author of the *Arcadia.* Cf. Symonds, *Renaissance in Italy* 5. 197, 211: "To Sannazzaro belongs the glory of having first explored Arcadia, mapped out its borders, and called it after his own name. He is the Columbus of this visionary hemisphere. . . . For English students the *Arcadia* has a special interest, since it begot the longer and more ambitious work of Sir Philip Sidney. Hitherto I have spoken only of its prose; but the book blends prose and verse in alternating sections."

26 24. *Boethius.* Cf. Morley, *First Sketch of Eng. Lit.,* pp. 24-5 : "Boethius, a Roman senator, lost the favour of Theodoric by a love for his country, which his enemies called treason, was imprisoned, and from prison led to execution, about the year 525. In prison he wrote his noble work called *The Consolation of Philosophy,* in five books of prose, mixed with verse. The first of its five books recognised as the great source of consolation that a wise God rules the world; the second argued that man in his worst extremity possesses much, and ought to fix his mind on the imperishable; the third maintained that God is the chief good, and works no evil; the fourth, that, as seen from above, only the good are happy; and the fifth sought to reconcile God's knowledge of what is necessary with the freewill of mankind."

26 34. *Melibæus'*. Cf. Virgil's *First Eclogue.*

27 1. *Tityrus*. See last note.

27 3. *Wolves and sheep.* Probably referring to Spenser, *Ninth Eclogue* (September) of the *Shepherd's Calender*. If so, it is easier to understand why Sidney's judgment upon Spenser's work (cf. 47 16–19) is so harsh.

27 7. *Strave.* Cf. 41 17, and the note on 1 27.

27 10. *Hæc memini*, etc. Virgil, *Ecl.* 7. 69–70: "These verses I remember, and how the vanquished Thyrsis vainly strove. From that day it has been with us Corydon, none but Corydon."

27 12. *Which*. But Sidney immediately passes over to personification, as in the characterization of the other species below.

27 14. *Heraclitus.* Cf. Seneca, *On Anger* 2. 10. 5: "Heraclitus, as often as he went forth a-doors, and saw about him such a multitude of evil livers, nay, rather, men dying wickedly, he wept, having compassion on all those that met him with a joyful and contented countenance."

27 23. *Omne vafer*, etc. Condensed from a couplet of Persius, *Sat.* 1. 116–7:

> Omne vafer vitium ridenti Flaccus amico
> Tangit, et admissus circum præcordia ludit.

Conington thus translates: "Horace, the rogue, manages to probe every fault while making his friend laugh; he gains his entrance, and plays about the innermost feelings." Gildersleeve, in his edition of Persius, would translate *præcordia* by 'heart-strings.' Gosson quotes the couplet, p. 31.

27 28. *Circum præcordia ludit.* See last note.

27 30. *Est Ulubris*, etc. Modified from Horace, *Epist.* 1. 11. 30, which has *te* for *nos*. Lines 25 to 30 are thus translated by Howes:

> For if 'tis wisdom gives content and ease —
> Not a fair prospect of expanded seas,
> Who roam abroad from shore to shore, shall find
> They change the climate only, not the mind.

Idly alert we traverse sea and land
In quest of happiness that lies at hand.
Let but good sense each fretful whim control
And tranquillize the tumults of the soul,
'Tis here — 'tis anywhere : you cannot miss;
And Ulubræ may prove the seat of bliss.

Ulubræ was a town of Latium proverbial for its desolation. Cf. Juvenal 10. 102; Cicero, *Familiar Letters* 7. 18. 3.

27 32. *Justly.* Cf. 47 28–9.

27 33. *Argument of abuse.* The first direct reference to Gosson's diatribe. Cf. 34 31, 37 30, 38 7 ff., 42 9–10, 43 4, 52 8, and especially 38 28.

28 1. *The comedy.* Cf. 28 26–27, 50 21.

28 8. *Wanteth a great foil.* Cf. Milton, *Areopagitica :* "Good and evil we know in the field of this world grow up together almost inseparably; and the knowledge of good is so involved and interwoven with the knowledge of evil, and in so many cunning resemblances hardly to be discerned, that those confused seeds which were imposed upon Psyche as an incessant labor to cull out and sort asunder, were not more intermixed. It was out the rind of one apple tasted, that the knowledge of good and evil, as two twins cleaving together, leaped forth into the world. And perhaps this is that doom which Adam fell into of knowing good and evil; that is to say, of knowing good by evil.

"As therefore the state of man now is, what wisdom can there be to choose, what continence to forbear, without the knowledge of evil? He that can apprehend and consider vice with all her baits and seeming pleasures, and yet abstain, and yet distinguish and yet prefer that which is truly better, he is the true warfaring Christian. I cannot praise a fugitive and cloistered virtue unexercised and unbreathed, that never sallies out and seeks her adversary, but slinks out of the race, where that immortal garland is to be run for not without dust and heat. Assuredly we bring not innocence into the world, we bring impurity much rather; that which purifies us is trial, and trial is by what is contrary. That virtue therefore which is but a youngling in the contemplation of evil, and knows not the utmost that vice promises to her followers, and rejects it, is but a blank virtue, not a pure; her whiteness is but an excremental whiteness; which was the reason why our sage and serious poet Spenser (whom I dare be known to think a better teacher than Scotus or Aquinas), describing true temperance under the person of Guion, brings him in with his palmer through the Cave of Mammon and the Bower of Earthly Bliss, that he might see and know, and yet abstain."

So Bacon, *De Augmentis* 7. 2 (*Works* 5. 17–18): "For it is not possible to join the wisdom of the serpent with the innocence of the dove, except men be perfectly acquainted with the nature of evil itself, for without this virtue is open and unfenced; nay, a virtuous and honest man can do no good upon those that are wicked, to correct and reclaim them, without first exploring all the depths and recesses of their malice. For men of corrupted minds presuppose that honesty grows out of an ignorance or simplicity of manners, and believing of preachers, school-masters, books, moral precepts, common discourses and opinions; so as, except they plainly perceive that you know as much of their corrupt opinions and depraved principles as they do themselves, they despise all honesty of manners and counsel." And see also Plutarch, *On Listening to Poetry* (*Morals* 2. 66): "And of this nature is Homer's poetry, which totally bids adieu to Stoicism, the principles whereof will not admit any vice to come near where virtue is, nor virtue to have any thing to do where any vice lodgeth, but affirms that he that is not a wise man can do nothing well, and he that is so can do nothing amiss. Thus they determine in the schools. But in human actions and the affairs of common life the judgment of Euripides is verified, that

> Virtue and vice ne'er separately exist,
> But in the same acts with each other twist."

28 12–13. *Demea*, etc. Characters in the plays of Terence, the Latin dramatist: respectively a parsimonious old man, a slave, a parasite, and a braggart.

28 20. *In pistrinum.* This phrase is borrowed from Terence and Plautus, in whom the master, if he wishes to bring a slave to terms, threatens to send him to labor in the mill. Thus Terence, *Andria* 1. 2. 28: "I'll hand you over, Davus, beaten with stripes, to the mill, even to your dying day." And Plautus, *Mostellaria* 1. 1. 16: "Before long you'll be handed over to the mill."

28 24. *His own actions.* Cf. Gosson, p. 31: "Now are the abuses of the world revealed; every man in a play may see his own faults, and learn by this glass to amend his manners." Gosson borrows this thought from Cicero. According to Donatus, "Cicero says that comedy is an imitation of life, a mirror of customs, an image of truth." Cf. Shakespeare, *Hml.* 3. 2. 23–27: "The purpose of playing, whose end, both at the first and now, was and is, to hold, as 'twere, the mirror up to nature; to show virtue her own feature, scorn her own image, and the very age and body of the time his form and pressure." Cf. also *Hml.* 3. 4. 19–20:

> You go not till I set you up a glass
> Where you may see the inmost part of you.

28 25. *By nobody be blamed.* See Shelley, *Defense of Poetry:* "In the drama of the highest order there is little food for censure or hatred; it teaches rather self-knowledge and self-respect. . . . But in periods of the decay of social life, the drama sympathizes with that decay." And again: "And it is indisputable that the highest perfection of human society has ever corresponded with the highest dramatic excellence; and that the corruption or the extinction of the drama in a nation where it has once flourished, is a mark of a corruption of manners, and an extinction of the energies which sustain the soul of social life."

28 28. *Covered with tissue.* Cf. Shakespeare, *Hml.* 3. 4. 145-150:

> Lay not that flattering unction to your soul,
> That not your trespass, but my madness speaks:
> It will but skin and film the ulcerous place,
> Whilst rank corruption, mining all within,
> Infects unseen. Confess yourself to heaven;
> Repent what's past; avoid what is to come.

28 30. *Admiration and commiseration.* Aristotle's 'awe and pity,' or 'fear (terror) and compassion,' as his words in the sixth chapter of the *Poetics* are variously translated. Cf. 50 22, 52 4.

28 32. *Gilden.* An Old English form. Cf. *Astrophel and Stella,* Sonnet 11, "gilden leaves."

28 33. *Roofs.* Apparently = Lat. *tecta,* dwellings.

28 34. *Qui sceptra,* etc. Seneca, *Œdipus* 705-6, which I translate:

> The savage tyrant, bearing sternest rule,
> Dreads those who dread him, and his fear recoils
> To plague the inventor.

29 2. *Alexander Pheræus.* Plutarch, *Pelopidas* 29, relates of this Alexander the incident to which Sidney alludes: "For he (i.e. Epaminondas) knew his savage disposition, and the little regard he paid to reason or justice; that he buried some persons alive, and dressed others in the skins of bears and wild boars, and then, by way of diversion, baited them with dogs, or despatched them with darts; that having summoned the people of Melibœa and Scotusa, towns in friendship and alliance with him, to meet him in full assembly, he surrounded them with guards, and with all the wantonness of cruelty put them to the sword. . . . Yet upon seeing a tragedian act the *Troades* of

Euripides, he went hastily out of the theatre, and at the same time sent a message to the actor not to be discouraged, but to exert all his skill in his part; for it was not out of any dislike that he went out, but he was ashamed that his citizens should see him, who never pitied those he put to death, weep at the sufferings of Hecuba and Andromache." Plutarch repeats this somewhat more dramatically in his *Fortune or Virtue of Alexander* (*Morals* 1. 492).

29 18. *Lauds of the immortal God.* Cf. 52 15 ff.

29 20. *Barbarousness.* Cf. Child, *Eng. and Scott. Popular Ballads*, Part VI. p. 305, note: "The courtly poet deserves much of ballad lovers for avowing his barbarousness (one doubts whether he seriously believed that the gorgeous Pindar could have improved upon the ballad), but what would he not have deserved if he had written the blind crowder's song down?"

Percy and Douglas. Cf. Child, *Ballads*, p. 305: "The song of Percy and Douglas, then, was sung about the country by blind fiddlers about 1580 in a rude and ancient form, much older than the one that has come down to us; for that, if heard by Sidney, could not have seemed to him a song of an uncivil age, meaning the age of Percy and Douglas, two hundred years before his day. It would give no such impression even now, if chanted to an audience three hundred years later than Sidney."

29 26. *Hungary.* Where Sidney was for a month or so, just before completing his nineteenth year (August or September to October, 1573). See Fox Bourne, *Memoir*, pp. 64–5.

29 33–35. *The lusty men,* etc. Plutarch, *Laws and Customs of the Lacedæmonians* (*Morals* 1. 90–91).

30 7. *Olympus.* By mistake for Olympia.

30 7-8. *Three fearful felicities.* Cf. Plutarch, *Alexander* 3: " Philip had just taken the city of Potidæa, and three messengers arrived the same day with extraordinary tidings. The first informed him that Parmenio had gained a great battle against the Illyrians; the second, that his racehorse had won the prize at the Olympic games; and the third, that Olympias was brought to bed of Alexander. His joy on that occasion was great, as might naturally be expected; and the soothsayers increased it by assuring him that his son, who was born in the midst of three victories, must of course prove invincible."

30 16. *Turnus.* A celebrated character in the last half of the *Æneid.* Cf. note on 24 20. *Tydeus.* See *Iliad*, Bk. 4. *Rinaldo.* See Ariosto, *Orlando Furioso.*

30 20. *Plato.* Cf. his *Phædrus* 250 (Jowett 2. 127): " For sight is

the keenest of our bodily senses; though not by that is wisdom seen;
her loveliness would have been transporting if there had been a visible
image of her, and the same is true of the loveliness of the other ideas
as well."

Tully. Cf. Cicero, *On Duties* I. 5. 15 : "You here perceive at least a
sketch, and, as it were, the outline of virtue; which, could we perceive
her with our eyes, would, as Plato says, kindle a wonderful love of
wisdom." Cf. also Sonnet 25 of *Astrophel and Stella :*

> The wisest scholar of the wight most wise
> By Phœbus' doom, with sugared sentence says,
> That virtue, if it once met with our eyes,
> Strange flames of love it in our souls would raise.

"The wight most wise by Phœbus' doom" is of course Socrates. Cf.
43 23.

30 26. *Sweet poetry.* Cf. 44 23; also 36 6, 41 8.

30 27. *Best.* Cf. Dryden, *Discourse on Epic Poetry* (near the beginning) : "An heroic poem (truly such) is undoubtedly the greatest
work which the soul of man is capable to perform. The design of it
is to form the mind to heroic virtue by example; it is conveyed in verse
that it may delight while it instructs."

31 10-11. *Melius Chrysippo et Crantore.* Horace, *Epist.* I. 2. 4.
The opening lines are (Howes' translation) :

> While in the schools of Rome, you, Lollius! plead,
> I at Præneste with new rapture read
> The tale of Troy divine, whose facts declare
> Where moral fitness lies — expedience where,
> Better than all the logic of the sage,
> Than Crantor's precepts or Chrysippus' page.

Chrysippus was a famous Stoic (282-209 B.C.). Cf. Cicero, *Character
of the Orator* I. 11. 50 : "For we see that some have reasoned on the
same subjects jejunely and dryly, as Chrysippus, whom they celebrate
as the acutest of philosophers; nor is he on this account to be thought
to have been deficient in philosophy, because he did not gain the talent
of speaking from an art which is foreign to philosophy."

Of Crantor Cicero says (*Tusc. Disp.* 3. 6. 12) : "Crantor, who
was one of the most distinguished men that our academy has ever
produced."

31 12. *Poet-whippers.* Cf. 32 14.

31 16. *Particularities.* Cf. 26 19 ff.

31 17. *Carping.* Cf. 32 17.

31 19. *Ancient.* Cf. 2 18–3 15.

31 21. *Learned.* Cf. 5 8–6 33. *Barbarous.* Cf. 4 21–5 7. Sidney here inverts the order, as indicated in the note on 11 2–3.

31 23. *Prophesying.* Cf. 5 12–16.

31 24. *Making.* Cf. 6 28–33.

31 27. *His own stuff.* Cf. 7 1–8 30.

31 29. *Description.* Cf. 9 9 ff. *End.* 13 1 ff.

31 31. *Goodness.* Cf. 26 3–11.

31 32. *Chief.* Cf. 13 1–2.

31 33. *The historian.* Cf. 22 7–10.

31 34. *The philosopher.* Cf. 22 14–23.

32 1. *Holy Scripture.* Cf. 9 17–26, 17 32 ff., 25 27 ff.

32 3. *Kinds.* Cf. 9 17 ff.

32 4. *Dissections.* Cf. 11 1 ff., 26 19 ff.

32 14. Μισομούσοι. Apparently coined by Sidney.

32 17. *Wandering.* Rambling.

32 19. *Through-beholding.* Cf. 18 3.

32 20. *Those kind.* Sidney usually employs the singular demonstrative with *kind.* Thus 32 15, 33 8, 52 11–12.

32 25. *The discretion of an ass.* Probably in allusion to the 102d chapter of Agrippa's work (see 32 30, below) entitled *A Digression in Praise of the Ass.*

32 26–27. *Comfortableness . . . plague.* Francesco Berni, an Italian author (ca. 1496–1535), wrote on these two subjects, debt and the plague. Cf. Symonds, *Renaissance in Italy* 5. 364. That on the plague is one of the best of the so-called *Capitoli*, in which such subjects were treated, and which he was so graceless as to invent, or rather revive. Such themes had been chosen by the sophists of the first Christian centuries as a means of exhibiting their intellectual dexterity and rhetorical skill, but it was reserved for Berni and his imitators to add touches of bestial obscenity of which their masters were incapable.

32 29. Another instance of Sidney's adaptation of the Latin authors to his purpose. The line in Ovid stands (*Art of Love* 2. 662) :

Ut lateat vitium proximitate boni,

which Sidney might have expressed by, "That vice lie hid in nearness of the good."

32 30. *Agrippa.* (Henry) Cornelius Agrippa, a German scholar (1486–1535). Emerson, *Essay on Books*, says : "Cornelius Agrippa 'On the Vanity of Arts and Sciences' is a specimen of that scribatiousness which grew to be the habit of the gluttonous readers of his time.

. . . They read voraciously, and must disburden themselves; so they take any general topic, as Melancholy, or Praise of Science, or Praise of Folly, and write and quote without method or end." Agrippa's fourth chapter is a diatribe against poetry, which Harington endeavors to refute (Haslewood, 2. 125 ff.).

32 31. *Erasmus*. The famous Dutch scholar (1467–1536). His *Encomium Moriæ*, or *Praise of Folly*, was written in 1509. It owes a part of its celebrity to the illustrations by Holbein.

33 5. *Scoffing cometh not of wisdom*. Cf. for example, Prov. 9. 8: " Reprove not a scorner, lest he hate thee; rebuke a wise man, and he will love thee." " Bacon, quoting Prov. 14. 6 (*Adv. Learning* 2. 21. 9), thus comments upon it: ' He that cometh to seek after knowledge with a mind to scorn and censure, shall be sure to find matter for his humor, but no matter for his instruction.' "

33 15. *Scaliger*. The second book of his *Poetics* is devoted to the Matter of Poetry, as he calls it, under which head he treats of metrical feet.

33 16. *Oratio*, etc. Cf. Cicero, *On Duties* 1. 16. 50: "Of this (i.e. human society) the bond is speech and reason (oratio et ratio), which by teaching, learning, communicating, debating, and judging, conciliate men together, and bind them into a kind of natural society."

34 7. *Throughly*. Common in Shakespeare. Cf. *Hml*. 4. 5. 136.

34 15. *Percontatorem*, etc. Horace, *Epist*. 1. 18. 69: "Avoid a curious man; he is sure to be a gossip." Quoted also by Bacon, *Adv. Learning* 1. 4. 8, and by him translated, "An inquisitive man is a prattler."

34 16. *Dum sibi*, etc. Ovid, *Rem. Love* 686: "While each one is satisfying himself, we are ever a credulous set."

34 30. *Mother of lies*. But cf. 38 27.

34 32. *Siren's*. Cf. Gosson, p. 20: "The siren's song is the sailor's wrack."

34 34. *To ear*. To plough. Alluding to Chaucer, *Knight's Tale* 28:

> I have, God woot, a large feeld to ere.

35 1. *In other nations*. Gosson, p. 23, illustrates these words: " C. Marius, in the assembly of the whole Senate at Rome, in a solemn oration giveth an account of his bringing up: he showeth that he hath been taught to lie on the ground, to suffer all weathers, to lead men, to strike his foe, to fear nothing but an evil name." For this oration cf. Sallust, *Jugurtha* 85.

35 4. *Shady idleness.* Cf. Milton, *Lycidas* 67–8:

> Were it not better done, as others use,
> To sport with Amaryllis in the shade?

35 6. *Banished.* Gosson, p. 20: " No marvel though Plato shut them out of his school, and banished them quite from his Commonwealth." Cf. Milton, *Areopagitica :* " Plato, a man of high authority indeed, but least of all for his Commonwealth, in the book of his Laws, which no city ever yet received, fed his fancy with making many edicts to his airy burgomasters. . . . By which laws he seems to tolerate no kind of learning but by unalterable decree, consisting most of practical traditions, to the attainment whereof a library of smaller bulk than his own dialogues would be abundant. And there also enacts, that no poet should so much as read to any private man what he had written, until the judges and law-keepers had seen it; but that Plato meant this law peculiarly to that Commonwealth which he had imagined, and to no other, is evident."

35 11. *Petere principium.* Beg the question. *For if,* etc. Cf. 13 1 ff., 22 14 ff.

35 20. *Out of earth.* Cf. 14 32.

35 21. *Should be.* Cf. Abbott's *Shakespearian Grammar,* § 328: " ' Should,' denoting a statement not made by the speaker. (Compare ' sollen ' in German.) "

35 24. *Though he would.* Cf. Harington (Haslewood, 2. 127): " But poets never affirming any for true, but presenting them to us as fables and imitations, cannot lie though they would."

35 28. *Physicians.* Cf. 38 16.

36 1. *Hardly escape.* Cf. 36 23–24, and Agrippa, *Vanity of the Arts and Sciences,* ch. 6: " Historians are at such variance among themselves, delivering several tales of one and the same story, that it is impossible but that most of them must be the greatest liars in the world ! "

36 5. *Authorities.* Cf. 13 29.

36 6. *Sweet Muses.* Cf. Scaliger, *Poetics* 5. b. 1 : " Hence therefore the poets invoke the Muses, that, inspired with their rage, they may complete what they have taken in hand."

36 8. *Should.* Cf. 19 9, 36 21.

36 11. *Nathan.* Cf. 25 27 ff.

36 16. *Among the beasts.* Cf. 18 18.

36 18. *Upon an old door.* Cf. 48 11–25, and Collier, *Hist. Eng. Dram. Poetry,* 3. 375 : " The practice of exposing to the eyes of the audience in the opening of a play where the action was laid continued down to the time of Davenant, and it is remarkably proved by the very first piece in which scenery was employed. . . . It was not only the custom to exhibit to the eyes of the audience the place of action, but the title of the play; one of the oldest instances of the kind is to be found in the piece last quoted (i.e. Kyd's *Spanish Tragedy*), which was written about 1588."

36 31. *John of the Stile*, etc. "Fictitious characters made use of by lawyers in actions of ejectment." Cf. Wheeler's *Noted Names of Fiction.*

37 4. *Reverend.* Sidney, like Shakespeare, employs the two spellings, *reverend* and *reverent.* I have normalized to the first. Cf. 57 12, and the variants.

37 9. *Wanton sinfulness.* Cf. the whole of Gosson's pamphlet.

37 10. *Abuse.* See Sidney's own concessions, 45 20–27, 50 18 ff., 51 19 ff.

37 14. *Cupid.* Cf. Harington (Haslewood, 2. 134): "Sith as Sir Philip Sidney confesseth, Cupido is crept even into the heroical poems."

37 24. *In setting forth*, etc. Cf. 43 22–32.

37 26. *Scurrility.* Cf. 50 18.

37 30. *But that*, etc. Sidney and Gosson, by their mutual concessions, approach each other very nearly at this point. See Gosson, p. 40: "And as some of the players are far from abuse, so some of their plays are without rebuke; which are as easily remembered as quickly reckoned." And again, p. 65: "He that readeth with advice the books which I wrote, shall perceive that I touch but the abuses of all these. When we accuse the physician for killing his patient, we find no fault with the art itself, but with him that hath abused the same." Cf. Harington's imitation of Sidney (Haslewood, 2. 134): "It may be said where any scurrility and lewdness is found, there poetry doth not abuse us, but writers have abused poetry."

37 32. Εἰκαστική. The distinction here made is from Plato's *Sophist* 235–6 (Jowett 4. 448–9): "I think that I can discern two divisions of the imitative art, but I am not as yet able to see in which of them the desired form is to be found.

Theætetus. Will you tell me first what are the two divisions of which you are speaking?

Stranger. One is the art of likeness-making; — generally a likeness is made by producing a copy which is executed according to the proportions of the original, similar in length and breadth and depth, and also having colors answering to the several parts.

Theætetus. But is not this always the case in imitation?

Stranger. Not always; in works either of sculpture or painting, which are of any magnitude, there is a certain degree of deception; for if the true proportions were given, the upper part, which is farther off, would appear to be out of proportion in comparison with the lower, which is nearer; and so our artists give up the truth in their images and make only the proportions which appear to be beautiful, disregarding the real ones." The first answer of the stranger defines εἰκαστική, the second φανταστική.

37 34. Φανταστική. Cf. *fantastically*, 18 24, and the last note. See also Puttenham, Bk. I. ch. 8: "For commonly whoso is studious in the art, or shows himself excellent in it, they call him in disdain a fantastical; and a light-headed or fantastical man, by conversion, they call a poet."

38 10. *Army.* The earliest recorded instance of this figurative use.

38 12. *That contrariwise*, etc. Cf. Shak., *Rom.* 2. 3. 17–26:

> For nought so vile that on the earth doth live
> But to the earth some special good doth give;
> Nor aught so good but, strained from that fair use,
> Revolts from true birth, stumbling on abuse.
> Virtue itself turns vice, being misapplied,
> And vice sometime's by action dignified.
> Within the infant rind of this small flower
> Poison hath residence, and medicine power;
> For this, being smelt, with that part cheers each part,
> Being tasted, slays all senses with the heart.

38 27. *Fathers of lies.* Cf. Gosson, p. 21: "Tully accustomed to read them with great diligence in his youth, but, when he waxed graver in study, . . . he accounted them the fathers of lies." See also Agrippa, *Van. of Arts and Sciences*, ch. 4: "And thus the best and wisest of men have always despised poesy as the parent of lies."

38 30. *Our nation.* Cf. Gosson, p. 34: "Dion saith that Englishmen could suffer watching and labor, hunger and thirst, and bear off all storms with head and shoulders; they used slender weapons, went naked, and were good soldiers; they fed upon roots and barks of trees, they would stand up to the chin many days in marshes without victuals, etc. . . . But the exercise that is now among us is banqueting, playing, piping, and dancing, and all such delights as may win us to pleasure or rock us asleep."

38 34. *No memory*, etc. Cf. 2 27 ff.

39 1. *Yet never.* Cf. 45 9.

39 3. *Chain-shot.* The earliest example of the word.

39 4. *Bookishness.* No earlier appearance of this word has been noted.

39 5. *Certain Goths.* The story is related by Gibbon, ch. 10: "We are told that in the sack of Athens the Goths had collected all the libraries, and were on the point of setting fire to this funeral pile of Grecian learning, had not one of their chiefs, of more refined policy than his brethren, dissuaded them from the design by the profound observation, that as long as the Greeks were addicted to the study of books they would never apply themselves to the exercise of arms. The sagacious counsellor (should the truth of the fact be admitted) reasoned like an ignorant barbarian. In the most polite and powerful nations, genius of every kind has displayed itself about the same period, and the age of science has generally been the age of military virtue and success." Gibbon derives it from Zonaras (12. 635), a mediæval Byzantine compiler (1081–1118 A.D.), who in turn transcribes, with slight changes, an anonymous continuer of the *Roman History* of Dio Cassius, perhaps of the age of Constantine. There were French (1561) and Italian (1564) translations of Zonaras which Sidney might have read, or he might have seen the account in Montaigne (1580), Bk. I. ch. 24. An interesting parallel is furnished by Florio's translation of this chapter of Montaigne. Dio (54. 17) tells of a similar reply made by the actor Pylades to Augustus.

39 20. *Horace.* The line is adapted from Horace, *Sat.* 1. 1. 63: "Jubeas miserum esse libenter" = "Cheerfully bid him go and be wretched," as the line was then interpreted. Sidney accordingly means: "I cheerfully bid him be a fool."

39 24. *Companion of the camps.* Cf. 45 10.

39 26. *Quiddity,* etc. Philosophical terms.

39 28. *Turks.* Cf. 4 21.

39 33. *First light.* Cf. 2 29.

40 2. *Fortune.* Cf. Plutarch, *Fortune or Virtue of Alexander* (*Morals* 1. 505): "To which grandeur if he arrived by the assistance of Fortune, he is to be acknowledged the greater, because he made so glorious a use of her. So that the more any man extols his fortune, the more he advances his virtue, which made him worthy of such fortune."

40 3. *Did not.* Had not.

40 4. *Left his schoolmaster.* Plutarch, *Alexander* 7, speaks of Alexander's writing to Aristotle from Asia.

40 5. *Took dead Homer.* Plutarch, *Alexander* 8: "The *Iliad* he thought, as well as called, a portable treasure of military knowledge;

and he had a copy corrected by Aristotle, which is called 'the casket copy.' Onesicritus informs us that he used to lay it under his pillow with his sword."

40 6. *Callisthenes.* Cf. Plutarch's account in his *Alexander,* 53, 55: "His great reputation naturally exposed him to envy; and he gave some room for calumny himself, by often refusing the king's invitations, and when he did go to his entertainments, by sitting solemn and silent; which showed that he could neither commend, nor was satisfied with what passed. . . . His death is variously related. Some say Alexander ordered him to be hanged; others, that he fell sick and died in chains," etc.

40 9. *Homer had been alive.* Probably referring to Cicero's statement, *Archias* 10. 24: "How many historians of his exploits is Alexander the Great said to have had with him! and he, when standing on Cape Sigeum at the grave of Achilles, said, 'O happy youth, to find Homer as the panegyrist of your glory!' And he said the truth, for if the Iliad had not existed, the same tomb which covered his body would also have buried his renown." A similar account of this incident is given by Plutarch, *Alexander* 15.

40 12. *If Cato misliked Fulvius.* Referring to Gosson, p. 21: "Cato layeth it in the dish of Marcus the noble as a foul reproach, that in the time of his consulship he brought Ennius the poet into his province." Cf. also Agrippa, *Van. of Arts and Sciences,* ch. 4: "And Q. Fulvius was accused by M. Cato, for that he, going proconsul into Asia, had taken Ennius the poet along with him to bear him company." These statements are based upon Cicero, *Tusc. Disp.* 1. 2. 3: "A speech of Cato's shows this kind of poetry to have been in no great esteem, as he censures Marcus Nobilior (i.e. Fulvius) for carrying poets with him into his province; for that consul, as we know, carried Ennius with him into Ætolia."

40 14. *Fulvius liked it.* Cf. Cicero, *Archias* 11. 27: "And lately that great man Fulvius, who fought with the Ætolians, having Ennius for his companion, did not hesitate to devote the spoils of Mars to the Muses."

40 15. *Excellent Cato Uticensis.* Great-grandson of Cato the Censor (95–46 B.C.). For his excellence cf. Sallust, *Catiline* 54: "Cato . . . made temperance, dignity, and, above all, austerity of behavior, his pursuit. He did not vie in wealth with the wealthy, nor in intrigue with the intriguer, but in courage with the man of action, in honor with the scrupulous, in self-restraint with the upright. He preferred to be good rather than to seem so; and thus, the less he pursued

renown, the more it attended him." And see, besides Plutarch, *Cato the Younger*, Longfellow, *Translation of Dante*, note on *Purg.* I. 31: "Here, on the shores of Purgatory, his countenance is adorned with the light of the four stars, which are the four virtues, Justice, Prudence, Fortitude, and Temperance, and it is foretold of him that his garments will shine brightly on the last day. And here he is the symbol of Liberty, since for her sake to him 'not bitter was death in Utica'; and the meaning of Purgatory is spiritual Liberty, or freedom from sin through purification, 'the glorious liberty of the children of God.'"

40 19. *Misliked*, etc. Cf. Plutarch, *Cato the Censor* 22, 23: "When Cato was very far advanced in years, there arrived in Rome two ambassadors from Athens, Carneades the Academic, and Diogenes the Stoic. . . . Upon the arrival of these philosophers, such of the Roman youth as had a taste for learning went to wait on them, and heard them with wonder and delight. . . . But Cato, from the beginning, was alarmed at it. He no sooner perceived this passion for the Grecian learning prevail, but he was afraid that the youth would turn their ambition that way, and prefer the glory of eloquence to that of deeds of arms. . . . And to dissuade his son from those studies, he told him in a louder tone than could be expected from a man of his age, and, as it were, in an oracular and prophetic way, that when the Romans came thoroughly to imbibe the Grecian literature, they would lose the empire of the world. But time has shown the vanity of that invidious assertion; for Rome was never at a higher pitch of greatness than when she was most perfect in the Grecian erudition, and most attentive to all manner of learning." Milton relates the same story in his *Areopagitica*.

40 20. *Fourscore years old.* Bacon, *Adv. Learning* I. 2. 9, says threescore: "As to the judgment of Cato the Censor, he was well punished for his blasphemy against learning, in the same kind wherein he offended; for when he was past threescore years old he was taken with an extreme desire to go to school again, and to learn the Greek tongue to the end to peruse the Greek authors, which doth well demonstrate that his former censure of the Grecian learning was rather an affected gravity than according to the inward sense of his own opinion." But cf. the words put in his mouth by Cicero, *Old Age* 8. 26: "Nay, they even learn something new; as we see Solon in his verses boasting, who says that he was becoming an old man, daily learning something new, as I have done, who, when an old man, learned the Greek language; which too I so greedily grasped, as if I were desirous of satisfying a long protracted thirst." Reid and Kelsey, in their edition of the *Cato Maior* (Boston, 1885) say, p. xx: "The ancients give us

merely statements that he only began to learn Greek 'in his old age.' "

40 21. *Belike.* Cf. 41 35.

40 25. *Scipio Nasica.* The Roman Senate, being charged by the Delphic oracle to select the best man of Rome to bring the statue of the Idæan mother from Pessinus to Rome, in 204 B.C. made their decision, and the choice fell upon Scipio Nasica. Cf. Livy 29. 14: "Publius Scipio, son of Cneius who had fallen in Spain, a youth not yet of the age to be quæstor, they adjudged to be the best of the good men in the whole state." See Mayor's edition of Juvenal, note on 3. 137. An anecdote illustrating the intimacy of Scipio with Ennius is found in Cicero, *Character of the Orator* 2. 68. 276.

40 30. *Sepulchre.* See Cicero, *Archias* 9. 22: "Our countryman, Ennius, was dear to the elder Africanus; and even on the tomb of the Scipios his effigy is believed to be visible, carved in the marble."

41 2. *Most poetical.* Cf. notes on 3 18 and 3 27, and Jowett, *Plato* 3. 139: "Why Plato, who was himself a poet, and whose dialogues are poems and dramas, should have been hostile to the poets as a class, and especially to the dramatic poets. . . ."

Fountain. Cf. 44 13.

41 6. *Natural enemy.* Cf. Plato, *Republic* 10. 607 (Jowett 3. 504): "Let this then be our excuse for expelling poetry, that the argument constrained us; but let us also make an apology to her, lest she impute to us any harshness or want of politeness. We will tell her that there is an ancient quarrel between philosophy and poetry. . . ."

41 14. *Force of delight.* Cf. 24 22.

41 20. *Had their lives saved.* Cf. Plutarch, *Nicias* 29: "Some there were who owed their preservation to Euripides. Of all the Grecians, his was the muse whom the Sicilians were most in love with. From every stranger that landed in their island they gleaned every small specimen or portion of his works, and communicated it with pleasure to each other. It is said that on this occasion a number of Athenians, upon their return home, went to Euripides, and thanked him in the most respectful manner for their obligations to his pen; some having been enfranchised for teaching their masters what they remembered of his poems, and others having got refreshments when they were wandering about after the battle, for singing a few of his verses. Nor is this to be wondered at, since they tell us that when a ship from Caunus, which happened to be pursued by pirates, was going to take shelter in one of their ports, the Sicilians at first refused to admit her; upon asking the crew whether they knew any of the verses of Euripides

and being answered in the affirmative, they received both them and their vessel." See also the Prologue of Browning's *Balaustion's Adventure.*

41 23. *Simonides.* A contemporary and rival of Pindar (556–468 B.C.). He resided for some time at the court of King Hiero in Sicily, and in the year 476 B.C. was instrumental in effecting a reconciliation between him and Theron. In his dialogue entitled *Hiero,* Xenophon introduces him as discussing with that monarch the advantages and disadvantages of kingly station.

Pindar. In 472 he visited the court of Hiero, but the length of his stay is uncertain. The indirect manner in which he imparted moral counsels to the tyrant is illustrated in his Third Pythian Ode, 68–71: "And then in a ship would I have sailed, cleaving the Ionian sea, to the fountain of Arethusa, to the home of my Aitnaian [Ætnæan] friend, who ruleth at Syracuse, a king of good will to the citizens, not envious of the good, to strangers wondrous fatherly."

41 26. *Was made a slave.* Cf. Mahaffy, *Hist. Grk. Lit.* 2. 161: "He gained his first practical experience of the effects of irresponsible monarchy from the elder Dionysius. Though introduced by Dion, the tyrant was so offended with his views, which were then probably a reflex of those of Socrates, that he delivered him up to the Spartan ambassador Pollis, who had him sold in the market of Ægina." See also Cicero, *Rab. Postumus* 9. 23: "We have heard that that great man, beyond all comparison the most learned man that all Greece ever produced, Plato, was in the greatest danger, and was exposed to the most treacherous designs by the wickedness of Dionysius, the tyrant of Sicily, to whom he had trusted himself. We know that Callisthenes, a very learned man, the companion of Alexander the Great, was slain by Alexander."

41 29. *One should do.* Evidently referring to Scaliger, *Poetics* 5. b. 1: "Let him look to see what foolish and filthy tales he introduces, and what opinions reeking with the vice which above all others is peculiar to Greece he ever and anon expresses. Certainly it were worth while never to have read Phædrus or the Symposium, and other monstrous works of this nature."

41 35. *Community of women.* Cf. the admirable discussion by Jowett, in his translation of Plato, of which I cite a mere fragment (3. 167): "What Plato had heard or seen of Sparta was applied by him in a mistaken way to his ideal commonwealth. He probably observed that both the Spartan men and women were superior in form and strength to the other Greeks; and this superiority he was disposed to attribute to the laws and customs relating to marriage."

42 7. *Twice two poets.* These are Aratus, Cleanthes, Epimenides, and Menander. The first two are quoted in Acts 17. 28, the third Titus 1. 12, and the fourth 1 Cor. 15. 33. The verse, "For in him we live, and move, and have our being," is found substantially in the *Phænomena* (cf. note on 44. 25) of Aratus, who lived in the third century B.C., and in the *Hymn to Zeus* of Cleanthes, whose lifetime fell somewhat later in the same century. Epimenides of Crete lived much earlier, in the sixth century B.C. It is to him that Paul is said by Chrysostom and others to refer in Titus 1. 12: "One of themselves, a prophet of their own, said, Cretans are always liars, evil beasts, idle gluttons." The quotation, which forms a complete hexameter in the original, is said by the early commentators to have been taken from his poem *On Oracles,* which has long since perished. The gnomic sentence, "Evil company doth corrupt good manners," 1 Cor. 15. 33, is from the *Thais* of the comic dramatist Menander (342–291 B.C.).

42 8. *Watchword upon philosophy.* Cf. Col. 2. 8: "Take heed lest there shall be any one that maketh spoil of you through his philosophy and vain deceit."

42 10. *Not upon poetry.* Cf. Scaliger, *Poetics* 5. a. 1: "And if he condemns some of their books, we are not for that reason to be deprived of the rest, such as he himself frequently employs to confirm the authority of his arguments."

42 13. *Would not have,* etc. Cf. Plato, *Republic* 3. 391 (Jowett 3. 265): "We will not have them teaching our youth that the gods are the authors of evil. and that heroes are no better than men; undoubt-edly these sentimen.s, as we were saying, are neither pious nor true, for they are at variance with our demonstration that evil cannot come from God. . . . And further they are likely to have a bad effect on those who hear them. . . . And therefore let us put an end to such tales, lest they engender laxity of morals among the young."

42 20. *Imitation.* Cf. 9 12.

42 27. *Atheism.* The first example of the word.

42 29. *Meant not in general.* Cf. Jowett, *Plato* 3. 146: "Plato does not seriously intend to expel poetry from human life. But he feels strongly the unreality of poets; and he is protesting against the degen-eracy of them in his own day as we might protest against the want of serious purpose in modern poetry, against the unseemliness or extrava-gance of some of our novelists, against the time-serving of preachers or public writers, against the regardlessness of truth, which to the eye of the philosopher seems to characterize the greater part of the world. . . . For there might be a poetry which would be the hymn of divine perfection, the harmony of justice and truth among men: a strain which should renew the youth of the world, as in primitive ages the poet was men's only teacher and best friend: which would find materials in the living present as well as in the romance of the past, and might subdue to the fairest forms of speech and verse the intractable materials of modern civilization: which might elicit the simple principles, or, as Plato would have called them, the essential forms of truth and goodness out of the variety of opinion and the complexity of modern society: which would preserve all the good of each generation and leave the bad unsung: which should be based not on vain longings or faint imaginings, but on a clear insight into the nature of man. Then the tale of love might begin again in poetry or prose, two in one, united in the pursuit of knowledge, or the service of God and man; and feelings of love might still be the incentive to great thoughts and heroic deeds as in the days of Dante or Petrarch; and many types of manly and womanly beauty might appear among us, rising above the ordinary level of humanity, and many lives which were like poems be not only written but lived among us."

42 31. *Qua authoritate,* etc. Scaliger, *Poetics* 5. a. 1: "Which authority (i.e. that of Plato) certain rude and barbarous persons desire to abuse, in order to banish poets out of the commonwealth."

43 13. *Inspiring.* Cf. Plato, *Ion* 534 (Jowett 1. 248): "For the poet is a light and winged and holy thing, and there is no invention in him until he has been inspired and out of his senses, and the mind is no longer in him: when he has not attained to this state, he is powerless and is unable to utter his oracles. . . . And therefore God takes away the minds of poets, and uses them as his ministers, as he also uses diviners and holy prophets, in order that we who hear them may know that they speak not of themselves who utter these priceless words in a state of unconsciousness, but that God is the speaker, and that through them he is conversing with us." See also 57 23, and cf. Spenser, *Shepherd's Calendar, October,* Argument: "In Cuddie is set out the perfect pattern of a poet, which, finding no maintenance of his state and studies, complaineth of the contempt of poetry, and the causes thereof; specially having been in all ages, and even amongst the most barbarous, always of singular account and honor, and being, indeed, so worthy and commendable an art; or rather no art, but a Divine gift and heavenly instinct not to be gotten by labor and learning, but adorned with both, and poured into the wit by a certain ἐνθουσιασμὸς and celestial inspiration, as the author hereof elsewhere at large discourseth in his book called 'The English Poet,' which book being lately come to

my hands, I mind also, by God's grace, upon further advisement, to publish."

43 18. *Sea of examples.* Cf. Shak. *Hml.* 3. 1. 59: "Sea of troubles." *Alexanders.* Cf. 40 4 ff., and Harington (Haslewood, 2. 122): "For who would once dare to oppose himself against so many Alexanders, Cæsars, Scipios, . . . that . . . have encouraged and advanced poets and poetry?"

43 19. *Scipios.* Cf. 40 25 ff.

43 20. *Roman Socrates.* Cf. Cicero, *On Duties* 1. 26. 90: "That equanimity in every condition of life is a noble attribute, and that uniform expression of countenance and appearance which we find recorded of Socrates, and also of Caius Lælius."

43 22. *Made by him.* Cf. Cicero, *To Atticus* 7. 3. 10: "The comedies of Terence are thought, on account of their elegance of diction, to have been written by C. Lælius." Terence himself, in the prologue to the *Heautontimoroumenos*, says: "Then, as to a malevolent old poet saying that he (i.e. Terence) has suddenly applied himself to dramatic pursuits, relying on the genius of his friends, and not his own natural abilities; on that your judgment, your opinion, will prevail." The reference to Lælius is thought to be still more explicit in the prologue to the *Adelphi.*

43 23. *Only wise man.* Cf. Plato, *Apology* 21 (Jowett 1. 353): "He (i.e. Chærephon) went to Delphi and boldly asked the oracle to tell him whether . . . there was any one wiser than I was, and the Pythian prophetess answered, that there was no man wiser."

43 24. *Æsop's Fables.* Cf. Plato, *Phædo* 60–61 (Jowett 1. 432–3), where Socrates says: "In the course of my life I have often had intimations in dreams 'that I should compose music.' The same dream came to me sometimes in one form, and sometimes in another, but always saying the same or nearly the same words: Compose and practise music, said the dream. And hitherto I had imagined that this was only intended to exhort and encourage me in the study of philosophy, which has always been the pursuit of my life, and is the noblest and best of music. The dream was bidding me do what I was already doing, in the same way that the competitor in a race is bidden by the spectators to run when he is already running. But I was not certain of this, as the dream might have meant music in the popular sense of the word, and being under sentence of death, and the festival giving me a respite, I thought that I should be safer if I satisfied the scruple, and, in obedience to the dream, composed a few verses before I departed. And first I made a hymn in honor of the god of the festival,

and then considering that a poet, if he is really to be a poet, should not only put together words, but should invent stories, and that I have no invention, I took some fables of Æsop, which I had ready at hand and knew, and turned them into verse."

43 29. *Teacheth the use.* In his *On Listening to Poetry* (*Morals* 2. 42–94).

43 32. *Guards of poesy.* *Guard* = ornamental border, ornament. Cf. Shak. *Ado* 1. 1. 288–9: "The body of your discourse is sometime guarded with fragments, and the guards are but slightly basted on." Plutarch is very fond of poetical quotation.

44 4. *Low-creeping.* Perhaps with reference to Horace's "serpit humi," *Art of Poetry* 28. Cf. *earth-creeping*, 58 5, and note on 55 25.

44 5. *Not being an art of lies.* Cf. 35 21–37 7.

44 6. *Not of effeminateness.* Cf. 38 29–40 32.

44 7. *Not of abusing.* Cf. 37 8–38 28.

44 8. *Not banished.* Cf. 42 9–43 15.

44 9. *Engarland.* Used by Sidney in Sonnet 56 of *Astrophel and Stella.*

44 22. *Musa,* etc. Virgil, *Æneid* 1. 12: "O Muse, relate to me the causes, tell me in what had her will been offended?"

44 25. *David.* Cf. 6 5, 9 19. *Adrian.* Roman emperor (76–138 A.D.). See Capes, *Age of the Antonines*, p. 54: "Poet, geometer, musician, orator, and artist, he had studied all the graces and accomplishments of liberal culture, knew something of the history and genius of every people, could estimate their literary or artistic skill, and admire the achievements of the past." And again, pp. 69–70: "Even on his deathbed he could feel the poet's love for tuneful phrase, and the verses are still left to us which were addressed by him to his soul, which, pale and cold and naked, would soon have to make its way to regions all unknown, with none of its whilom gaiety:

Animula, vagula, blandula,
Hospes comesque corporis,
Quæ nunc abibis in loca,
Pallidula, rigida, nudula,
Nec ut soles dabis jocos."

These lines have been translated by Byron, and loosely paraphrased by Pope, with the admixture of Christian sentiment.

Sophocles. The Greek tragic poet (496–406 B.C.). Probably placed here because of the commands with which his fellow-citizens entrusted him. Cf. Mahaffy, *Hist. Grk. Lit.* 1. 280–1: "The Athenian public were so delighted with his *Antigone* that they appointed him one of the ten generals, along with Pericles, for the subduing of Samos . . . He was (in 443 B.C.) one of the *Hellenotamiæ*, or administrators of the public treasury — a most responsible and important post. He sided with the oligarchy in 411, if he be the Probulus (i.e. member of the council) then mentioned."

Germanicus. The nephew and adopted son of the emperor Tiberius, and commander of an expedition against the Germans (15 B.C.–19 A.D.). Besides more original poems, he composed a translation of the *Phæ-nomena*, a didactic poem by the Greek poet Aratus. Cruttwell, *Hist. Rom. Lit.* p. 349, calls it "elegant and faithful, and superior to Cicero's in poetical inspiration."

44 27. *Robert, King of Sicily.* Robert II. of Anjou (1275–1343 A.D.). Of him we are told by Paulus Jovius, *Elogia* (Basle, 1575): "He bore with marvellous fortitude the death of his only son, con-soling himself with . . . the best literature, in which he became so proficient that he was wont to say that he preferred it to the possession of his kingdom. He was a munificent patron to the professors of the highest learning, and took so much pleasure in light and graceful poetry that he was desirous, in addition to the many other marks of his favor which he had previously bestowed upon Francis Petrarch, to confer upon him with his own hands the honor of the laureateship, the same which Petrarch preferred afterwards to receive at the Capitol in Rome." Cf. Symonds, *Renaissance in Italy* 2. 252: "Robert of Anjou was proud to call himself the friend of Petrarch, and Boccaccio found the flame of inspiration at his court."

44 28. *Francis of France.* The critic Sainte Beuve says of him: "Fascinated by every species of noble culture of the arts and the intel-lect; admiring and appreciating Erasmus as well as Lionardo da Vinci and Primaticcio, and bent, as he himself was accustomed to avow, upon adorning with them his nation and his kingdom; a fosterer of the ver-nacular, by employing it in documents of state; and the founder of free higher education outside of the Sorbonne; he justifies, in spite of many errors and vagaries, the title awarded him by the gratitude of his contemporaries. The service he rendered consists less in this or that particular institution of his creation than in the spirit with which he was animated and which communicated itself to every one about him."

King James of Scotland. Probably James I. (1394–1437), author of *The King's Quair*, the poetical disciple of Lydgate, Gower, and especially of Chaucer. Cf. Warton, *Hist. Eng. Poetry* 3. 121: "This unfortunate monarch was educated while a prisoner in England, at the command of our Henry IV., and the poem was written during his captivity there. The Scottish historians represent him as a prodigy of erudition. He civilized the Scottish nation." Sidney may have derived his information in part from the historian Buchanan (cf. 44 33).

With the foregoing cf. Meres (Haslewood, 2. 155–6): "Among others in times past, poets had these favorers, Augustus, Mæcenas, Sophocles, Germanicus, — an emperor, a nobleman, a senator, and a captain; so of later times poets have these patrons, — Robert, King of Sicily, the great King Francis of France, King James of Scotland, and Queen Elizabeth of England."

44 29. *Bembus.* According to Symonds, *Renaissance in Italy* 2. 410, "the fullest representative of his own age of culture" (1470–1547). See also Symonds, 5. 264–5 : "He was untiring in his literary industry, unfailing in his courtesy to scholars, punctual in correspondence, and generous in the use he made of his considerable wealth. At Urbino, at Venice, at Rome, and at Padua, his study was the meeting-place of learned men, who found the graces of the highest aristocracy combined in him with genial enthusiasm for the common interests of letters."

Bibbiena. 1470–1520. He is best remembered by his comedy, the *Calandra*, which is modelled upon the *Menæchmi* of Plautus.

44 30. *Beza.* A famous Biblical scholar (1519–1605). His poetry is not remarkable either for quantity or quality, and consists of some verses composed in youth, a translation of certain Psalms, and a comedy, all of which are now forgotten.

Melanchthon. 1497–1560. Scaliger, *Poetics* 308. c. 1, praises his poems on the eclipses of the sun and the moon.

44 31. *Fracastorius.* 1483–1553. He spent the greater portion of his life at Verona, "enjoying high reputation as a physician, philosopher, astronomer, and poet." Symonds, *Renaissance in Italy* 2. 477.

Scaliger. 1484–1558. The author of the *Poetics,* and other learned works. He also composed Latin poetry of no particular celebrity.

44 32. *Pontanus.* Cf. note on 10 2. Besides the poem there mentioned, Pontanus wrote pastorals, elegies, odes, etc. Symonds says of him (*Renaissance in Italy* 5. 220) : "In Pontano, as in Poliziano, Latin verse lived again with new and genuine vitality."

Muretus. A French scholar (1526–1585), who wrote hymns, besides certain juvenile verses. It is not a little remarkable that Sidney should pay him this honor, since he must have been abhorrent to all good Protestants as the eulogist of the Massacre of St. Bartholomew.

44 33. *George Buchanan.* A Scotch author (1506–1582). Besides

other original poems, and translations from the Psalms and Euripides into Latin verse, he wrote two Latin tragedies, *Jephthah* and *John the Baptist.* His chief other works are a *History of Scotland* and a treatise on *Government in Scotland,* both in Latin. Of his *John the Baptist* there is an English translation in Peck's *New Memoirs of Milton.*

With the foregoing cf. Meres (Haslewood, 2. 156): "As in former times two great cardinals, Bembus and Bibbiena, did countenance poets, so of late years two great preachers have given them their right hands in fellowship, Beza and Melanchthon. As the learned philosophers Fracastorius and Scaliger have highly prized them, so have the eloquent orators Pontanus and Muretus very gloriously estimated them. As Georgius Buchananus' *Jephtha* amongst all modern tragedies is able to abide the touch of Aristotle's precepts and Euripides' examples " . . .

44 34. *Hospital of France.* Michel de l'Hospital (1504-1573), Chancellor of France, the type of moderation in an age of violence and intolerance. His works include a number of Latin poems. He gives a pleasing picture of his occupations after his retirement from court, in a letter quoted by Villemain, *Études d'histoire moderne,* pp. 327-8: "There my amusements are of a rather serious nature, whether I hold in my hands the works of Xenophon, or the divine Plato pours into my ears the words of Socrates. I frequently amuse myself with re-reading the great poets, a Virgil or a Homer. I like to follow up the reading of a tragic poet by that of a comedy, mingling sadness and gaiety, sportiveness and grief. But to me there is no work comparable to the Holy Scriptures. There is none in which the mind reposes with so sweet a contentment, and in which it finds so sure a refuge from every ill. These are the studies in which I should like to pass all the remaining moments of my life."

Than whom. Cf. Lounsbury, *Hist. Eng. Lang.* p. 236.

45 5. *Only.* Note the position of this word.

45 6. *Hard welcome.* Cf. Puttenham, Bk. I. ch. 8: "But in these days, although some learned princes may take delight in them, yet universally it is not so. For as well poets as poesy are despised, and the name become of honorable, infamous, subject to scorn and derision, and rather a reproach than a praise to any that useth it."

45 13. *Mountebanks.* Cf. Sidney's letter to his brother, quoted in Fox Bourne, *Memoir,* p. 222: "I think ere it be long, like the mountebank in Italy, we travellers shall be made sport of in comedies."

45 16. *Hath rather be.* A notable example of a disputed construction. *Troubled in the net.* *Odyssey* 8. 266–366.

45 22. *Epaminondas.* Cf. Plutarch, *Political Precepts (Morals* 5,

125-6): "Epaminondas being by the Thebans through envy and in contempt appointed telearch, did not reject it, but said that the office does not show the man, but the man also the office. He brought the telearchate into great and venerable repute, which was before nothing but a certain charge of the carrying the dung out of the narrow streets and lanes of the city, and turning of water courses. . . . Though he who in his own person manages and does many such things for himself may be judged mean-spirited and mechanical, yet if he does them for the public and for his country, he is not to be deemed sordid; but on the contrary, his diligence and readiness, extending even to these small matters, is to be esteemed greater and more highly to be valued."

45 33. *Queis,* etc. Sidney makes one line out of parts of two. The original (Juvenal 14. 34-5) has:

> Quibus arte benigna
> Et meliore luto finxit præcordia Titan.

The sixteenth century editions must more frequently have had *queis* instead of *quibus*, since Montaigne (Bk. I. ch. 24) also has this reading. In English the passage will run: "Whose hearts the Titan has (formed with kindlier art, and) moulded out of better clay." The Titan is Prometheus.

46 4. *Paper-blurrers.* Cf. 57 8.

46 6. *In despite of Pallas.* Against the grain. Lat. *invita Minerva, invita Pallade.* Cf. Ovid, *Fasti* 3. 826: "Nor will any one be able to make nea·'y the sandals for the foot if Pallas is unpropitious, even though he we.·· more skilful than Tychius; and even if, compared with ancient Epeus, h. should excel him in handicraft, yet if Pallas is displeased, he will be but a bungler." See also Horace, *Art of Poetry* 385: "But you, my friend, will say and do nothing against the bent of your genius." Still another instance will be found in Cicero, *On Duties* 1. 31. 110.

46 9. *Myself.* Cf. 55 6.

46 13. *Look themselves.* Note the construction.

46 14. *Unflattering glass.* See note on 28 24.

46 15. *Must not be drawn.* Cf. note on 13 4.

46 18. *Divine gift.* So Harington (Haslewood, 2. 123): "He doth prove nothing more plainly than that which M. Sidney and all the learneder sort that have written of it do pronounce, namely, that it is a gift and not an art."

46 22. *Orator,* etc. The orator is made, the poet is born.

46 23. *Manured.* Cultivated, tilled.

46 34. *Matter . . . and words.* Cf. Bacon, *De Augmentis* 2. 13 (*Works* 4. 315): "Now poesy . . . is taken in two senses; in respect of words or matter. In the first sense it is but a character of speech; for verse is only a kind of style and a certain form of elocution, and has nothing to do with the matter; for both true history may be written in verse and feigned history in prose. But in the latter sense, I have set it down from the first as one of the principal branches of learning, and placed it by the side of history; being indeed nothing else but an imitation of history at pleasure. . . . I dismiss from the present discourse satires, elegies, epigrams, odes, and the like, and refer them to philosophy and arts of speech. And under the name of poesy, I treat only of feigned history." Cf. his *Adv. Learning* 2. 4. 1.

47 3. *Quicquid,* etc. Ovid's verse (*Tristia* 4. 10. 26) is:

Et quod tentabam dicere, versus erat,

or, translated: "And whatever I tried to express, the same was poetry." Another reading, which has only a single authority in its favor, is *conabar* for *tentabam*. Both editions of Sidney have *crit*, thus changing the preterit into a future, and one, Ponsonby, has *conabor*, to agree with the change from *erat* to *erit*. It is accordingly difficult to decide which tense Sidney meant to set down, especially since he is otherwise inexact in the quotation of this line, as in other places. The form of our text is that quoted by Mercs (Haslewood, 2. 157).

47 8–9. *Either . . . or.* Note the peculiar construction.

47 11. *Mirror of Magistrates.* Cf. Brooke, *Eng. Lit.*, pp. 60–1: "The *Mirror of Magistrates*, 1559, for which he (i.e. Sackville) wrote the *Induction* and one tale, is a poem on the model of Boccaccio's *Falls of Princes*, already imitated by Lydgate. Seven poets, along with Sackville, contributed tales to it, but his poem is the only one of any value. . . . Being written in the manner and stanza of the elder poets, this poem has been called the transition between Lydgate and Spenser. But it does not truly belong to the old time; it is as modern as Spenser."

47 17. *Allow.* Sanction, commend.

47 20. *Not . . . but.* Note the peculiarity.

47 22. *In prose.* Cf. Plato, *Republic* 10. 601 (Jowett 3. 496): "And I think that you must know, for you have often seen what a poor appearance the tales of poets make when stripped of the colors which music puts upon them, and recited in prose."

47 24. *Another.* Adapted by Harington (Haslewood, 2. 131): "One doth, as it were, bring on another."

47 30. *Gorboduc.* Cf. Morley, *First Sketch*, pp. 332 ff.: "An un authorised edition of it was published in 1565, as *The Tragedy of Gorboduc.* . . . The authorised edition of it did not appear until 1571, and in that the name of the play appeared as *Ferrex and Porrex.* The argument was taken from Geoffrey of Monmouth's 'History of British Kings,' and was chosen as a fit lesson for Englishmen in the first year of the reign of Elizabeth. It was a call to Englishmen to cease from strife among themselves, and knit themselves into one people, obedient to one undisputed rule. Each act is opened with a masque, or dumb-show; and as the play was modelled on the Tragedies of Seneca, there was at the close of every act except the last a chorus. Except for the choruses, Sackville and Norton used the newly-introduced blank verse as the measure of their tragedy. . . . Thus our first tragedy distinctly grew out of the life of its own time, and gave expression to much that lay deep in the hearts of Englishmen in the first years of Elizabeth's reign." For the argument of the play see Warton, *Hist. Eng. Poetry* 4. 256.

47 31. *As.* That.

47 34. *Notable morality.* Cf. Warton, *Hist. Eng. Poetry* 4. 260: "Sir Philip Sidney . . . remarks that this tragedy is full of 'notable moralitie.' But tragedies are not to instruct us by the intermixture of moral sentences, but by the force of example and the effect of the story. In the first act, the three counsellors are introduced debating about the division of the kingdom in long and elaborate speeches, which are replete with political advice and maxims of civil prudence. B[ut] this stately sort of declamation, whatever eloquence it may display, and whatever policy it may teach, is undramatic, unanimated, and unaffect-ing. Sentiment and argument will never supply the place of action upon the stage. . . . But we must allow, that in the strain of dialogue in which they are professedly written, they (i.e. the speeches) have uncommon merit, even without drawing an apology in their favor from their antiquity; and that they contain much dignity, strength of reflec-tion, and good sense, couched in clear expression and polished numbers."

48 5. *For where*, etc. Cf. Symonds, *Shakspere's Predecessors*, p. 258: "These canons the Italians had already compiled from passages of Aristotle and of Horace, without verifying them by appeal to the Greek dramatic authors. They were destined to determine the practice of the great French writers of the seventeenth century, and to be accepted as incontrovertible by every European nation, until Victor Hugo with Hernani raised the standard of belligerent Romanticism on the stage of Paris."

48 8. *Aristotle's precept.* Cf. the *Poetics*, ch. 5: "Tragedy sceks to bring the action within the compass of a single revolution of the sun, or to vary but slightly from that limit." See the quotation from Milton in the note on 50 5.

48 9. *There is . . . days.* This construction is common in Shakespeare, as in *Cæs.* 3. 2. 29, "There is tears for his love," or *Macb.* 2. 3. 146, "There's daggers in men's smiles."

48 12. *Asia.* Cf. Cervantes, *Don Quixote*, Bk. I. ch. 48: "What greater folly can there be in the subject of our debate, than to see a child appear in swaddling-clothes in the first scene of the first act, and in the second a goodly aged man with a beard? . . . What shall I say also of their observance of the time in which are to happen the acts which they present, except that I have seen a comedy in which the first act opened in Europe, the second in Asia, the third in Africa; and, had there been four acts, the fourth would have ended in America, and the play would have travelled to all the four parts of the world."

48 15. *Telling where he is.* Cf. Collier, *Hist. Eng. Dram. Poetry* 3. 375: "Sometimes the fact appears to have been communicated in the prologue, and at others it was formally announced by one of the actors. When old Hieronimo, in Kyd's *Spanish Tragedy*, is about to present his play within a play to the King and Court, he exclaims, 'Our scene is Rhodes.'"

48 29. *Groweth a man.* Whetstone had already, in his dedication to *Promos and Cassandra* (printed 1578), uttered a similar racy censure (Hazlitt's *Shak. Lib.* Part II. Vol. 2, p. 204, or Collier's *Hist. Eng. Dram. Poetry* 2. 422): "The Englishman in this quality is most vain, indiscreet, and out of order: he first grounds his work on impossibilities; then in three hours runs he through the world, marries, gets children, makes children men, men to conquer kingdoms, murder monsters, and bringeth gods from heaven and fetcheth devils from hell." Cf. also the note on 48 12.

48 35. *Matter of two days.* The next three or four lines are somewhat obscure. The play mentioned contains in one sense matter of two days, inasmuch as Phædria is sent away for that length of time; but he actually returns within the day, and the action is completed within that time. One is tempted to believe that Sidney meant the *Heautontimorumenos*, concerning which see Dryden, *Essay of Dramatic Poesy* (Arnold's ed., 31 16–21): "The unity of time even Terence himself, who was the best and most regular of them, has neglected. His *Heautontimorumenos*, or Self-Punisher, takes up visibly two days, says Scaliger, the two first acts concluding the first day, the three last the day ensuing." *Yet far short.* We should expect 'yet not far short.' The time is actually not far from fifteen years.

49 2. *Played in two days.* If this means that two days, or parts of two days, were occupied in the representation, it would seem to be an inaccurate statement, unless it is to be understood of the *Heautontimo-rumenos.* Cf. the note on p. 158 of the Bohn translation: "Madame Dacier absolutely considers it *as a fact beyond all doubt* that the Roman audience went home after the first two acts of the play, and returned for the representation of the third the next morning at daybreak. Scaliger was of the same opinion, but it is not generally entertained by commentators."

49 3. *And though Plautus.* Possibly referring to the *Captivi,* in which some commentators have detected a violation of the unity of time. Between the end of the second and the beginning of the fourth act, one of the characters, Philocrates, "has taken ship from the coast of Ætolia, arrived in Elis, procured the liberation of Philopolemus, and returned with him, all in the space of a few hours. This, however, although the coast of Elis was only fifteen miles from that of Ætolia, is not at all consistent with probability; and the author has been much censured by some commentators, especially by Lessing, on account of his negligence. It must, however, be remembered that Plautus was writing for a Roman audience, the greater part of whom did not know whether Elis was one mile or one hundred from the coast of Ætolia." (Note in Bohn's translation.) Cf. also the note on 50 14.

49 7. *Laws of poesy.* Cf. note on 18 25.

49 16. *Pacolet's.* Cf. Wheeler, *Noted Names of Fiction :* "A character in the old romance of 'Valentine and Orson,' who owned an enchanted steed, often alluded to by early writers."

49 17. *Nuntius.* Messenger. Cf. what Moulton, *Anc. Class. Drama,* p. 145, says of the Messenger's Speech: "This is a device by which one of the incidents in the story, occurring outside the unity of place, and thus incapable of being acted, is instead presented in description, and treated with a vividness and fulness of narration that is an equiva-lent for realisation on the stage."

49 20. *Ab ovo.* From the egg, or, more freely, from the first course of the meal; in general, from the beginning. The quotation is from Horace, *Sat.* 1. 3. 6.

49 23. *Story.* From the *Hecuba* of Euripides. Sidney's choice of this play may be accounted for by Mahaffy's statement, *Hist. Grk. Lit.* I. 344: "The *Hecuba* has always been a favorite play, and has not only been frequently imitated, but edited ever since Erasmus' time for

school use." Notwithstanding Sidney's praise, the unities are somewhat violated in it. Cf. Mahaffy, as above: "It treats of the climax of Hecuba's misfortunes, the sacrifice of Polyxena at the grave of Achilles, and the murder of Polydorus, her youngest son, by the Thracian host, Polymestor. . . . It is to be noted that the scene being laid in Thrace, and the tomb of Achilles being in the Troad, the so-called unity of place is here violated, as often elsewhere in Greek tragedy. . . . The narrative of her (Polyxena's) death . . . forms a beautiful conclusion to the former half of the play, which is divided, like many of Euripides', between two interests more or less loosely connected."

50 5. *Kings and clowns.* Cf. Whetstone (as in note to 48 29) : "And — that which is worst — their ground is not so unperfect as their working indiscreet; not weighing, so the people laugh, though they laugh them, for their follies, to scorn; many times, to make mirth, they make a clown companion with a king; in their grave councils they allow the advice of fools; yea, they use one order of speech for all persons, a gross indecorum." To the same effect Milton in his preface to *Samson Agonistes :* "This is mentioned to vindicate tragedy from the small esteem, or rather infamy, which in the account of many it undergoes at this day with other common interludes; happening through the poet's error of intermixing comic stuff with tragic sadness and gravity, or introducing trivial and vulgar persons, which by all judicious hath been accounted absurd, and brought in without discretion, corruptly to gratify the people. . . . The circumscription of time wherein the whole drama begins and ends, is, according to ancient rule and best example, within the space of twenty-four hours."

But cf. Moulton, *Shak. as a Dram. Artist*, pp. 219–220 : "The institution of the court fool is eagerly utilised by Shakespeare, and is the source of some of his finest effects; he treats it as a sort of chronic Comedy, the function of which may be described as that of translating deep truths of human nature into the language of laughter."

50 9. *Tragi-comedy.* Cf. Mahaffy, *Hist. Grk. Lit.* 2. 411 : "Greek tragedy, being essentially religious, became in the hands of its greatest masters so serious a thing, that the relief of humorous or low scenes was hardly permitted. Aristotle indeed gives us to understand in his sketch of its history that this was not so originally, that it arose from a satyric representation, of which the grotesque side was preserved in the satyric afterpiece, when banished from serious tragedy. This severance was exaggerated by the French school of the seventeenth century, who are far more particular than the less artificial Greek masters in avoiding the lower side of human nature. And such, too, was the

opinion of Milton, but happily for us Shakespere gave the law for a
wider conception, and since his day, even in theory, the comic or
humorous element is admitted and even admired as a merit of contrast
in our tragedies." Shakespeare, however, was not the first to proclaim
this law. It was already virtually announced by Plato, *Symposium* 223
(Jowett 2. 74) : "The chief thing which he remembered was Socrates
compelling the other two to acknowledge that the genius of comedy
was the same as that of tragedy, and that the true artist in tragedy was
an artist in comedy also." The explanation of this harmony or identity
is thus given by Everett, *Poetry, Comedy, and Duty*, p. 166: "The
circumstances which suggest the comic are very naturally those which
are, to a greater or less extent, really tragic. The tragic is, like the
comic, simply the incongruous. . . . Thus it is that there is nothing
tragic that may not to some persons, or to some moods, be comic.
Take the great tragedies themselves. Take the story of Œdipus : A
man goes forth to meet another, whom he does not know, and kills
him; this stranger turns out to be his father. He falls in love with a
woman that he meets, and marries her; she proves to be his mother.
Shall we have out of all this a tragedy or a comedy? This depends
upon the taste of the author, or of the audience for whom he writes."

The historical process is thus commented upon by Moulton, *Shak.
as a Dram. Artist*, pp. 292–3: "The exclusive and uncompromising
spirit of antiquity carried caste into art itself, and their Tragedy and
Comedy were kept rigidly separate, and indeed were connected with
different rituals. The spirit of modern life is marked by its compre-
hensiveness and reconciliation of opposites; and nothing is more important in dramatic history than the way in which Shakespeare and his
contemporaries created a new departure in art, by seizing upon the
rude jumble of sport and earnest which the mob loved, and converting
it into a source of stirring passion-effects. For a new faculty of mental
grasp is generated by this harmony of tones in the English Drama. If
the artist introduces every tone into the story he thereby gets hold
of every tone in the spectators' emotional nature. . . . Moreover it
brings the world of fiction nearer to the world of nature, which has
never yet evolved an experience in which brightness was dissevered
from gloom."

Lope de Vega had already anticipated the latter part of Moulton's
justification. Lessing says, *Dramatic Notes*, No. 69 (Bohn's tr., p.
394): "Although Lope de Vega is regarded as the creator of the
Spanish theatre, it was not he who introduced the hybrid tone. The
people were already so accustomed to it, that he had to assume it

against his will. In his didactic poem concerning the art of making new comedies, he greatly laments the fact." The words of Lope de Vega, as quoted by Lessing (p. 395), are as follows: "It is therefore somewhat difficult to me to approve our fashion. But since we in Spain do so far diverge from art, the learned must keep silent on this point. It is true that the tragic fused with the comic, Seneca mingled with Terence, produces no less a monster than was Pasiphae's ' Minotaur.' But this abnormity pleases, people will not see any other plays but such as are half serious, half ludicrous, nature herself teaches this variety, from which she borrows part of her beauty."

A wise caveat is uttered by Shelley, *Defense of Poetry:* "The modern practice of blending comedy with tragedy, though liable to great abuse in point of practice, is undoubtedly an extension of the dramatic circle; but the comedy should be as in King Lear, universal, ideal, and sublime." Cf. also Ulrici, *Shakespeare's Dram. Art* 1. 368–370; Schlegel's *Dram. Lit.*, pp. 369–371; *Hamlet* 2. 2. 415–420.

50 10. *Apuleius.* A writer of the second century A.D. His *Metamorphoses*, or *Golden Ass*, is here referred to. See Bohn's translation, or Dunlop, *History of Fiction.*

50 14. *Amphytrio.* Cf. the prologue to this play: " I'll tell the subject of this tragedy. Why do you contract your brows? . . . This same, if you wish it, from a tragedy I'll make to be a comedy, with all the lines the same. . . . I'll make this to be a mixture — a tragicomedy. For me to make it entirely to be a comedy, where kings and gods appear, I do not deem right. What then? Since here the servant has a part as well, just as I said, I'll make it to be a tragicomedy."

50 15. *Daintily.* Almost = rarely. Cf. 53 33. *Hornpipes and funerals.* Cf. Shakespeare, *Hml.* 1. 2. 12–13:

> With mirth in funeral and with dirge in marriage,
> In equal scale weighing delight and dole.

50 20. *Loud laughter.* Cf. *Hml.* 3. 2. 42–8: "And let those that play your clowns speak no more than is set down for them; for there be of them that will themselves laugh, to set on some quantity of barren spectators to laugh too, though in the mean time some necessary question of the play be then to be considered."

51 7. *Against the bias.* A figure taken from the game of bowls (cf. *Phil. Soc. Eng. Dict.* s.v. *bias*). See Shak. *Shr.* 4. 5. 24–5:

> Well forward, forward! thus the bowl should run.
> And not unluckily against the bias.

Also *Rich. II.* 3. 4. 4–5:

> 'Twill make me think the world is full of rubs,
> And that my fortune runs against the bias.

51 11. *Alexander's picture.* Cf. Plutarch, *Alexander* 4: "The statues of Alexander that most resembled him were those of Lysippus, who alone had his permission to represent him in marble. The turn of his head, which leaned a little to one side, and the quickness of his eye, in which many of his friends and successors most affected to imitate him, were best hit off by that artist. Apelles painted him in the character of Jupiter armed with thunder, but did not succeed as to his complexion. He overcharged the coloring, and made his skin too brown; whereas he was fair, with a tinge of red in his face and upon his breast."

51 13. *Hercules.* Millin, *Mythologische Gallerie*, No. 454 (2d ed., Berlin 1836), thus describes the picture to which Sidney may refer, though it must be remembered that he had never visited Rome: "Hercules is represented in an ancient mosaic of the Capitoline Museum at Rome as naked from his waist up, the lower part of his body being clothed in the attire of a woman. Into the waist of the dress is stuck a distaff, from which he is pulling the thread with one hand, while the other is engaged in twirling the spindle. His countenance is sorrowful and downcast. Beside him are his shield and club, while on the ground near by lie an overturned vase, a thyrsus, and bunches of grapes, symbolical of the Bacchic orgies in which he has been indulging with Omphale. Two Cupids, one of whom is crowned with a chaplet of oak-leaves, are playing with a fettered lion, while a third is playing on a Pan's-pipe." See also the illustration of the Farnese group at Naples in Mrs. Clement, *Handbook Legend. and Myth. Art*, p. 456. Cf. Ovid, *Fast.* 2. 304 ff.; *Her.* 9. 53 ff.

51 18. *Scornfulness.* Used in the passive rather than the active sense, and hence nearly = disgracefulness. Cf. 51 20, and Shakespeare, *Lucrece* 520, "The scornful mark of every open eye." See also Abbott's *Shak. Gram.* § 3.

51 23. *Aristotle.* See his *Ethics*, 4. 9. 82 (Williams' tr., p. 113): "The witty man will not indulge in every kind of ridicule. For all ridicule is a species of abuse, and legislators, inasmuch as they forbid certain forms of abuse, ought perhaps also to have forbidden certain forms of ridicule. And the man of culture, who is liberally-minded, will bear himself according to these rules, and be, as it were, a law unto himself. Such then is the man who observes the correct mean, — whether it is

tact which we are to say that he has, or wit: whereas the buffoon can never resist the ridiculous, and, provided only that he can raise a laugh, will spare neither himself nor anyone else, and will say things which no gentleman would ever say, and sometimes even things to which no gentleman would submit to listen."

51 28. *Jest at strangers.* As, for example, in Shakespeare's *Merry Wives of Windsor.*

51 31. *Nil habet,* etc. From Juvenal, *Sat.* 3. 152–3: "Poverty, bitter though it be, has no sharper pang than this, that it makes men ridiculous."

51 34. *Thraso.* A boastful captain in *The Eunuch* of Terence.

Self-wise-seeming schoolmaster. Perhaps Sidney has in mind Master Rhombus, a character in his own masque, *The Lady of May.* Another example would be Holofernes, in *Love's Labor's Lost.*

52 1. *Traveller.* Cf. Shakespeare, *A. Y. L.* 4. 1. 33–38: "Farewell, Monsieur Traveller: look you lisp and wear strange suits, disable all the benefits of your own country, be out of love with your nativity and almost chide God for making you that countenance you are, or I will scarce think you have swam in a gondola."

52 4. *Buchanan.* Cf. 44 33. See the *Dict. Nat. Biog.* under his name: "In the 'Baptistes' especially the virtue of liberty, the fear of God rather than of man, and the infamy of the tyrant, are the themes."

52 13. *So good minds.* Sidney, after writing the lyrics of his *Astrophel and Stella,* ha l "so good mind" given him, if we may judge from his noble sonnet:

> Leave me, O Love, which reachest but to dust,
> And thou, my mind, aspire to higher things;
> Grow rich in that which never taketh rust;
> What ever fades, but fading pleasure brings.
> Draw in thy beams, and humble all thy might
> To that sweet yoke where lasting freedoms be,
> Which breaks the clouds, and opens forth the light
> That doth both shine and give us sight to see.
> O take fast hold; let that light be thy guide
> In this small course which birth draws out to death;
> And think how evil becometh him to slide,
> Who seeketh heaven, and comes of heavenly breath.
> Then farewell, world; thy uttermost I see;
> Eternal Love, maintain Thy life in me.

Splendidis longum valedico nugis.
[I bid a long farewell to splendid toys.]

Boccaccio (*De Genealogia Deorum*, p. 252) extols Petrarch's Eclogues for celebrating the praises of the true God.

52 21. *Banner.* Cf. Song of Solomon 2. 4: "His banner over me was love." *Unresistible.* Irresistible.

52 26. *North-west and by south.* Cf. Shakespeare, *Hml.* 2. 2. 396–7: "I am but mad north-north-west: when the wind is southerly I know a hawk from a handsaw."

52 29. *Energia.* This is the Latinized form of the Greek *energeia*. Cf. Quintilian, 8. 3. 89; Aristotle, *Rhet.* 3. 11. Apparently the word had not yet become Anglicized. *Energy* does not occur in Shakespeare.

52 32. *Material.* Cf. 46 34.

52 34. *Well worse*, etc. Sidney is castigating Gosson, though he no doubt had others in mind also.

52 35. *Matron eloquence.* He is here ringing the changes, in Gosson's own style, upon the latter's words, *School of Abuse*, p. 20: "Pull off the vizard that poets mask in . . . you shall perceive their sharp sayings to be placed as . . . chaste matrons' apparel on common courtesans."

53 4. *Coursing of a letter.* Cf. Shak., *LLL.* 4. 2. 56: "I will something affect the letter, for it argues facility."

53 5–6. *Dictionary . . . flowers.* Cf. Sonnet 15 of *Astrophel and Stella :*

> You that do search for every purling spring
> Which from the ribs of old Parnassus flows,
> And every flower, not sweet perhaps, which grows
> Near thereabouts, into your poesy wring;
> Ye that do dictionary's method bring
> Into your rimes, running in rattling rows.

Cf. also Sonnet 3:

> Or Pindar's apes flaunt in their phrases fine,
> Enameling their pride with flowers of gold.

53 7 ff. *But I would*, etc. Sidney is still ridiculing Gosson, and in this sentence apparently travestying his style. Gosson was at once or in succession versifier, prose-printer, scholar, and preacher, and obnoxious to Sidney. For proof of the latter statement part of a letter from Spenser to Gabriel Harvey may be quoted, bearing date of October 16, 1579: "New books I hear of none, but only of one that, writing a certain book called *The School of Abuse*, and dedicating it to Master Sidney, was for his labor scorned, — if at least it be in the goodness of

that nature to scorn. Such folly is it, not to regard aforehand the inclination and quality of him to whom we dedicate our books." This letter may be found in Grosart's ed. of Spenser, 9. 261–271.

53 14. *Nizolian.* Adjective formed from the name of the Italian lexicographer Nizzoli, or, in Latinized form, Nizolius (1498–1566), whose Ciceronian lexicon was published at Basle about 1530, and has been frequently reprinted.

53 14. *Keep Nizolian paper-books.* As Speron Sperone (1500–1588) is related to have done. See his own account in Symonds, *Renaissance in Italy* 5. 254 : " Using the greatest diligence, I composed a rhyming dictionary or vocabulary of Italian phrases, in the which I classed by the alphabet every word those two authors had used; moreover I collected in another book their divers ways of describing things, as day, night, anger, peace, hate, love, fear, hope, beauty, in such wise that not a single word or thought came from me which had not its precedent in their sonnets and novels."

53 16. *Devour.* Cf. Du Bellay, *Defense and Illustration of the French Tongue* (A.D. 1549), Bk. I. ch. 7 : " By what means then have the Romans been able so to enrich their language as to make it almost equal to the Greek? By imitating the best Greek authors, transforming themselves into them, devouring them, and after having thoroughly digested them, converting them into blood and nutriment."

53 17. *Sugar.* Cf. Shakespeare's *A. Y. L.* 3. 3. 31 : " To have honey a sauce to sugar."

53 24. *Vivit,* etc. Sidney apparently quoted from memory (see the Variants). I have restored the true reading of Cicero, *Catiline* 1. 2: " He lives. Lives? ay, he comes even into the senate," etc.

53 30. *Too much choler.* I suspect that Sidney here intends a pun upon *choler* and *color.* Shakespeare frequently plays tricks with the word *choler.* If my supposition is correct, Sidney uses *color* in the sense of figure of speech, rhetorical ornament, artifice, as in Chaucer, *Prologue of the Franklin's Tale :*

> Colours ne knowe I non, withouten drede,
> But swiche colours as growen in the mede,
> Or elles swiche as men dye with or peynte.
> Colours of rethoryke been to queynte.

If this surmise is correct, we must understand: " When it were too highly rhetorical to simulate anger."

53 31. *Similiter cadences.* A partial Anglicization of Quintilian's *cadentia similiter* (9. 4. 42), a translation of the Greek rhetorical term

ὁμοιόπτωτα, which is allied to, and frequently identical with, the *similiter desinentia* or ὁμοιοτέλευτα, which we call 'rime.' An example
occurs in Cicero, *Quintius* 23. 75: "Ut, si veritatem volent retinere,
gravitatem possint obtinere." Another example may be taken from
Apuleius, *Flor.* 21: "Camporum rivos et collium clivos." The use of
this figure in prose was censured by the best critics of antiquity, as by
Quintilian in the passage cited, though it is allowed under certain circumstances. Cicero mentions it, *Character of the Orator* 3. 54. 206:
"The use of words, also, which end similarly, or have similar cadences,
or which balance one another, or which correspond to one another."
Cf. also his *Orator* 34. 135, and De Mille, *Rhetoric*, § 264. With
respect to the employment of these figures by Demosthenes, my col-
league, Professor Goodell, kindly gives me this statement: "It is safe
to say that both figures occur so seldom that when one is used it produces, as in 6. 21, all the effect of which such a figure is capable."
That in 6. 21 (Second Philippic) is as follows: οὐ κρατηθέντες μόνον
ἀλλὰ καὶ προδοθέντες ὑπ' ἀλλήλων καὶ πραθέντες.

54 3. *Seeming fineness.* Cf. Bacon, *De Augmentis*, Bk. VII. ch. 1:
"Seneca says well, 'Eloquence is injurious to those whom it inspires
with a fondness for itself, and not for the subject'; for writings should
be such as should make men in love with the lesson, and not with the
teacher."

54 5. *Similitudes.* Cf. *Astrophel and Stella*, 3. 7–8:

> Or with strange similes enrich each line,
> Of herbs or beasts which Ind or Afric hold.

54 12. *Most tedious prattling.* Hinting again at Gosson; cf. his
School of Abuse throughout. A single specimen may answer: "The
fish remora hath a small body, and great force to stay ships against
wind and tide; ichneumon, a little worm, overcomes the elephant; the
viper slays the bull, the weasel the cockatrice; and the weakest wasp
stingeth the stoutest man of war." And these are just one-third of the
number of similes employed to illustrate the truth that small things are
capable of producing great results. Bacon deplores the perpetuation
of errors in natural history through this means (*Adv. Learning* 2. 1. 3.):
"If an untruth in nature be once on foot, . . . what by reason of the
use of the opinion in similitudes and ornaments of speech, it is never
called down." Drayton says that Sidney

> did first reduce
> Our tongue from Lyly's writing, then in use, —
> Talking of stones, stars, plants, of fishes, flies,
> Playing with words and idle similes.

54 16. *Antonius.* 143–87 B.C.

54 17. *Crassus.* 140–91 B.C.

54 18. *Pretended.* Cf. Cicero, *Character of the Orator* 2. 1. 4 : " But there was such peculiarity in each, that Crassus desired not so much to be thought unlearned as to hold learning in contempt, and to prefer, on every subject, the understanding of our countrymen to that of the Greeks; while Antonius thought that his oratory would be better received by the Roman people if he were believed to have had no learning at all." Quintilian, 2. 17. 6, calls Antonius "dissimulator artis."

54 19. *Because.* In order that. See the peculiar uses in 48 3, 53 21.

54 21. *Credit.* Aristotle, *Rhet.* 2. 1 : "It is a highly important element of proof that the speaker should enjoy the credit of a certain character, and should be supposed by his audience to stand in a certain relation to themselves." *Persuasion.* Aristotle, *Rhet.* 1. 2 : " Rhetoric may be defined as a faculty of discovering all the possible means of persuasion in any subject."

54 32. *Art.* The jingle on this word is perhaps intended as ridicule of the Euphuists. The modern fashion was originated, or at least reinforced, by the Spaniards (see Landmann, *Der Euphuismus*, Giessen 1881), and accordingly we find Cervantes ridiculing it in *Don Quixote*. In ch. 1 (Duffield's tr.) we have : "The reason of the unreason which is done to my reason in such manner enfeebles my reason that with reason I lament your beauty." But such collocations, which are often adduced as examples of barbarism in language, are recommended to the world by the example of Cicero. Thus, *On Friendship* 1. 5 : "But as then I, an old man, wrote to you, who are an old man, on the subject of old age; so in this book I myself, a most sincere friend, have written to a friend on the subject of friendship"; this is still more striking in the original : "Sed ut tum ad senem senex de senectute, sic hoc libro ad amicum amicissimus scripsi de amicitia." Cf. also *Limits of Good and Evil* 5. 6. 16, but especially *Character of an Orator* 1. 41. 186 : " For nothing can be reduced into a science unless he who understands the matters of which he would form a science has previously gained such knowledge as to enable him to constitute a science out of subjects in which there has never yet been any science." If for 'science' we substitute 'art,' the tone of the original will be more accurately reproduced, since this is the term actually employed by Cicero. If Sidney is not here indulging in parody, he probably is modeling his sentence on that of Cicero last quoted.

55 10. *Matter and manner.* Cf. 46 34.

55 25. *Compositions.* Cf. 8 2, note. Sidney employs them not only in his more ornate prose, but in this, a comparatively sober style. Among the more noticeable, because the more poetical, of such epithets are: death-bringing 9 32, dull-making 58 4, earth-creeping 58 5, fine-witted 14 13, heart-ravishing 5 16, honey-flowing 52 34, ink-wasting 57 8, low-creeping 44 4, never-leaving 9 33, old-aged 14 12, self-devouring 17 4, soon-repenting 17 3, sweet-smelling 8 1, through-beholding 32 19, through-searching 18 3, well-accorded 29 15, well-enchanting 23 24 (cf. well-raised 50 22, well-sounding 47 32, well-waiting 21 10, well-weighed 56 3), winter-starved 53 6, wry-transformed 51 34. Many of these seem to be translated directly from Latin or Greek, rather than borrowed from the French. Thus, death-bringing = mortifer (used by Cicero as well as Virgil); earth-creeping, low-creeping = χαμαιτυπής, χαμαιπετής; honey-flowing = mellifluous, μελίγηρυς, μελίγλωσσος, μελίρρυτος, etc. That Sidney was capable of thus translating is proved by his coinage of Greek compounds (cf. 22 18, 32 14). Other compounds used in the *Defense* are: after-livers 27 9 (after-thinker used by Grote), before-time 38 33, best-measured 33 21, far-fet 25 11, 53 2, fore-backwardly 46 30, fore-conceit 8 15, good-fellow 24 33, high(est)-flying 5 35, 46 24, light-giver 2 22, many-fashioned 42 18, many-formed 12 8, new-budding 52 19, often-assaulted 38 17, paper-blurrers 46 4, poet-apes 57 5, poet-haters 32 14, poet-whippers 31 12, school-art 41 10, school-name 24 29, small-learned 54 28, virtue-breeding 57 1, war-stratagem 20 31. Those in -like are: ass-like 43 9, courtesan-like 53 1, learner-like 1 11, man-like 35 3, much-like 20 19, planet-like 58 5, soldier-like 29 28. Compositions of three words are: self-wise-seeming 51 34, too-much-loved 8 2. With respect to the employment of compound epithets, there has been and is much diversity of taste and practice. Aristotle condemns it, *Rhet.* 3. 3: "Faults of taste occur in four points of style. Firstly, in the use of compound words, such as Lycophron's 'many-visaged heaven,' 'vast-crested earth,' and 'narrow-passaged strand.' . . . There are instances too in Alcidamos, e.g. . . . 'he thought their zeal would prove end-executing,' . . . or 'steel-gray the ocean's basement'; for all these are terms which, as being compound, have a certain poetical character." Yet this principle has been frequently disregarded in ornate English prose, especially when impassioned. Take, for example, such a sentence from Ruskin as this: "The low bronzed gleaming of sea-rusted armor shot angrily under their blood-red mantle-folds" (*Mod. Paint.* Part IX. ch. 9). Or this (Part VI. ch. 10): "To them, slow-fingered, constant-hearted, is entrusted the weaving of the dark, eternal tapestries of the hills; to them, slow-pencilled, iris-dyed, the tender framing

of their endless imagery." And I open the last number of *Harper's Magazine* (March, 1890) to find Dr. Charles Waldstein, in a paper on *The Restored Head of Iris*, expressing himself thus: "There may be more true life in stone than in the sound of the waving reeds, and the shout of dying men, when heard re-echoing through the riotous brain of truth-ignoring posterity." If these are examples of good English prose, Sidney's use of compounds may well be pardoned, if not applauded. But on this supposition, what shall we say to the authority of Aristotle and the views held by many modern rhetoricians and stylists? With respect to compound epithets in general, and especially in poetry, they have been rare when Latin influence has been in the ascendant, and have multiplied under the stimulus of a revived Teutonism or Hellenism. The oldest English and modern German are here at one with the flexible Greek, and antagonistic to the more prosaic Latin. Chaucer has but few compounds; Cynewulf, Chapman, and Tennyson have many. See Coleridge's remarks on the subject in his *Biographia Literaria*, ch. 1.

55 28. *Now of versifying,* etc. For the attempt to revive classical metres in English, see Church, *Spenser*, pp. 18–28.

56 9. *For the ancient.* Sidney seems not to have emancipated himself from the notion that the ancient metres could be reproduced in the modern languages by means of quantity, as well as imitated by means of accent.

56 17. *Rime.* Here apparently = (accentual) rhythm, metre, as in Minsheu's *Guide into the Tongues* (London, 1627). In 56 23, "the very rime itself," the modern meaning is resumed (cf. 55 33, 56 3). See also Webbe's *Discourse of English Poetry* (Haslewood, 2. 55–6): "The falling out of verses together in one like sound is commonly called in English, rime, taken from the Greek word ῥυθμός, which surely in my judgment is very abusively applied to such a sense. . . . For rime is properly the just proportion of a clause or sentence, whether it be in prose or metre, aptly comprised together, . . . and is proper not only to poets, but also to readers, orators, pleaders, or any which are to pronounce or speak anything in public audience. There be three special notes necessary to be observed in the framing of our accustomed English rime. The first is that one metre or verse be answerable to another, in equal number of feet or syllables, or proportionable to the tune whereby it is to be read or measured. The second, to place the words in such sort as none of them be wrested contrary to the natural inclination or affectation of the same, or, more truly, the true quantity thereof. The third, to make them fall together mutually in

rime, that is, in words of like sound, but so as the words be not dis-
ordered for the rime's sake, nor the sense hindered."

56 19. *Observe the accent.* Cf. Daniel, *Defense of Rime* (Haslewood,
2. 198) : "And though it doth not strictly observe long and short syllables, yet it most religiously respects the accent; and as the short and
the long make number, so the acute and grave accent yield harmony —
and harmony is likewise number; so that the English verse then hath
number, measure, and harmony in the best proportion of music, which,
being more certain and more resounding, works that effect of motion
with as happy success as either the Greek or Latin."

57 1. *So that*, etc.   Cf. 31 30–32.

57 3. *Since the blames*, etc.   Cf. 44 3–8.

57 4. *Since the cause*, etc.   Cf. 44 14–53 6.

57 6. *Since, lastly*, etc.   Cf. 55 10–56 35.

57 12. *Rimer.*   Cf. *Shak. Ant.* 5. 2. 215–6:

> Scald rimers
> Ballad us out of tune.

Cf. Harington (Haslewood, 2. 123): "The common sort, that . . .
rather in scorn than in praise bestow the name of a poet on every base
rimer and ballad-maker." Cf. Egger, *Hellenisme* 1. 318, 357.

57 15. *That no*, etc.   Cf. Scaliger, *Poetics* 104. a. 2: "By none of
the precepts of the philosophers can you become better or more courteous than from the reading of Virgil."

57 17. *Clauserus.*   Conrad C. Clauser (ca. 1520–1611). A German
scholar.   His edition of Cornutus and Palæphatus appeared at Basle in
1543.

57 18. *Cornutus.*   A Stoic, the teacher of Persius, the Roman satirist,
honored and beloved by him, but banished by Nero on account of his
upright life.

57 22. *Mysteries.*   Cf. Harington (Haslewood, 2. 127–8): "The
ancient poets have indeed wrapped as it were in their writings divers
and sundry meanings, which they call the senses or mysteries thereof.
. . . The men of greatest learning and highest wit in the ancient
times did of purpose conceal these deep mysteries of learning, and as
it were cover them with the veil of fables and verse for sundry causes.
One cause was that they might not be rashly abused by profane wits."

57 24. *Landino.*   A Florentine humanist (1424–1504). Commen-
tator on Dante, Horace, and Virgil, translator of Pliny, lecturer on
Petrarch, and author of the *Camaldolese Discussions*, in which the
active and the contemplative life are compared.   Cf. Symonds, *Renaissance in Italy* 2. 338 ff.

57 25. *Divine fury.* Cf. 43 14.

57 32. *Libertino patre natus.* From Horace, *Sat.* 1. 6. 6: "The son of a freedman."

57 33. *Herculea proles.* Professor Gildersleeve (*Am. J. Phil.* 12. 123) refers to Ovid, *Fast.* 2. 237.

57 34. *Si quid*, etc. Virgil, *Æneid* 9. 446 : "If aught my verse can do."

58 4. *Cataract of Nilus.* Cf. Cicero, *Vision of Scipio :* "The ears of mankind, filled with these sounds (i.e. the music of the spheres), have become deaf, for of all your senses it is the most blunted. Thus the people who live near the place where the Nile rushes down from very high mountains to the parts which are called Catadupa are destitute of the sense of hearing, by reason of the greatness of the noise." Montaigne tells the story, Bk. I. ch. 22.

58 8. *Mome.* Dolt, blockhead. Cf. Shak. *Err.* 3. 1. 32. *Momus.* The ancient personification of censure and mockery.

58 10. *Midas.* Cf. Ovid, *Metam.* 11. 146–193. *Bubonax.* Probably for Bupalus. Cf. Pliny, *Nat. Hist.* 36. 12: "Bupalus and Athenis were very celebrated in their art (i.e. sculpture), and were contemporary with the poet Hipponax, who certainly lived in the sixtieth Olympiad. . . . Hipponax was remarkably ugly, and the two artists, by way of a joke, exposed his portrait to the ridicule of the public. The indignation of Hipponax being aroused by this act, he directed against them the bitterness of his poems to such effect that, according to some writers, they hanged themselves in despair; but this opinion is false." We have seen that Sidney often misquotes, whether intentionally or otherwise. Here he has apparently confused the two names Bupalus and Hipponax, and thus blended them into the one, Bubonax.

58 12. *In Ireland.* Cf. Shak. *A. Y. L.* 3. 2. 186: "I was never so berimed since Pythagoras' time, that I was an Irish rat." Also Ben Jonson, Apology of *Poetaster :*

> Or I could do worse,
> Armed with Archilochus' fury, with iambics
> Should make the desperate lashers hang themselves,
> Rime them to death, as they do Irish rats
> In drumming tunes.

Add Mallory's note (*Yale Studies in English* 27. 137).

VARIANTS.

The following variants are based upon a collation of the reprints by Arber and Flügel, which are presumed to be literal transcripts of the editions printed in 1595 by Olney and Ponsonby respectively. How far these do actually represent the two earliest texts I am in no position to state, but the errors, if any, must be few and unimportant. Except for the rejection of *his* as the possessive sign of the noun, I have rarely ventured, in the construction of the text, to reject the authority of both the early copies. These instances will all be found recorded in their proper places, and are mostly confined to cases where the retention of the older forms would have occasioned a manifest transgression of grammatical concord, or where a form, like Pindarus, 41 23, would have constituted a noticeable exception.

It must be understood that no attempt has been made to note mere differences of spelling and punctuation. This would have been impracticable without greatly increasing the bulk of the volume, and would have served no useful purpose that could not be quite as readily served by consulting the reprints which I have used.

1 1. *Edward Wotton.* P. E.W.
1 21. *the.* O. a.
1 28. *be.* O. are.
2 1. *Pugliano's.* O. Pugliano his.
2 8. *since.* O. sith (and always, except 23.7).
2 15. *latter.* P. later.
2 19. *inveigh.* P. envey.
2 23. *by.* P. omits.
2 24–25. *they now.* P. you.
2 28. *her.* P. his.
2 29. *Hesiod.* O. Hesiodus.
2 34. *to their.* P. to the.
2 35. *may.* P. nay.
3 10. *Boccace.* P. Bocace.

3 14. *as in.* P. as.
3 18. *masks.* P. mask.
3 24. *hidden.* O. hid.
3 31. *standeth.* P. stands.
3 32. *feigneth.* P. feigns.
3 32. *to speak.* P. speak.
4 3. *knoweth.* P. knows.
4 8. *the.* O. omits.
4 10. *stole.* P. stale.
4 24. *goeth.* P. goes.
4 27. *areytos.* P. arentos.
4 32. *exercise.* O. exercises.
5 18. *any.* P. any of.
5 22. *making.* P. as it is reported by many.

5 26. *although.* O. which although.

5 27. *that.* P. omits.

5 33. *the.* P. by the.

6 3. *further.* P. farther.

6 4. *vates.* P. vatis.

6 7. *of.* O. omits.

6 20. *fear.* O. fear me.

6 28. *called.* P. named.

6 28. *ποιητήν.* O. a poet.

6 30. *ποιεῖν.* O. poiein.

6 35. *any.* O. my.

7 1. *unto.* O. to.

7 6. *set.* O. setteth.

7 7. *do.* P. doth.

7 9. *musician.* P. musicians.

7 12. *and passions.* P. or passions.

7 28. *into.* O. omits.

7 34. *within.* O. only within.

8 7. *cunning.* P. comming.

8 13. *any.* P. every.

8 14. *each.* O. the.

8 18. *hath.* P. had.

8 32. *far.* P. omits.

8 33. *argument.* P. arguments.

9 7. *the more.* O. more.

9 13. *his.* P. the.

9 13. *μίμησις.* O. mimesis.

9 17. *general.* O. several.

9 19. *inconceivable.* P. unconceivable.

9 23. *Franciscus.* P. F.

9 28. *Greeks.* P. Greek.

9 29. *James'.* P. Paul's. O. James his.

9 35. *and.* P. omits.

10 3. *judgment.* O. judgments.

10 7. *free.* O. omits.

11 5. *sort of verse.* O. sorts of verses.

11 18. *wrote.* O. writ.

12 7. *clay.* O. clayey.

12 8. *of.* O. of the.

12 17. *by.* P. omits.

12 21. *into.* P. in.

12 26. *each.* P. omits.

12 28. *called.* P. omits.

12 28. *ἀρχιτεκτονική.* O. arkitectonike.

12 33. *further.* O. farther.

13 5. *poet is worthy to have it before any.* O. poet's nobleness by setting him before his.

13 6. *as.* P. omits.

13 7. *thinketh.* P. thinks.

13 23. *contain.* O. containeth. P. contains.

13 24. *extendeth.* P. extends.

13 27. *giveth.* P. gives.

13 31. *of.* P. omits.

13 33. *thousand.* P. 1000.

13 35. *goeth.* P. goes.

13 35. *runneth.* P. runs.

14 3. *virtuous.* P. virtue's.

14 4-5. *testis . . . vitæ.* O. lux vitæ, temporum magistra, vita memoriæ.

14 17. *confirming.* O. conferring.

14 18. *by story.* P. by stories.

14 21. *maketh.* P. makes.

15 2. *and Justice.* P. omits.

15 2. *seeketh.* P. seeks.

15 12. *in that.* P. in the.

15 18. *arguments.* O. argument.

15 33. *in.* P. by.

16 8. *an.* O. the.

16 11. *conceit.* O. conceits.

16 14. *that.* O. the.

16 17. *definitions.* O. definition.

16 17. *virtues or.* O. virtue.

16 28. *said.* O. P. say. Ed. of 1598, said.

17 7. *Gnatho.* O. P. Gnato.

17 10. *states.* O. seats.

17 23. *poesy.* P. poetry.

17 26. *attained.* O. obtained.

18 4. *Lazarus in.* O. Lazarus being in.

18 7.   *mine.* O. my.

18 18.   *make.* P. makes.

18 19.   *those.* O. these.

18 22.   *bringeth.* P. brings.

18 27.   φιλοσοφώτερον. P. φιλοσοφωτερων. O. philosophoteron.

18 27.   σπουδαιότερον. P. σπουδαιοτερων. O. spoudaioteron.

18 28.   *studiously serious.* P. omits.

18 29.   καθόλου. O. Katholou.

18 31.   καθ' ἕκαστον. O. Kathekaston.

18 34.   *marketh.* O. marks.

19 11.   *in Xenophon.* O. of Xenophon.

19 17.   *foul and.* P. full.

19 27.   *Quintus.* P. Q.

19 33.   *it hath.* P. hath it.

20 7.   *poetically.* O. poetical.

20 11.   *a poet.* P. an poet.

20 12.   *do concur.* P. did.

20 12.   *do both.* P. doth both.

20 34.   *pleaseth.* P. please.

21 2.   *yet.* P. so yet.

21 5.   *history.* O. histories.

21 6.   *gotten.* P. got.

21 9.   *setteth.* P. sets.

21 19.   *historian.* P. history.

21 29.   *sixteen hundred.* O. P. 1600.

21 33.   *literas.* P. litteras.

22 2.   *occidendos.* P. occidentos.

22 3.   *you.* O. your.

22 6.   *injustice.* O. unjustice.

22 9.   *deserveth.* P. deserves.

22 12.   *poet.* P. poets.

22 16.   *teach.* O. doth teach.

22 18.   φιλοφιλόσοφος. O. philophilosophos.

22 21.   *both.* O. omits.

22 21.   *and the.* P. and.

22 26.   γνῶσις. P. γνόσις O. gnosis.

22 26, 27.   πρᾶξις. O. praxis.

22 27.   *cannot.* P. can.

23 7.   *since.* O. seeing.

23 14.   *conceit.* O. conceits.

23 18.   *very.* O. omits.

23 32.   *of the.* O. of.

23 33.   *rhubarb.* P. rhabarbrum. O. rubarb.

24 2.   *Æneas.* O. and Æneas.

24 4.   *valor.* P. value.

24 14.   *and.* P. of.

24 16.   *wisheth.* P. wished.

24 17.   *do.* P. doth.

24 17.   *those.* O. the.

24 24.   *virtue.* P. virtus.

24 26.   *Boethius.* P. Poetius.

25 10.   *either.* O. omits.

25 14.   *behaves.* P. behave.

25 23.   *ever.* P. only.

25 29.   *murder.* O. P. murther (and always).

26 6.   *ensueth.* P. ensue.

26 13.   *or.* P. and.

26 14.   *a.* O. an.

26 17.   *defectious.* P. defectuous.

26 22.   *like.* P. omits.

26 23.   *Sannazzaro.* O. Sanazzar. P. Sanazara.

26 35.   *lords and.* O. lords or.

27 5.   *contention.* P. contentons.

27 12.   *it.* P. in.

27 13.   *bewaileth.* O. bewails.

27 17.   *lamentation.* P. lamentations.

27 19.   *who.* O. which.

27 24.   *till.* O. until.

27 33.   *argument.* P. arguments.

27 33.   *answer after.* P. after answer.

28 11.   *an.* P. omits.

28 16.   *comedian.* P. comedient.

28 17.   *evil.* P. the evil.

28 22.   *to.* O. omits.

28 24.   *find.* P. see.

28 28.   *ulcers.* O. vicers (misprint?).

28 35. *auctorem.* O. P. autho-rem.

29 5. *blood.* P. bloods.

29 16. *giveth.* O. gives.

29 19. *mine.* O. my.

29 22. *it is.* O. is it.

29 27. *such.* P. such-like.

29 28. *valor.* P. valure. O. valour.

29 29. *think.* P. think one of.

29 33. *be.* O. be the.

30 2. *matters rather.* P. rather matters.

30 15. *it.* P. him.

30 19. *through.* O. throughout.

30 22. *setteth.* O. sets.

30 28. *kind.* P. kinds.

30 33. *he.* P. be (misprint?).

30 35. *the.* P. omits.

31 2. *human.* O. P. humane.

31 8. *most.* O. not.

31 10. *even.* P. omits.

31 18. *learnings.* O. learning.

31 21. *nor.* O. nor no.

31 27. *only.* P. only, only.

31 29. *his end containeth.* P. nor end containing.

31 31. *and.* O. and to.

31 31-32. *of it.* O. omits.

31 35. *and.* P. omits.

31 35. *leaveth.* O. leaves.

32 6. *triumphant.* O. triumph-ing.

32 11. *be.* O. may be.

32 14. μισομούσοι. P. μυσομου-σοι. O. mysomousoi.

32 21. *a.* O. omits.

32 27. *commodity.* P. commod-ities.

33 11. *humor.* O. humors.

33 11. *is riming.* P. in riming.

33 20. *considereth.* O. consid-ers.

33 29. *treasurer.* P. treasure.

33 34. *one.* O. one word.

33 35. *accusing.* O. accuseth.

34 10. *word.* O. words.

34 10. *needeth.* P. needs.

34 11. *a.* P. omits.

34 15-16. *as, Percontatorem. . . . sumus.* O. omits.

34 19. *mathematic.* P. mathe-matics.

34 33. *fancies.* O. fancy.

34 35. *ear.* O. erre.

35 6. *had overshot.* O. outshot.

35 14. *poesy.* O. poetry.

35 32. *affirmeth.* O. affirms.

36 4. *writeth.* O. writes.

36 6. *into.* P. unto.

36 14. *thinketh.* O. thinks.

36 14. *wrote.* O. writ.

36 19. *at that.* P. to the.

36 24. *may.* O. omits.

36 25. *but.* O. omits.

36 30. *proveth.* O. proves.

36 31, 32. *of the.* O. a.

36 32. *putteth.* O. puts.

37 1. *chess.* P. chestes.

37 10. *the only.* P. only.

37 15. *ambitiously.* P. amba-tiously.

37 24. *forth.* P. for.

37 25. *whatsoever.* P. what.

37 32. εἰκαστική. P. ρικαστική. O. eikastike.

37 33. *things.* P. thing.

37 34. φανταστική. O. phantas-tike.

37 35. *that.* P. omits.

38 5. *Goliath.* P. Golias. O. Goliah.

38 10. *do.* P. to (misprint?).

38 15. *receiveth.* P. receives. O. conceiveth.

38 27. *say.* P. said.

38 31. *upon.* P. omits.

39 9. *in.* O. on.

39 11. *these.* P. those.

39 16. *digression.* P. disgression.

39 31. *opposed.* P. apposed.

40 8. *was ever.* O. ever was.

40 18. *never.* O. never well.

40 20. *fourscore.* O. 80.

40 30. *sepulchre.* P. sepulture.

40 30. *Cato's.* O. Cato his.

40 33. *that.* O. now.

40 33. *Plato's.* O. P. Plato his.

41 13. *shops.* P. shop.

41 17. *strave.* O. strove.

41 21. *where.* O. when.

41 23. *Pindar.* O. P. Pindarus.

41 28. *cavillations.* O. cavillation.

41 34. *doth.* O. did.

42 6–8. *who . . . prophet.* P. omits.

42 8. *setteth.* P. sets.

42 29. *construe.* O. conster. P. consture.

42 31. *atque.* P. atq.

42 32. *republica.* P. rep.

43 1. *the.* P. omits.

43 4. *unto.* O. to.

43 5. *unto.* P. to.

43 14. *forenamed.* O. aforenamed.

43 21. *Heautontimoroumenos.* O. P. Heautontimorumenon.

43 27. *needs.* O. need.

43 33. *his.* O. her.

43 34. *that.* P. to have showed.

44 9. *our.* P. the.

44 12. *held.* O. had.

44 12. *ill-savored.* O. ill-favoring.

44 15. *it.* P. omits.

44 19. *proceedeth.* P. proceeds.

44 19. *wit.* P. with (misprint?).

44 19. *others.* O. other.

44 22. *memora.* P. memoria.

44 24. *thousand.* P. thousands.

45 6. *find.* P. sinde (editor's misprint?).

45 7. *lamenteth, decketh.* P. laments, decks.

45 26. *men.* O. omits.

45 30. *post.* P. pass.

45 34. *outflowings.* O. outflowing.

46 9. *but.* O. but I.

46 19. *hath.* P. have.

46 21. *is it.* P. is.

46 26. *wings.* P. wrings.

47 3. *conabar.* P. conabor.

47 3. *erat.* O. P. erit.

47 4. *any.* O. an.

47 7. *Cressida.* O. Cresseid. P. Creseid.

47 11. *reverend.* O. reverent. P. reverent an.

47 15. *eclogues.* O. P. eglogues.

47 19. *Sannazzaro.* O. Sanazar. P. Sanazara.

47 19. *I do.* O. do I.

47 26. *tinkling.* O. P. tingling.

47 27. *reason.* P. reasons.

47 33. *Seneca's.* O. P. Seneca his.

48 1. *truth.* O. troth.

48 9. *and many.* P. and.

48 14. *cometh.* P. comes.

48 19. *and.* P. omits.

48 29. *falleth.* O. falls.

49 3. *have.* O. hath.

49 4. *hit.* P. hit it.

49 5. *containeth.* P. contains.

49 15. *it.* P. in (misprint?).

49 25. *Trojan.* O. P. Troyan.

49 28. Arber's original reads by Hecuba; P. Hecuba.

49 35. *leaving the rest.* P. the rest leaving.

50 1. *needs.* O. need.

50 6. *the clown.* O. clowns.

50 23. *comedians.* P. comedients.

50 25. *it.* P. is (misprint?).

51 4. *and.* O. or.

51 9.	*sorry.* O. sorry, yet.		54 14.	*whit.* P. with (misprint?).

51 9. *sorry.* O. sorry, yet.

51 14. *in.* P. in a.

51 17. *procureth.* P. procures.

51 20. *stir.* O. stirreth.

51 71. *mixed.* P. mix.

51 33. *a heartless.* P. and a heartless.

51 34. *wry-.* O. awry-.

52 14. *fruits.* O. fruit.

52 22. *enough.* O. enow.

52 34. *that.* P. it that.

53 2. *far-fet.* P. far-set.

53 2. *that many.* O. they may.

53 23. *used.* P. useth.

53 23. *as.* O. omits.

53 24. *Vivit?* P. et vincit.

53 24. *vero etiam.* O. P. omit.

53 24. *in senatum venit.* O. senatum venit. P. in senatum venit, imo in senatum venit.

53 27–28. *in choler do.* O. do in choler.

53 30. *too.* O. to too.

53 30–54 4. *How well . . . their fineness.* O. omits.

54 5. *Now.* O. Fow.

54 7. *may.* O. omits.

54 14. *whit.* P. with (misprint?).

54 23. *knacks.* O. tracks.

54 26. *than.* O. than to speak.

54 28. *small-.* O. smally.

55 3. *the.* O. this.

55 3. *digression.* P. disgression.

55 15, 16. *wanteth.* P. wants.

55 18. *in.* O. of.

55 23. *conceits.* P. conceit.

55 34. *more.* O. most.

56 1. *tune.* P. time.

56 5. *obtaineth.* O. obtains.

56 17. *for.* O. for the.

56 27. *the Italians term.* P. Italian.

56 28. *is.* O. omits.

56 33. *already I find.* O. I find already.

56 34. *triflingness.* P. triflings.

57 4. *it is.* P. is.

57 24. *Landino.* O. P. Landin.

57 33. *Herculea.* O. Hercules.

58 1. *Beatrice.* O. P. Beatrix.

58 4. *cataract.* O. cataphract.

58 7. *of.* P. omits.

58 13. *send.* P. sent.

58 14. *get.* P. yet (misprint?).

INDEX OF PROPER NAMES.